FINDING
DOLPHIN'S COVE

Kellie Hailes declared she was going
[...] hen she grew up. It took a while
for her to get there, with a career as a radio copywriter, freelance copywriter and beauty editor filling
the dream-hole, until now. Kellie lives in Auckland,
New Zealand, with her patient husband and very
entertaining daughter. When the characters in her
head aren't dictating their story to her, she can be
found taking short walks, eating good cheese and
hanging out for her next coffee fix.

Also by Kellie Hailes

The Great Christmas Escape
The New Beginnings Bridal Boutique
Snowed in at Snowflake B&B
Sunrise at Strawberry Farm

FINDING HOME
IN
DOLPHIN'S COVE

Kellie Hailes

This edition first published in Great Britain in 2021 by Orion Dash,
an imprint of The Orion Publishing Group Ltd.,
Carmelite House, 50 Victoria Embankment
London EC4Y 0DZ

An Hachette UK Company

1 3 5 7 9 10 8 6 4 2

A CIP catalogue record for this book
is available from the British Library.

ISBN (Paperback): 978 1 3987 0917 1
ISBN (eBook): 978 1 3987 0724 5

The Orion Publishing Group Ltd
Carmelite House
50 Victoria Embankment
London, EC4Y 0DZ

An Hachette UK company

www.orionbooks.co.uk

For Dad, who gave me my love of the sea.

For Dad, who gave me my love of the sea.

Chapter One

It wasn't so much that she'd just been shat on by a seagull
that annoyed Kenna Sanders, it was that the seagull had
chosen to relieve itself three whole seconds before Kenna
was due to open up shop and start her new life as the
owner and manager of Fishful Thinking, Dolphin's Cove's
best – and only – bait shop.

Not *just* Dolphin's Cove's bait shop. *Her* bait shop.
Left to her by the grandmother she barely knew, along
with a cottage she'd apparently spent time in as a toddler,
before her mother had decided their life was better spent
elsewhere. So much so, that they'd not once returned; not
even for a visit.

Glancing up at the brilliant blue sky, Kenna shook her fist
in the direction of the circling seagulls, whose cries smacked
of 'Haha, did you think coming home would be easy?'

Of course she'd not thought things would go swim-
mingly. At least, not initially. Not while she was still
finding her feet in the quaint Cornish village, but she'd
hoped to at least get the door to the shop open while still
looking presentable.

Heaving in a lungful of the pungent, briny air, Kenna
closed her eyes for the count of five.

She could do this.

She could manage a store.

She could ingratiate herself with the local villagers.

She could create the home she'd dreamed of, but never felt in her heart.

'It's 6.01. You're late.'

Kenna opened her eyes and spun round, ready to tell the man with the unimpressed tone that he could hold his horses for one hot minute, that the bait wasn't going anywhere.

Her mouth opened, but no words came out. She shut it, breathed in once more, then opened her mouth again in readiness to give him a polite dressing-down.

Still no words.

Great. She must look like a gawping fish. At least she'd look like one of the locals . . . well, if she suddenly grew a tail, fins and was covered in scales.

'6.02.' He tapped the chunky black watch on his wrist, his thick black brows rising, emphasising his point. 'Unless you're not Kenna, in which case you're breaking and entering and I'll have to call the authorities.'

Mr Impatient may have been ridiculously attractive with his head of lush, wavy raven-coloured hair that was tied up in a manbun, penetrating umber-brown eyes and shoulders that were so wide they'd look out of place on anyone who didn't have the height he had to put them into perspective, but his blunt, bordering on rude, manner was making his hotness level decline at a rapid rate.

'I *am* Kenna, so you can forget about calling the police. And you are?' Kenna turned her back on His Royal Rudeness, slotted the key in the door's lock and pushed it open, cringing at the shriek of rusty hinges.

'Your business partner.'

'My what now?' Kenna jumped out of the way as her supposed business partner strode into the shop, opened the old fridge-freezer that sat next to the cash register and

2

began pulling out bags of bait. 'I think you've got the wrong place. I don't have a business partner.'

'Sonia didn't have her lawyer tell you?' He dumped the bait into a cool box. 'Of course she didn't. God, even in death your gran likes to keep me on my toes.'

He straightened up and thrust his hand out.

Large, strong, capable-looking. On any other man she'd be imagining his hand grasping her waist as she was picked up and thrown over one of those ridiculously big shoulders, then carted off to bed. On this guy?

After his rude welcome, she'd sooner eat the bait in his coolbox than let him touch her like that.

The hand dropped and was followed by an unbothered shrug. 'Fine. Don't shake my hand. Don't open the shop. In fact, why don't you just take those no-good-for-being-on-your-feet-all-day blue shoes and put them to good use by walking out the door and leaving the running of this place to me. Or better yet, we could close the place up and call it done.'

Kenna fought the urge to glance down at her ballet flats that, up until two seconds ago, she'd thought were perfect shoes for running a fishing supplies store. Flat, comfortable and not blue – but aquamarine – to match the sign hanging out the front, which was now more of a faded and flaked shade of aquamarine than the brilliant, bright shade she'd seen in the picture the lawyer had shown her.

Still, as shabby and tired as the sign was, it wasn't anything that couldn't be fixed with a bit of sanding and a lick of fresh paint.

She tilted her chin and pulled herself up to her full height of just over five foot six. There was no way she was going to let the brute before her bully her into submission or out of her shop. 'I'm not going anywhere. This was Gran's place, she left it to me in her will, and it's now my job to run it. Which means closing it is not an option.'

'She left *her* share to you. And you're doing a bang-up job of running it by opening late. The early bird gets the worm has a whole other meaning around these parts. Early birds sell the worms, and don't go out of business. You really ought to have opened up at five.'

Five? Kenna's brain fuzzed at the thought. Even at this time of day she was barely functioning. At five in the morning she was a snoring zombie.

'And do you know you've got seagull shit on your head?' He shook his head and clucked his tongue in a blatant show of disgust. 'I should've sold my share of this place when I had the chance. Gotten out before the going went even more to hell.'

He dragged his hand over his eyes. His shoulders slumped like the weight of the world had been placed upon them. Or perhaps the weight had already been there, and he was tired of carrying it.

Kenna tried to process their short but fraught conversation while taking in the shop. She noted the dust nestled along the windowsills, the webs in the corners of the room, the spaces on shelves and along the wall where stock ought to be.

'So what you're saying is that you also own this place? And that it's in trouble?' *That the shop wouldn't automatically bring her the simple, secure life she'd hoped for.*

Kenna pressed her lips together as exhaustion, caused by a combination of a ten-hour trip on the bus from Leeds, followed by a fretful night's sleep at a local B&B, along with the crushing disappointment that the security, the happiness, the reason to be that she thought she'd find here, was non-existent.

4

'The state of the shop isn't enough of an answer?'

Kenna didn't think a person could look any less impressed, but her newly discovered co-owner somehow managed it.

'I don't know. I mean . . . It's rather gloomy in here. Hard to see. Probably because the windows are filthy.' Kenna shook her head as annoyance dashed away her embarrassment. Why was she letting this random guy get under her skin? 'But it's nothing that a bit of elbow grease can't fix.' She hoped. 'Anyway, I need to get the store open, and then . . .' She spotted what looked worryingly like mice droppings by the counter. 'Then I need to get my elbows into action. Have you even bothered to run a rag over the dust, like, ever? Or was that women's work? Did you leave it up to Gran?'

Not waiting for an answer, deciding she'd proved her point that she could give as good as she got, Kenna spun on her heel and marched towards the door at the back of the small store that she assumed led to a storeroom and bathroom. She pushed it open and nearly gagged as she inhaled, needing fresh air, only to breathe in more dust combined with the nose-wrinkling stench of a toilet in desperate need of a scrub.

'Honestly?' she said to no one in particular. Was it really that hard to squirt a bit of bleach and then run a brush around a toilet bowl?

Having worked for a cleaning company after leaving school, experience had taught her that it was, in fact, for some people, that hard. Luckily she could handle a rancid bathroom, as well as a truckload of dust and grime.

'I don't believe in "women's work". I believe in work.'

The dim room further darkened as her newly discovered co-owner filled the doorway. Was the man part-giant on top of being a total grump?

'And Sonia wouldn't let me touch a cleaning product. She once caught me trying to pick up a cloth and the spray bottle – third shelf down to the right, if that's what you're looking for – and she slapped my hand so hard it stung for half a day.'

Was that a note of affection she heard in his voice? Despite her irritation, a smile crept upon Kenna's lips. She hadn't known her grandmother all that well. Or even remotely well. What she did know of her was from the rare occasions her mother had brought her up. *Four foot ten and full of spit and fire*, her mother had said. Almost admiringly. Definitely begrudgingly. And not without a hint of warning: Kenna's grandmother was to be kept at not just arm's, but country's length for their own good.

According to her mother, her grandmother had been indomitable. Had never let anyone get in her way or tell her what to do. Legend had it – or at least the tale her mother had told her – was that when her husband had cheated on her, then come back begging for forgiveness, she'd booted him out – literally – deciding she'd rather raise their child on her own than put up with a no-good, cheating scoundrel. Locals had tried to gently suggest that it would be hard for her to go it alone, but whenever the subject had been broached she'd told them to pull their heads in. When they said she couldn't raise a child *and* take a job on a fishing boat, she'd told them to bugger off. When they'd said she couldn't raise a child, work on the boat and start up a shop she'd not said a word – only given them the two-finger salute.

Kenna's smile morphed into a fully fledged grin. 'From the stories I've heard, she really did sound like quite the woman.' *I only wish I'd been able to spend time with her. Get to know her.* In a way not tainted by her mother's opinion.

Tears rose, blurring the shelves before her. She blinked them away, not wanting to show weakness in front of a stranger – in front of anyone. If only her grandmother's feisty spirit had softened when it came to her mother, to her. Perhaps then they'd never have had to leave the village; her mother tired of having every aspect of her life picked over and found wanting. Tired of searching for signs of affection, only to find derision. Disappointment.

'You've no idea, Kenna. She was terrifying. Nothing I did was right. Nothing you do will be right. Anything you do wrong she'll blame on me. We're best just to stay away.'

And stay away they had. Her mother refusing to step foot in Dolphin's Cove, even to attend the funeral. Kenna too afraid of what she'd discover if she visited as an adult – of how *she* would be found wanting. How? More like how many ways.

She'd just scraped by in school.

Hadn't gone to university.

She wasn't an entrepreneur.

She rarely stood up for herself.

And when life looked like it was getting too hard she picked up and moved on. Much as her mother had done before her.

It was how, together, she and her mother had bounced from town to town, job to job, never settling for too long, keeping those who could be friends at a distance, always upping and leaving before anyone could find a flaw in their personality or work ethic. The two of them a team who stuck together no matter what. Until now.

Kenna may not have met her grandmother, but it seemed the shadow of her ways had followed Kenna around anyway, with her grandmother's impact on her mother now impacting Kenna herself.

7

For the first time, she'd rebelled against her mother's pleas to avoid Dolphin's Cove, causing their first real argument. She'd hated how they'd yelled, how her mother had begged her to stay, how she'd refused and, finally, how they'd left things – Kenna getting on the bus with no hug or words of advice from her mother; just her suitcase and a head full of worry, determination and certain knowledge that this was her chance to find out who she was, to rediscover her roots, to ground herself once and for all. An opportunity she couldn't let go by.

She fisted her hands as she caught sight of a pair of grandmother foot-sized wellies. A symbol of strength. Of what could be achieved when you dug in, when you didn't listen to what others had to say, when you followed your dreams and lived life on your own terms.

Kenna had no idea why her grandmother had left the business – well, her half of it – to her, but she had, and Kenna wasn't going to give it up or walk away from it. She was going to channel her grandmother's ways, and that meant standing up to the man behind her.

'Mum always said Gran had a quick hand.' She reached for the cleaning products and turned back around. 'Don't know that she'd get away with that kind of thing these days.'

'She swiped me up the back of the head a week before she died.' He shrugged. 'I don't think she cared much for what other people thought. It was one of the many reasons I liked her.'

Despite the thick beard that hid a good half of his face, despite the gloominess of the room, Kenna could swear she saw his cheeks pinken. A thought struck her. Out of the blue. Like a lightning bolt on a sunny day.

Did her grandmother and this hulking man have a thing going on? Were they *involved*?

It wasn't the maddest thought. Sure, he would have to be half Gran's age, at least, but that wouldn't have stopped the grandmother she'd been told tales of. And even in her late sixties, if the photo in the funeral booklet was anything to go by, she was a very handsome woman. Her small stature was made up for by sharp cheekbones and a strong nose, paired with voluptuous lips and piercing green eyes – looks Kenna had inherited, albeit with a touch more height thanks to her long-gone father. The inability to find a decent, stable man apparently being a trait of the Sanders women.

If she really put her mind to it, she could see the two of them together.

Although clearly it could only have been a physical attraction, because so far he wasn't giving off anything personality-wise that Kenna found attractive.

'Do you even have a name?' The words blurted from her mouth before she could stop them. 'Or are you hoping that by not giving me one I'm going to give up and go away?'

His lips kicked up into a smile, revealing fleshy pads of cheek that softened his overall appearance, and made him somehow even more attractive.

'You caught that, huh?'

'I'm the granddaughter of a fishing-supply store owner. I catch a lot of things. It's in my DNA,' retorted Kenna. 'So? Are you going to duck and dive the question or just tell me?' She matched his smile. 'Because I'm not going anywhere.'

'Really? You think so?' He leaned against the doorway, shoved his hands into his cargo shorts pockets and crossed one booted foot over the other. 'Well then, Kenna Sanders, let me tell you what you're in for, because it's clear your grandmother's lawyer has done nothing more than say "Congratulations, you've won a fishing-supply store".'

9

Kenna's gut twisted. Why did she have a feeling she was about to be brought down to reality with the kind of bump that would leave her unable to sit for a week?

Mr No Name lifted his clenched hand and cocked his thumb.

'The business is failing. Your gran's temperament didn't sit well with the locals. Many prefer the fishing supplies store one village over. On top of that, her health meant it became harder for her to get here early enough, and she refused to get help in. This meant . . .'

Kenna hated how he was speaking to her. Slowly. Patiently. Like one would talk to a child who refused to do as they were told. Part of her wanted to reach over and pinch his lush lips shut. Another part knew that she needed to hear the truth if she was going to make a go of things here.

His index finger rose. 'This meant that we lost the few regular customers we had. Also, the fishing charter business is barely ticking over. The tourists can't easily find us because we don't have a website – I don't know how to make one and Sonia had no interest in modern technology. And, further to that, since your gran died things have slowed down even more because I've been trying to be in two places: here and on the boat.'

Another finger lifted.

'This means we have minimal cash flow.'

Another finger.

'We can't afford new stock.'

And, finally, his little finger.

'And your gran's lack of customer service meant any words spoken about Fishful Thinking are not what you could call glowing, and I don't know if that's something that can be easily repaired with a fresh face at the counter.'

He shrugged. 'Frankly, I think people need to calm down. Sonia was a good woman. People ought to be as open as her. At least when it came to her, you knew where you stood.'

And there was that pinkening of the cheeks again.

Just what kind of relationship did they have? Colleagues by day and lovers by night? Kenna shook the thought from her head. Now was not the time to be thinking about her grandmother's sex life. Hell, there was *never* a time to think about that.

'So even if we were to try and make things work here, tourists aside, there are a fair few locals – also known as our bread and butter – who would sooner give up their nightly beer than cross the threshold of this place again.' He lowered his hand and his shoulders rose then fell in a silent sigh. 'So what I'm saying is that there's no point in sticking around. The business is failing. My thoughts are to sell the business, take what we can get, and for you to go back to wherever you came from.'

Go back? There was more of a chance of her taking a running jump off the wharf right now than there was of her heading back to Leeds and listening to her mother say 'I told you so'.

No, where there was a will there was a way. And she had all the will in the world to find a way to make this work.

'You know, I'm good with customers. I've had tons of experience working in shops. Counter work mostly, but I can stock a shelf and tidy up after myself. I've also worked as a cleaner in offices and in private homes, so getting this place in tip-top shape will be easy.'

He exhaled a long, pointed sigh. 'That's all well and good, but what experience do you have on the water? Have you fished? Do you know anything about rods and reels, or which bait or lure fish prefer?'

Kenna's heart and hopes sunk. 'Well, no. Not so much. I have vague memories of Mum taking me fishing when I was little.' *Brilliant sunlight blinding her to the blue waters. The thrill of the tug on a line. The laughter at lifting a sprat, then sending it back to where it came from.* She chose not to mention her memory of their last fishing adventure, which had ended with the reel in the drink and her mother cross with her for being so careless, knowing it would add to her new business partner's already lacklustre thoughts on her ability to help run the business. 'But I can learn. I'm a quick learner. I've picked up enough skills with all my different jobs that I reckon there's not much I can't do if I put my mind to it.'

'You've had lots of different jobs? Is that your way of saying you're going to leave me in the lurch? Get bored and take off? Because there's no point in this going any further if you're not going to stick around. Better just to put the business on the market now.'

'I'm not saying I'm going to leave you in the lurch. There's a difference between this place and all the others I worked at. This is mine, and from the sounds of it . . .' An idea began to form in her mind. 'Things are going slow, right?'

He nodded.

'So that means you have time to teach me the ropes. Or the lines. Or the reels. Or whatever it is that needs teaching.' Kenna raised her brows and forced her eyes as wide and pleadingly as she could.

'Why do I feel like you're about to start up with the "pretty pleases" and the "with sugar and cherries on top"?'

'Because maybe I am?'

His lips quirked to the side.

Triumph surged through her. This was it. She was getting through to him. He was going to say yes. She would have a proper career. A home to make her own. A life to live that wasn't dictated by loyalty to her mother, but of her own choosing.

His broad shoulders, attached to ridiculously burly arms, rose and fell once more.

She had him. Success ahoy!

'No. Can't do it.' He shook his head, turned from her and sloped back into the shop. 'I'm not pinning my hopes on someone I don't know. Who I can't trust. I've lost enough as it is to waste time on someone who will only see me lose more.'

Anger rose fast and fearsome, heating Kenna's blood. How dare he make it sound like the shop's failing was all her grandmother's fault? He could've turned things around at the shop. Could've put in the hard yards the way her grandmother apparently had to get it going. Instead he'd obviously thought his job was to simply go out on the water and be Mr Aye Aye Captain. Well he could take his pirate hat and stick it where the sea didn't sparkle.

Gritting her teeth, Kenna stormed into the shop to find him halfway out the door.

'Stop right there.' She whipped her arm out and grabbed his elbow, pulling him to a stop. 'You don't get to make the decisions just like that. This business is half mine. And I'm wholly not leaving. Whether you like it or not, I'm not going anywhere. You're stuck with me, for better or worse.'

He twisted around, glanced at her hand clasped around his elbow, then glanced back up.

'For better or worse, huh?' His lips twitched.

Great, so he was going to laugh at her. Perfect. Still, he wasn't . . . yet . . . so she may as well continue spouting her grand plan.

'So . . . My plan – whether you like it or not – is to straighten this place up. Make her look like someone cares. Then I'm going to give her a facelift. New paint on the sign outside, sand the windowsills and refinish those, then do something with the counter. Then I will find a way to bring the community back to the shop. But first?'

Kenna paused. Unsure what to do first. She wrinkled her nose as the whiff of something putrid hit her nostrils.

'First, I'm going to clean the toilet. Then I'm not just going to save this business, I'm going to make it a success. But before I do any of that . . .' She thrust her hand out towards her new business partner's hand, ready to shake it. 'I would really like to know the name of the person I'm going to be working with. So . . . Hi, I'm Kenna Sanders, your new business partner, and you are?'

14

Chapter Two

Kyran averted his eyes from his so-called newly appointed business partner, then quietly cursed as he immediately found his gaze drifting back towards her.

A man couldn't be blamed for being a touch trans-fixed. Even from his spot on the wharf, a good twenty metres away from where Kenna stood, he could see her bicep muscles flex as she attacked the grimy windows with vigour, sending her swingy yellow skirt lifting and swaying with each movement. Something that could be considered alluring – if you could tolerate the infuriating mix of perki-ness and stubbornness that came with the person wearing it.

He turned his attention back to winding a rope and sighed, long and heavy, and wished he could close his eyes, have a nap and wake up to his old reality. The one that had Sonia in it. The two of them rubbing along together, running the business as they each saw fit. Trusting each other to do what was best.

And where had that got him?

He glanced over at Fishful Thinking once more, only to see Kenna lift herself up on tiptoes as she wiped the upper area of the window, revealing a length of firm-looking thigh. If her skirt rode even an inch higher she'd be revealing a whole lot more. Not that he was interested in seeing that much of her. Or interested in her, full stop.

'She's the spit of her grandmother, is she not?'

Kyran turned to see Old Man Henry leaning up against a wharf post, his customary dead cigarette hanging out the corner of his mouth.

'She's nothing like her. Smiles too much, for one.'

'Ah, but then so did Sonia, back in the day. Life and soul of the party, she was. Would have us up dancing at the pub. Singing all sorts of songs. She was never the same after her mister took off with the barmaid. Then, after her kid took off, her frown became all but fixed to her face.' Old Man Henry shook his head. 'It was sad to see such a bright light fade. The closest to happy I ever saw her after that was when she and you were having a laugh. And, let's be honest, the way you two shared a bit of humour was more in a grunting way than a proper belly-chuckle.'

Kyran threw the perfectly coiled length of rope into his boat. 'I can't imagine that Sonia. The one I knew could crack a joke, but was full of salt and bluster. It's why I stuck around – I always knew where I stood with her.'

'Well, from the ruckus I heard as I wandered by this morning, you know where you stand with her grand-daughter too. I don't remember the last time I saw someone brave enough to take a stand against you. Most people take one look at you and run the other way.'

'Wandered by and overheard us, ay?' Kyran lifted his brows in obvious disbelief. 'We weren't that loud.'

Old Man Henry shrugged unapologetically. 'I heard fighting words. Muffled, to be fair. But thought I ought to hang around in case you needed a hand.'

'Is that so?' Kyran couldn't help but grin. Dolphin's Cove was a quiet spot and its residents were fond of the odd snippet of gossip. Some, like Old Man Henry, had the ability of a bloodhound to scent it out. 'Anyway, I've got this whole thing under control. It won't be long before I see the back of her.'

Old Man Henry snorted. 'Good luck with that. You mark my words. That young lass is going to stick around. The only people who choose to settle in these parts are the people who have nowhere else to go. You'll not be getting rid of her anytime soon.'

Kyran could almost smell the unwanted advice in the air. He held his breath and waited, knowing trying to avoid it was an impossibility.

'My advice? You go make good with that one. She's got the spunk of her grandmother. The determination too. With her help you could achieve the glory days of Fishful Thinking once again, and maybe even make enough to upgrade this decrepit excuse of a vessel.'

'"Decrepit excuse"?' Kyran shot Old Man Henry a 'how dare you look', then twisted round to look at *Fishful Thinking Too*. 'Don't listen to him, my girl. You're perfect as you are.' Kyran turned his attention back to Old Man Henry. 'You don't know what you're talking about, Henry. She runs. She's seaworthy. Most of the time. And if there's a hiccup here and there, it's nothing I can't handle myself. She does the job.'

'That she does, my lad. For the time being.' Old Man Henry pulled a lighter out of his battered old jeans' pocket and relit his cigarette, gave it a few puffs, then set a beady eye on Kyran. 'And as loyal as you are to her, one day you might have to let her go – for your own good.'

Unspoken words passed between them. The kind that spoke of years gone by, and past pain that Kyran would rather keep buried. Would prefer never to think about again. Not that it meant he didn't. Not a day went by when he didn't wonder how his life might have been different if he'd been raised by another family, in another town. If he'd not fallen in love. If he'd not had his heart broken after making the biggest mistake of his life. Broken? Shattered would be a more accurate word. Not that he could blame anyone but himself for that.

Despite knowing that Old Man Henry's advice was coming from a good place, Kyran wasn't taking a pittance of it. He was done with love. Any version of it, from familial to romantic. The joy of giving yourself over to it wasn't worth the agony of seeing it disappear, of watching it die. He shook his head and blocked the thoughts of the past from his mind, knowing going down that path wouldn't help his current mood.

'I hear what you're saying, Henry. But I think for the time being I'll stick with old *Fishful Thinking Too*, here. I don't think she'll let me down anytime soon.' Kyran shrugged, knowing if he didn't give Old Man Henry an inch he'd hang around until he forced a mile. 'Still, you've got a point about trying to make things work with Sonia's granddaughter. Sonia would have my guts for garters if I gave up on this place too easily. I'll go over and talk to her and see if we can come to some sort of agreement. Preferably one that sees her do her thing, while I do mine.'

'Good lad.' Old Man Henry nodded his head approvingly, picked up his cool box and rod and shuffled off down the wharf, his fist waving at a seagull that hovered above him, in the way gulls had when they wanted what you had, or were thinking of bombing or defecating on you.

Kyran smiled to himself as Old Man Henry waved his fist once more at the gull, then turned in the direction of the pub. There were few things you could count on in life: the tide's turning, the moon waxing and waning, and Old Man Henry heading to the pub for a pint after a spot of fishing.

What couldn't he count on? The woman who was now back inside and attempting to whisk cobwebs away with an old feather duster. Old Man Henry could say she was the spit of Sonia, inside and out, but he no more knew Kenna than anyone in these parts did.

After their conversation earlier, she struck Kyran as flighty. Quick to rush in, quick to leave. Sure, she could say she wanted to tidy up the old place, but did she have what it took to dig in? To put in the elbow grease along with the hard yards?

He shook his head as his hand found purchase in his mop of hair and gave it a frustrated tug.

There was only one way to find out.

'I see you've become acquainted with the work of our freeloading guests.' Kyran pressed his lips together, keeping back a smile, as Kenna flapped the duster in the direction of the cobwebs once more. Her face was screwed up like she thought she was going to be attacked for disturbing the homes of those that made them.

He probably ought to tell her that she could whisk the webs away every day but they'd only be reconstructed the next. Strangely enough, he'd never seen an actual spider in them. Who knew where the eight-legged scuttlers went during the day, but they always came back at night and made themselves at home once again. Perhaps they just liked knowing there was a place that was theirs no matter what. And that place wasn't their web, but the shop.

He could relate to that. Except his home hadn't been the shop, or even his beloved boat, but Sonia.

And now she was gone.

'You know, you could stand there with a smirk on your face or you could move those tree trunks you call legs and help me.'

Gone, and yet not. That was a very Sonia-like instruction Kenna had just issued. And if she really did take after the ways of her grandmother, Kyran knew it would be best to do as he was told or risk a quick hand slapping the upside of his head. Or worse, a web-filled duster pushed into his face.

Crossing the shop, he squatted down, grabbed a clean, dry rag, dunked it in the bucket of lukewarm soapy water at Kenna's side, and began wiping down the web-free parts of the window frame.

'So you were serious when you said you wanted to clean the shop up?' He waited for Kenna to cast him a soul-withering glance for questioning something she'd already said she'd do, as Sonia would have done. In Kenna's case, her look wasn't so much withering as 'well, duh'.

Given time – and possibly the life scars that Sonia had accrued – Kyran could see how Kenna's expression could one day become as harsh as Sonia's. Though he hoped it never would. The last thing he wished on another was for them to experience the pain he had, or Sonia had; for people to lose their faith and hope in others, in all that life had to offer because of the circumstances that had been dealt to them.

'I was serious. Hence why I'm battling a case of the guilts at destroying spider homes.' She rolled her eyes good-naturedly. 'I was also serious about trying to find a way to get the locals on board, which is why to distract myself from feeling guilty about being a spider-home destroyer, I've been having thoughts about how we could raise our profile in a meaningful way. Like maybe host an event. A festival of some sort. A way to garner interest in what we do here, while also bringing the village together.'

Kyran halted cleaning as he processed what Kenna had just said. How had she gone from expecting him to work with her to deciding they needed to plan an event, together?

'Are you telling me that you expect me to find time in my day-to-day schedule to help you plan an activity?'

Kenna gifted him another withering 'duh' look. 'No. I'm not that much of an idiot to think you'd want to help out after our conversation earlier. By "we" I meant the shop. The business. My side of things.' Her nose screwed up as she shook her head a little. 'So there's no need to look like you want to bite my head off.'

Kyran cursed himself for being so quick to jump to conclusions. So much for trying to make good with Kenna. 'Sorry. I'm used to dealing with Sonia. We didn't mince our words. It was one of the rules we had that helped us keep the business from completely combusting.'

Rules that also included no lies, and no prying into the other's personal affairs. The latter rule being easy to keep as neither of them ever had any, preferring to keep themselves to themselves. Then there was the biggest rule, the one Sonia had chosen to flout: no keeping anything from the other because you thought it was 'for their own good'.

His heart twisted as fresh grief washed over him. If only Sonia hadn't kept her cancer diagnosis hidden from him. If only she'd revealed it before it was too late. Maybe he could've done something. Anything. Not just sat there helplessly, watching her body give up, before saying goodbye to the second person in his life that he'd loved, then lost.

Stubborn old bat. He twisted around, dunked the rag in the bucket then wrung the excess water out. *I miss you.*

'Is that rag meant to be a metaphor for my neck?' Kenna ducked into his line of vision, a fine line marring the smooth skin between her brows. 'Are you wishing you could wring it? Get rid of me that way?'

He swiped the rag along the dust-laden sill. 'Hardly. There are far more efficient ways of disposing of people when you've got the big wide yonder lapping at your front door.'

A sharp prod struck his side.

He glanced down to see Kenna's elbow beating a retreat. 'Cheeky.'

Kyran shrugged, and tried not to think about how Kenna's grandmother had been fond of prodding him whenever he gave her stick. Tried not to think about how Old Man Henry might be right; that he and Kenna could work together. Pick up where he and Sonia left off. Make a go of things.

'Well, if anything it's good to see you know your way around a rag.' Kenna dunked her rag into the bucket and began wiping the grime off the windows, leaving long streaks in her wake. 'I wouldn't have picked it. Thought your talk about Gran not letting you clean was just that. Talk. Like you were trying to make yourself look good in front of your new business partner.' She turned to him and smiled.

'Who's being cheeky now?' Kyran returned her smile, and their eyes met, locked. His breath caught in his chest and, despite trying, it was like his body had forgotten how to function. How to inhale. Exhale.

Her green gaze had hooked him with its sparkle, its good humour, but what held him was its undercurrent of determination, of strength. A refusal to let his gruff exterior get in the way of what needed to be done.

He could get used to having those eyes around.

The thought sent prickles, hard and fast, down his spine. He broke the tense moment, and the equally uncomfortable feelings it triggered, by turning his attention back to wiping the window sill.

He was missing Sonia and their easy camaraderie. That was all. Kenna had the look of her, the eyes of her. But that didn't make her the same person.

A soft exhalation met his ears, and a touch of guilt eddied in his gut. Who was he to judge Kenna and find her wanting without a fair trial? Who knew? She could do the impossible and prove him wrong. Prove not to be as flighty as her quick steps and easily found smile suggested. Prove to be every bit as good, as solid a person as her grandmother.

She had a hard act to follow, but he ought to give her a chance to trudge down that path. Or storm down it, as Sonia had. More than that, it would be unfair of him not to give her a chance to try and save the business that had helped save him from himself.

'Is there a way that I can convince you that my being here and working with you isn't the worst idea ever?'

Kyran heard a heart of steel wrapped in a velvet voice in Kenna's tone. A quiet challenge.

One he knew he had to take up. Not for himself, but for the woman who was no longer here. If Sonia wanted Kenna to run the shop there was a reason for it, and the least he could do for the woman who'd given him so much, who'd given *him* a chance, was do the same for her granddaughter.

'We're going to have to come up with some rules. They don't have to be the same as what Sonia and I followed, but we'll need to mutually agree on them.' He soaked the rag once more, wrung it out and continued cleaning the sill.

A pointed ahem filled the space between them. 'Are you going to tell me the rules you have in that head of yours, or am I going to have to read your mind? Or figure the rules out by screwing up every little thing I do until the mysterious rules become clear? You know, like a process of elimination.'

'Do you breathe?' Kyran shook his head, both amused and bemused, and also a touch bewildered. 'You've been go-go-go from the moment you got here. First with the cleaning plans, then with this mad festival idea, and now you're diving head-first into a future you know nothing about. Couldn't know anything about since you've not set foot in this shop once in your entire life.'

'As far as you know,' Kenna muttered.

Her face remained forward, focused on the window pane, but even Kyran could see his words had an effect. Her shoulders were hitched and hunched forward, as if she was hiding something. Unwanted feelings she preferred didn't rise to the surface? Feelings that didn't bear thinking about?

He inwardly huffed at himself. No. That was his way. He was projecting his feelings onto her. Kenna was too forward, too free, too open to be touched by hurt. She was probably tired or overwhelmed, or something . . . Probably sick of him and his ways. Sonia had always said he was a bit like olives – you didn't care for them the first time you tasted them, but, over time, once you'd forced yourself to eat them often enough, you got used to them. Then, eventually, you couldn't imagine life without them.

The sill blurred before him and he blinked furiously, refusing to let emotions – sadness, grief, loneliness – overwhelm him. Refusing to let Kenna see a hole in his closely woven net.

24

'I'd know if you'd been here.' He went back to work cleaning. 'You're kind of hard to miss.'

Her shoulders straightened out, her chin lifted. 'I'll take that as a compliment.'

'Take it however you want.' He shrugged like her being noticeable was no big deal, which it wasn't. He noticed people all the time. It didn't mean he felt anything for them, or wanted to get to know them better. 'So if we are going to work together we'll need rules like promising to respect each other's boundaries. And we need to be honest. Blatantly so. Sonia had no time for sugar-coating the truth, and neither do I. If – I don't know – the till doesn't balance one day and you've stuffed up the money, tell me. If I somehow damage the boat and need to pay for repairs, I'll tell you.'

'Do you damage the boat often?' Kenna's eyes met his. 'Is this your way of preparing me for lots of expenses?'

Kyran shook his head. 'Never. Not once. She's not the youngest boat around and needs regular maintenance, but my boat is my baby and I treat her with care.'

'I get that.' Kenna's fingertips trailed along the now clean windowsill. 'This is my baby now, and I'm going to get her the best clothes, the finest food and give her the kind of disposition that will see people coming from all over to upgrade their rod, get bait for fishing, or . . . I don't know . . . buy a lifejacket or three. You might even say, I'm going to lure them in . . .' Kenna's brows waggled up and down as a grin raised her cheekbones high and showed off the finest spray of lines on each side of her eyes.

Kyran pressed the palm of his hand to his face and groaned. 'That's a terrible joke.'

'You might think so, but those surly lips of yours are lifting. You didn't completely hate it.'

He closed his eyes as he shook his head and, at the same time, dipped his rag back into the bucket.

Warm, soft skin brushed his, sending a zing of something unexpected up his arm, to his chest, where it tingled like the after-effects of an electric shock.

His eyes flew open to see the back of his hand brushing Kenna's. The air in his chest held – trapped by surprise. And terror.

Did some primal part of him, something cellular find Kenna . . . attractive?

Worse . . . Was he *attracted* to her?

I mean, sure, she was a good-looking woman. There was no denying that. All long, curling brunette hair, curvaceous hips and, er . . .

He refused to let his gaze roam her way, to linger on her other shapely areas . . .

But it was one thing to appreciate good genetics, and entirely another to feel a connection. A wanting. Yearning.

He yanked his hand out of the bucket and started furiously wiping the sides of the window frame. Yearning? Ridiculous. It was static electricity, or two magnets opposing each other, pushing each other away – through electrical means. Yeah, that was it.

And if that *wasn't* it? Then it was grief. Pure and simple. He missed Sonia. She was a huge part of his life, and now she was gone, with the only reminder of her being the dilapidated shop and the woman kneeling next to him, who was now wiping the upper areas of the window with a renewed vigour that bordered on manic.

Had she felt the frisson between them too? Was she as disturbed by the feeling as he?

Didn't matter. All he knew was that he had to finish up

in a way that appeared natural and get out of there. Get away from zips and zaps, tingles and shocks.

'Those boundaries?' Kenna tugged at his sleeve to get his attention. Her lips pursed in a way that could be called adorable or cute or endearing, but definitely wasn't in Kyran's book. 'Could they be pushed a little so that you might actually bother to tell me your name? I tried to wheedle it out of that older gentleman who spent a good amount of today hanging about, but he told me you'd tell me when the time was right. And if we're doing this, working together, I think that means the time is most definitely right.'

Her brows raised, and Kyran feared if he didn't tell her they'd never fall back in place.

'It's Kyran. Kyran Walsh.'

'Kyran.' His name rolled off her tongue slowly, like she was feeling it out. Savouring it. 'Thank you. Pleased to properly make your acquaintance, Kyran Walsh.'

For the second time that day she offered him her hand.

Despite his fear of touching her again, he met her hand out of a need to be polite, to show the manners Sonia would have expected of him. A zizz of warmth hit his skin as they shook, reminding him of their weird connection moments ago. One he wasn't interested in exploring or feeling again any time soon.

Letting go of her hand, he pushed himself up, dropped the rag in the bucket, then made a show of wiping his damp hand on his shorts.

'Well, I'd better go and check on the boat.' With a nod he opened the shop's door, stepped into the bright sunshine, inhaled the briny air, and hoped it would erase the sight of Kenna's smile, the feel of her skin against his, the way she stirred something in him he didn't want to think about, let alone feel.

He exhaled as he made his way to his boat. His safe haven. His peace of mind.

The last time he'd felt a physical connection to another he'd ended up a broken man. Then, when he'd dared allow an emotional connection with Sonia, he'd found himself back at square one. Hurt. Pained. Unwilling to feel. Blocking the flow of emotion the second it rolled over him.

Kyran wasn't sure – no, he *knew* – he didn't have it in him to try attraction, caring or love, in any form, ever again. Because while he'd been built back up once before, he knew the rubble of his heart post-Sonia could never be reconstructed again.

Chapter Three

Kenna dumped the last bucketful of dirty water into the storage room's sink, set it down on the still-to-be-mopped floor, then wiped the droplets of splashback from her face with the sleeve of her T-shirt.

'Yuck.' She grimaced, then wrinkled her nose as she caught a whiff of her overly ripe armpits. 'Mental note to self: buy a better deodorant.'

Picking up her mobile from the bench, Kenna groaned as she caught sight of the time. Her stomach gurgled in response, then cramped in an effort to remind her that she'd just spent eight solid hours cleaning without a single bite to eat.

She'd spied a small cafe a minute's walk from the shop on her way in that morning. Who knew what the food was like, but at this point she'd be happy with fish eyeball soup if it calmed the burgeoning thunderstorm in her gut.

Kenna scanned the room for a mirror, not wanting to introduce herself to the local community looking a fright. Seeing none on the walls, she ducked into the bathroom in the hopes there'd be one above the sink. There wasn't. Of course there wasn't. Her mother had said Kenna's grandmother had no time for vanity, and Kenna could hardly imagine Kyran running his fingers through his beard or swishing his length of hair this way and that, then throwing it up into a manbun before heading out to take customers fishing.

She mentally face-palmed herself as she remembered the technology that had shown her the time could also show her the state of her face.

Keying in her mobile's passcode, she brought up the camera and flicked it to selfie mode.

Oh, god. She needed more than a shower and a fresh spritz of deodorant. She needed a hair brush, her straighteners, some dry shampoo, oh and about a million litres of concealer to hide the dark circles under her eyes.

Shutting the camera down, her mobile lit up with an incoming call. Her mum.

Kenna toyed with the idea of not answering, but knew she couldn't do it. She hated the way she'd left her mother on bad terms. They'd been so close all these years, supporting each other, having each other's backs. To the point that it had sometimes felt like they were more like sisters than mother and daughter, which had only made her mother's attempt to put the hard word on her about leaving even more difficult. The sudden morphing from friend to parental figure had been jarring, causing Kenna to only dig her heels in more.

Sighing as she stabbed at the screen to answer the call, Kenna promised herself that should her mother try and persuade her to return, she'd not let it rile her. She'd hold her ground but do so without an argument erupting.

'Hi, Mum.'

'Kenna, my love. How are you? How was the trip?'

Kenna's fears that her mother would be in a combative mood ebbed away as she heard the concern in her tone. This phone call wasn't a guilt trip, it was simply a check-in.

'Good thanks, Mum. Got here fine. Bus ride was long. The B&B is nice. I'm just at work now.'

Kenna waited for her mother to ask her about the shop, about her first impression of Dolphin's Cove, but was met with a long silence, which ended in a sharp intake of breath.

'Are you sure this is what you want, Kenna? To be working in a bait shop in the middle of nowhere, where you know no one.'

Kenna went to interrupt, to tell her mother that she was worrying about nothing, but her mother rushed on before she could get a word in.

'I mean, you have friends here in Leeds. You have a job at the cafe. Your room is still here. I know you wanted me to, but I haven't rented it out. I can't even bring myself to write up an ad for it. Not when I keep expecting you to walk in through the front door.'

Kenna closed her eyes and tried to ignore the frustration growing within her. So much for her mother calling just to check in.

'My friends are more like acquaintances, Mum. You know that. A year living in a place isn't long enough to make close friends, not when I'm either working or spending time with you. And I don't have a job anymore. I gave it up to come here, remember?'

'Well, you could have it back. I'm sure I could talk to Mr Seddon. He liked you. Told me this morning you were the best worker he's had in a long time.'

'He liked that he paid me next to nothing and that I didn't mind cleaning the grease trap.' Kenna shook her head. 'And I want you to rent out my room. Who knows, whoever moves in could become a friend. Maybe something else . . .' Kenna let the sentence hang, hoping her mother would realise that her moving away was also a chance for her to start afresh too. To find new friends. Maybe even love.

31

'But of all the places to go, Kenna, you went to the one place I'd warned you off. I'm just so worried for you.'

Sadness, mixed with guilt, swirled through her, and Kenna did her best to send it away. As much as she missed her mum, as bad as she felt for leaving her, she couldn't let this chance of living life on her terms, her way, go by. Not without giving it everything she had.

'You don't have to worry about me, Mum. I have a business to run here. I have Gran's cottage to live in. Gran has given me a chance to make something of myself. It's an opportunity I can't ignore. I'd be an idiot to.'

Kenna pushed her fisted hand between her brows to stop the throbbing that had sprung up. So much for having a nice, civil conversation.

'Are you saying I'm an idiot for leaving Dolphin's Cove, Kenna? Because you know I had no choice. I've told you what your grandmother was like. She drove me to it. I did it for us, remember? It was either stay and have her dictate the rest of our lives, or leave and at least try to live.'

'And that's what I'm doing here, Mum. I'm trying to live. So, please, just let me, okay?'

A sigh met Kenna's ears. One that hinted at surrender. Kenna crossed her fingers and hoped.

'I'm not meaning to make this difficult, Kenna. I just need to know you'll be okay, and that if you're not you'll let me know so I can get you out of there.'

Kenna worried her lip, and considered putting on a brave front, but she knew her mother would see straight through it.

'Honestly, Mum, I have no idea what I'm doing. I've never run a bait shop before. I know nothing about fishing. But I'm sure I can figure it all out, and I'm hoping that by being here I can find out who I am, where I come from, and maybe even find a place where I feel like I belong.'

'Because you don't belong with me?'

Her mother's voice was taut with unshed pain. Kenna could almost hear the tears brimming in her eyes.

'I belong with you always, Mum. In spirit and in heart. But I didn't belong in Leeds. Or Gloucester. Or Manchester. Or anywhere else we've lived. Those were your dreams, your new homes. I want a chance to see if Dolphin's Cove can be mine.'

A long silence followed, and Kenna could just imagine her mother tugging at her ear the way she did whenever she was upset.

'Oh, Kenna, I wish there was a way I could make you change your mind, but I suspect it would have had as much effect as when *my* mother tried to stop me.'

'Like mother, like daughter, hey, Mum?' Kenna's stomach growled once more, reminding her she'd been about to hunt down some food.

'Unfortunately, so it would seem.'

Kenna knew her mother was no happier about the situation, but at least this time they'd avoided raised voices and hurtful words.

'Look, Mum, I have to go, but we'll talk later. I'm just a phone call away. And I promise everything here will be fine.' *It has to be, because if I don't belong here then I'm scared I won't belong anywhere.*

'Okay, my love. But please do call if you need anything. Anything at all. I'm only a few rings away.'

'Okay, Mum. Love you.'

'Love you, too.'

Hanging up, Kenna placed the mobile on the washbasin, while trying to not let the remorse she felt at leaving her mother alone overwhelm her. Two peas in a pod they'd been for so long, but the pod had begun to feel uncomfortably tight in recent years and, while she'd never admit it to her mother, she'd been wondering about finding a way to save enough money to move out of the flat they'd shared for some time.

Her grandmother would never know it, but in leaving her business and cottage to Kenna, she'd given her a lifeline. One she intended making the most of, and right now that meant finding a good place to eat.

Flipping her head upside down, Kenna released her bedraggled mop from its ponytail then twirled it round until it was in a contained topknot. Righting herself, she took a wad of toilet paper, wet it and swiped it under her offensive-smelling armpits. It wouldn't take away the stench on her shirt, but hopefully it would tone down the smell somewhat. There was nothing she could do about her shadowy under eye area, but at least being upside down for a bit would've brought colour to her cheeks and made her look a little less pummelled by lack of sleep and life in general.

Locking up the shop, she made her way to the cafe, smiling as she pushed open the doors to a jangle of bells that announced her arrival.

Kenna glanced around, taking an immediate shine to the place. It was small, simple, but homely, with net curtains hanging at the halfway mark of the window, bookended by blue and white striped curtains. Simple blonde-wooden tables, bleached by the sun and dotted with rings from the mugs of customers past, lined the walls of the cafe, with a couple of tables placed in the middle of the room. Seated around them were comfortable-looking chairs made of the same wood. Not too flashy, not run-down either – it was the kind of place where you could pull up a chair, grab a magazine or a book from the little lending library in the corner and spend an hour or two whiling away the day.

Assuming the food was good. And the coffee.

She couldn't speak for the latter, but the former had to be well worth trying if the empty state of the cabinets were anything to go by.

'Bit late in the day if you're after something to eat, sweets. But I can rustle up a hot chocolate, tea, coffee, juice, even a milkshake, if you'd like?'

Kenna turned her attention to the warm, welcoming voice. It belonged to a petite woman, who looked to be in her early thirties, wearing a cornflower-blue apron with 'Coffee, Tea and Sea' emblazoned on the front.

'There's a bit of caramel slice out the back, if you'd like? It's an off-cut, and I wouldn't usually offer it to customers, but you've the look of a local.'

Before Kenna had a chance to say yay or nay the woman turned, her brown bob swinging with the movement, and bustled into the back room.

You've the look of a local.

Happiness stole through her at the words. It was a sign that she'd been right to come here. That she was home. No more moving. No more change. No more looking for a place to call hers. Dolphin's Cove was her place. Where she belonged. The chunk of caramel slice on a simple white plate being set in front of her proved it.

'Can I recommend a good, strong pot of tea to go with this? Helps cut through the sweetness.'

'That sounds perfect, thank you.' Kenna took the plate and sat at the table by the window so she could watch the world passing by. Get a further sense of the place where she was putting down roots. This time for good.

'There you go.' The woman set the silver teapot on the table, along with a small silver jug of milk. 'I'm Marie, by the way.'

35

'Kenna. Kenna Sanders.' Kenna raised her hand and gave a flourish from head to hip. 'Hence the look of a local.'

'Ah, Sonia's granddaughter. She mentioned she had one out in the great wide yonder. How are you enjoying Dolphin's Cove?'

Kenna smiled as she poured herself a cup of tea and added a dash of milk. 'So far, so good.' *If you ignore my business partner, who is barely tolerating my presence.*

Kenna went to bite into the slice, but stopped as the doorbell jangled once more.

Speak of the devil. She forced herself to keep smiling, to not show the hurt she'd felt at Kyran all but running out the door earlier. She'd thought they'd made strides in finding common ground, but his upping and leaving to 'check on the boat' when she could've used his help cleaning had made their agreeing to work together feel like lip service.

Marie turned around, and even though her face was half hidden, Kenna could see a hint of wide smile that sent her cheekbones sky high.

'Well, look what the cat dragged in.'

'"Look what the cat dragged in?"' Kyran snorted. 'Is that how you treat your best customer?'

'Best? More like the customer I've had to put up with for far too long.'

'Oh, you're horrid to me.' His lips turned down into a frown. 'And here I thought I was your oldest friend.'

'Oldest being the important word in that sentence.' Marie grinned. 'Remind me to get you a cane for your next birthday, okay?'

'And I'll get you a motorised wheelchair,' retorted Kyran.

Envy circled forth from deep within Kenna's subconscious as she watched the two interact with such ease; the feeling taking her by surprise.

Was that what she was missing? A relationship as close as the one between Marie and Kyran? Did she want to know someone so well, for *them* to know her so well, that they felt they could tease her, joke with her, be truly comfortable with her in the way two people who'd known each other for ever could be?

'You're. An. Idiot.' Marie's index finger prodded at Kyran's chest with each word, punctuating the point.

'And you'd be lost without me.' Kyran tipped his head, a small smile showing through the bushiness of his beard. 'Anyway, admit it, I'm your best customer.'

'You're my favourite, not my best. There's a difference.' Marie straightened out her apron and tutted. 'Honestly. I don't know why I've kept you around as long as I have.'

'Because you like my face.' Kyran laughed as Marie rolled her eyes at him.

Kenna turned her attention to the caramel slice, not wanting Kyran to see how fascinated she was by his interaction with Marie. Seeing him be so fun, so easy-going . . . She'd not imagined he had it in him. Would have never guessed it based on their two encounters that day. But part of her hoped that maybe, given time, their relationship could develop into something as open and friendly as the one he shared with Marie.

Silence settled on the room, and Kenna tried not to squirm as the feeling of being watched came over her. As casually as she could, she raised her eyes to see Kyran regarding her with his deep, dark eyes that gave nothing away.

'Finished up for the day?'

Kenna nodded. 'All that cleaning made me hungry.'

Despite their casual conversation, the atmosphere thickened, tension crackled. Their stillness belying the energy

37

that ran between them, like two gunslingers circling each other, prepared at any moment to fight.

Marie backed away from the table. 'Kyran, Kenna, I can see you've met. I'll leave you two alone, hey? Just, um, play nice, okay? I don't fancy having to tidy up overturned tables and chairs, or clear up broken crockery.'

The twinkle in Kyran's eyes returned briefly as he looked in Marie's direction. The amusement disappeared as quickly as it had appeared when he refocused his attention on Kenna.

For half a second Kenna was tempted to throw the tepid contents of her cup of tea in his direction just to get a reaction out of him; anything to stop feeling like a bug under a Kyran-shaped microscope. Remembering Marie's words, although said in jest, she moved her hand away. No way was she wasting good tea on that man. Or making an enemy of a person who seemed as nice as Marie. And it probably – definitely – wasn't the best idea to further antagonise the person she was to work with.

His words back at the shop came to mind. He liked honesty, openness. That she could do.

'Did I say something back at the shop to offend you?' She sat back in her chair and forced herself not to cross her arms defensively over her chest. 'I thought by agreeing on ground rules we'd come to some sort of steady ground, calmer waters, that kind of thing, but then you left in a hurry, and I struggle to believe you suddenly needed to check on your boat. I mean, I know me being on the scene's probably a surprise to you, and I'm sorry about that, truly, but I'm in this for the long haul, which means I want us to not be second-guessing what we think of each other or what we say to each other.'

'Okay,' he nodded. 'Fair enough.'

Fair enough? That was all he was giving her? After she'd laid all her thoughts out on the table?

'So, *did* I say something back at the shop to offend you?'

'No,' Kyran shrugged. 'I just had to check the boat.'

'Truly?' Kenna clenched her fists, glad the table was hiding them. Why was he being so obtuse? Why, if he was so interested in honesty, was he not being more open?

'Absolutely.'

'You're not lying?'

Kyran didn't reply, instead fixing her with a look that had her mentally zip her lips. A look that told her he didn't appreciate being called a liar by a person who'd known him all of a few hours.

Quick footsteps saw them look up to see Marie striding out from the kitchen.

'There you go, sweets.' Marie pressed a brown paper bag into Kyran's hands. 'Cheese scone as requested.' Marie's gaze flicked between Kyran and Kenna, and her brow furrowed. 'Now off you go. You've got better things to do than hang around here and annoy my newest customer. Besides, I need to close up.'

'Close up?' Kyran indicated the clock on the wall. 'There's still nearly an hour until you shut.'

'Well, time is ticking and you'll just get crumbs everywhere and make extra work for me. I've seen how you eat. Pigs are tidier.' Marie's arms crossed and her toe tapped impatiently. Her brows rose higher with every passing second.

'Women.' Kyran rolled his eyes up towards the ceiling. 'I'll never understand them.'

Nodding his head in thanks to Marie, he meandered towards the door at a pace that only served to send Marie's sudden impatience into overdrive if the inhalation raising her chest was anything to go by.

39

Kenna glanced around the cafe. It was already spick and span. Not a speck of dust or a splodge of sauce on a table top to be seen. To her trained eye, all Marie had to do was finish clearing out the cabinet, mop the floor and she would be fine. Which begged the question: why was she so keen to get rid of Kyran when it was clear they were good friends?

Kyran swung the door open with deliberate slowness, his lips pressed into a tight smile aimed at Kenna. 'See you at work tomorrow? Six on the dot?'

'I think you mean five,' Kenna shot back, pairing her words with her own tight, overly polite smile.

Without a backward glance, Kyran left the shop, and Kenna's shoulders inched down.

'Sorry about him. He's not good with change.' Marie sank into the seat opposite Kenna. 'And I feel it's my duty to let you know that because he's not going to make life easy for you. At least not until he gets to know you.'

Kenna rubbed her fist over her forehead as weariness set in. 'I'd already guessed that. Well, the part about him not making life easy for me. I didn't know about the change bit.'

She left the sentence in the air, hoping Marie would fill in the gap.

'I'll give you some advice. If you want it, that is.'

Kenna took a sip of her tea, then set the cup back down. 'Advice would be good. I feel – no – I *know* I'm going to need it.'

Marie's finger traced a ring pattern on the table, her eyes not meeting Kenna's, giving Kenna the impression that Marie felt like she was betraying Kyran by talking to Kenna.

'Kyran's not had the easiest life, which has made him not the easiest person to get to know. But he's not a bad person. He's just . . .'

'Closed off.' Kenna nodded as understanding dawned upon her. She and Kyran were similar, but where she kept people at bay with sunlight and smiles, he preferred the stormy clouds and thundering rain approach.

'Exactly.' Marie met her gaze. 'He's not one to let people into his life unless he's known you for a good, long time, but that doesn't mean he can't be worked with. The key to getting his respect is to not back down. To give as good as you get. To prove your worth through your actions rather than your words. Take the business seriously. Don't half-arse it, and you'll be fine.'

Kenna nodded. 'Understood. And all of that is exactly what I planned to do. Is there anything else I should know?'

Marie fixed Kenna with an unflinching stare. 'Don't try to pull him out of his shell. Not if you want him to ever come out of it. And,' Marie held up her index finger, 'don't just up and leave him without warning. Out of everything you could do, that would be the worst.'

Kenna waited for Marie to elaborate, but no further words of explanation came.

'I know he comes across as difficult, but once you get to know him, once he has your trust, he's as loyal as they come. And there's a lot to be said for a loyal man.'

Kenna stared at the caramel slice. Her appetite had disappeared with the knowledge that her new life wasn't going to be as cut and dry as she'd hoped. 'Why do I feel like I've an uphill battle in front of me?'

'Because you do.' Marie reached out and patted her hand.

A small show of comfort that Kenna appreciated.

'Just be strong. Prove him wrong by showing him he's wrong.'

Feeling like Marie wouldn't judge her for doing so, Kenna let out a long sigh. 'Oh well, at least I only have to deal with him during the day. It's not like I have to live with him or anything like that.'

Marie's brows drew together, then just as quickly smoothed out. 'Right, yes. Indeed. You'll be fine, Kenna. You've got the air of Sonia about you. Perhaps even the same spark she had, and those two were thick as thieves, which means there's hope for you and Kyran yet. Just give him time.'

'Thanks, Marie. I really do appreciate you helping me figure out the lay of the Kyran land.'

'No problem. Least I can do.' With a smile, Marie stood and headed back to the kitchen.

Sitting back in her seat, Kenna took in the sparkling sea, the brilliant blue sky painted with streaks of white cloud and the gulls circling over the wharf. She'd known in coming to Dolphin's Cove she'd have a steep learning curve ahead of her with getting to know the ropes of the business, but it turned out it was more than rods and reels and bait and hooks that she had to swot up on. The village, and the people in it, had its own tides, its own undercurrents, and if she was going to last, if she was going to stay, she was going to have to learn when to go with the flow, and when to fight against it.

The one thing that wasn't going to happen? No surrender. No escape. She was all in.

For better. For worse.

For richer. For poorer.

For Gran.

For herself.

Chapter Four

Kenna struggled to understand the sight that greeted her upon arrival at her grandmother's cottage. Initially charmed by its stone wall and slate roof exterior, complete with climbing blush-pink roses that looked to be doing their best to cover every inch of the property, her delight had quickly disappeared on finding Kyran standing in the kitchen at the age-worn wooden bench, preparing a meal. In what was meant to be her home. One in which, she'd assumed, she'd be living alone.

How could a gift from the universe so quickly feel like a cosmic joke?

'So what you're saying is that you live here?' Kenna cringed inwardly at how daft she sounded. 'That you lived with Gran?'

'That I do, and that I did. We rubbed along well together. It made sense.' Kyran went back to chopping an onion.

Kenna gripped the edge of the dining table, wishing she could just as easily get a grip on this new turn of events.

'Well, that was good for you both. I'm glad she had company, but I'm here now, so . . .'

'So?' Using the side of the knife, Kyran pushed the perfectly even pieces of onion next to a pile of thinly sliced leeks, then set about mincing three cloves of garlic.

'Well . . .' Was he being so oblivious on purpose? In order to wind her up? Or had Kyran truly not realised that there was no way she would be living with him in her grandmother's house. *Her* house, she amended. 'Well now that I'm here, you'll have to move. I imagine you'll no more want to live with me than you want to work with me.'

'I won't lie, the jury is still out on how much I want to work with you. But I have a feeling you might not get much of a say in the living arrangements. There . . .' He used the tip of the knife to guide her attention towards an envelope that sat upon the small square dining table. 'That's for you.'

Reluctantly, Kenna picked up the envelope, noting her name written in her grandmother's elegant scrawl. *Kenna*, complete with a curling flourish appearing from the end of the 'a'.

'Do you already know what it says?' Kenna regretted her words the moment they were out. Could she sound any more untrusting?

'If you're asking if I opened it, I haven't. And I don't know what it says. Sonia's lawyer just asked that I made sure you got it once you arrived.' He shrugged as he sloshed oil into a frying pan then added the garlic, leeks and onions.

Kenna stared at the envelope, afraid of the possibility, or the potential, that the contents within could see her new life be as easily ripped away as it had been gifted to her.

Although, working and apparently living with a man who looked like he'd rather eat the raw onion he'd just scraped into the pan than spend time in a room with her, was hardly what she'd call a gift.

With fingers that trembled more than she'd have liked, Kenna carefully opened the envelope and pulled out a sheet of heavy cream paper. The date at the top was a few days before her grandmother had passed away but, despite

44

the timing, the strength of her character was visible in the
steadiness of her penmanship.

Leaning against the dining room table, using it for
support, Kenna took in the words before her:

Dear Kenna,

I sense my time is coming to a close.

*Do I have regrets? Only one. Not that I drove my family
from the village, but that I never drew them back in again.*

*I don't see your mother returning. Dolphin's Cove holds
too many painful memories for her. You, however, I hope,
will find a good home here. The shop is yours, as you know.
As is the cottage, which you are to share with Kyran.*

*There is an envelope in the top drawer of my duchess.
Please give it to Kyran. And be good to him. I know his
first impression isn't the best, but give him time and I know
he'll bring you the same joy he brought me.*

Take care.

Gran

Acidic, foul-tasting bile burned its way up her gullet into
her mouth. Did her grandmother have it in her head that
Kenna and Kyran would hook up? Would have a relationship too? And what was with all the women in the village
trying to tell her Kyran was a good man once you got to
know him? Was he secretly a warlock, capable of casting
adoration spells on all women who entered his sphere?
Well, good luck getting her to think he was some kind
of wonderful.

'From the look on your face I'd guess you've just received
bad news?' Kyran poured rice into the pan and began
swishing it round with a wooden spoon. 'Though it's not
like Sonia to give bad news after the fact. She was straight
up through and through.'

Kenna folded the letter and shoved it back in the envelope, wishing it was winter so she could toss it in the kitchen's hearth that would've surely been burning hot and strong. The words she'd read – and the meaning attached to them – needed to be erased from not just her mind, but the world.

'No, no. Not bad news. Just a touch . . . unexpected.'

Kyran nodded, seemingly uninterested as he sloshed white wine into the rice and onion mixture.

'There's something I've got to do though.' Kenna cringed at what was to come. 'So don't go anywhere. I'll be back in a sec.'

Kyran waved the wooden spoon in the air. 'Wasn't planning to.'

Screwing her nose up at him behind his back, Kenna spun round and raced down the hall to her grandmother's bedroom. A simple space that due to its spartan, almost masculine state, could easily been mistaken for Kyran's room, except it had that empty feel and the scent of dust and neglect that came with an unoccupied space.

Spotting the duchess – oak, stained dark brown without any fancy accoutrements gracing its top – Kenna pulled open the top drawer. Sure enough, lying upon precisely folded handkerchiefs, was the envelope. Kenna's fingers hovered over it as she considered not giving it to Kyran. Of evicting him with the excuse that she didn't need a flatmate.

Guilt sent the thought scurrying. Kyran had clearly adored Sonia, and she him. This was as much his place as it was Kenna's. More. Because he'd lived here longer. Tended to her grandmother at the end of her life. Been there when her mother had chosen not to. Which meant he had every right to read the contents of the envelope,

46

and to decide how his future, with or without Kenna in it, would look.

Scooping it up, she marched down to the kitchen and thrust it in Kyran's direction. 'Here. Gran wants you to read this.'

Kyran shook his head. 'Can't. I'm at a critical risotto-making point. Adding and stirring stock.'

Impatience raced through her. Why couldn't he just make things between them easy? Just do as she asked, for once. Make a simple request an easy one. Hell, a smile wouldn't go astray.

'You read it to me.'

And just like that, all her bluster and irritation was doused.

'You'd trust me to read a private letter?'

A short shrug followed. 'I don't have anything to hide. And I don't imagine Sonia could say anything in there that would shock me.'

We'll see about that.

Smug satisfaction made opening Kyran's envelope a much calmer experience than when she'd opened her own. He was going to freak out when he heard the news. For two reasons. One – in a few seconds he'd discover himself to be a half-owner of the cottage. Two – he'd discover he'd be sharing it with her, and that would surely if not shock him, then shake up his controlled, detached nature.

Kyran,

What? No 'my love'? No 'my everything?' Kenna was surprised by the lack of endearment. Perhaps he and her grandmother weren't the types to say sweet things to each other. Maybe their sweet things happened elsewhere.

She mentally gagged at the thought, then instantly repressed it. She wasn't going there. Wasn't imagining

Gran with Kyran, Kyran with Gran, or her with Kyran the way it sounded like her grandmother wanted her to be with him.

'You've gone all quiet. Is it that bad?' Kyran asked as he poured another ladle of stock into the mixture, followed by more efficient spoon-swishing.

'No, I'm fine. It's fine. Sorry. Frog in my throat.'

Kenna made a small performance of clearing the non-existent blockage and went back to reading the note.

You're going to hate me for this, and for that I refuse to apologise.

You have been a good friend to me for so long.

Friend? Was that it? Was that all they were? Kenna refocused on reading the words before she further alerted Kyran to her brain's meanderings.

You were the closest thing I had to family, and I shall miss you. Which is why I'm leaving you a half-share of my cottage, and the company of my granddaughter.

'She what?' 'What the hell?' The two erupted in outrage at the same time. Their gazes connected, both wide-eyed, confused and more than a touch horrified.

Kenna blinked rapidly then got back on track. There were more words to be read, and surely they couldn't have been any worse than the admission her grandmother had just made, confirming her suspicions, her fears – that she was offering her granddaughter up to a man like she was nothing more than a piece of fruit in a bowl.

If either one of you chooses to leave, you forfeit your share of the house and business to the other. It's all been arranged with my lawyer. There is no point arguing.

I trust you to communicate this part of the arrangement to Kenna. And I ask that you treat her as you would me. And live a good life. The life you always ought to have lived.

48

My best,
Sonia

'She is the most infuriating woman in the world. Even in death.' Kyran swore as he dug the wooden spoon into the pan and lifted up a spoonful of burned rice. 'And she's managed to ruin my dinner.'

'Our dinner, right?' Kenna placed the letter back in the envelope and set it down on the table. 'A half-share of the cottage means I get a half-share of dinner?'

Kyran reached into a ceramic pot that held kitchen utensils, pulled out a fish scraper and began lifting the burned patch of risotto from the pan, while scraping the unburnt parts to the side. 'Not in my experience. I'm not looking for the kind of flatmate that you share meals with. Sonia knew that. That's why we got along so well. We had our shared interests with the business, but she and I knew when to let each other be.'

'Flatmates? Just flatmates? That's all you were?'

Kyran quit scraping up the burnt bits. His mouth fell open for a split second before he recovered his unruffled, sardonic persona. 'You didn't think we were lovers, did you?'

Kenna turned her gaze to her feet, one of which was twisting back and forth as embarrassment set in. 'Well, it wouldn't be the worst, would it? Or the first time that a fabulous older woman and a . . . er . . .' She pressed her lips together seconds before 'handsome' left her mouth. 'A younger man got together. Stranger things have happened at sea.'

'Perhaps.' Kyran lifted out the last of the ruined mixture, then stirred butter and parmesan cheese into the concoction that now had a light brown hue rather than a dark-brown speckled appearance thanks to his handiwork. 'But there's nothing I've seen at sea that would be stranger than Sonia

49

and I being an item. She had no time for men.' Picking up a lemon and grater, he zested a little rind into the mix.

'But you're a man. And she had enough time for you that you owned a business together and lived together.'

Kyran snorted. 'To Sonia I was a boy. The grandchild she never got to enjoy. Or perhaps the second-chance child, since I know she had many regrets around how she raised her own.'

A fresh bout of nausea stirred in Kenna's gut. 'Oh, don't say that. That makes it sound like you could be my uncle. Or brother. Family. I don't want you to be family.'

'Well, of course not. It would make what Sonia was clearly hoping to have happen between us revolting, don't you think?'

Kyran's lips quirked into the closest thing Kenna had seen to a real smile since they'd met. For a second her heart did something springy and odd, like it had found a trampoline in her chest and decided to go for a bounce.

Shock, it was just shock. Surely.

Definitely.

She'd not thought the man could do anything other than glare or show disdain, so of course her body was going to react oddly to this new and unexpected expression.

'Quite. It would have made what certainly won't happen between us beyond wrong.'

'Well at least we both agree on that.' Picking up the pan like it weighed nothing, Kyran tipped the creamy mixture into a bowl.

An ominous rumble broke the silence that had settled upon the room. Kenna clutched her stomach and closed her eyes. As good as Kyran's meal had looked, even after being burnt on the bottom, she hadn't thought she was *that* hungry, but clearly her stomach had other ideas.

Two clanks met her ears followed by the scraping sound of wood on metal.

'Sonia didn't happen to say in your note what would happen if one of us died, perhaps of . . . I don't know . . . starvation? Would that forfeit the arrangement she's forced upon us?'

Despite hearing the tease in his tone, ire rose up in Kenna then immediately died when she saw two bowls of risotto, each with a scattering of parsley on top, placed on the table, forks next to both of them, and a chair pushed out ready and waiting for her to sit.

'I really want to say that you're the most infuriating man I've ever met, but I don't want to be rude to the person who is about to share the meal he made for himself with me.'

Kyran lifted his fork and dug it into the risotto. 'Call me infuriating if you want. It won't be the worst description that's been hurled in my direction.' His eyes closed as he took a bite. A small frown appeared between his brows. 'Needs more salt.'

Kenna forked the risotto into her mouth and let the creamy, lemony mix settle upon her taste buds for a moment. 'Tastes perfect to me.'

Amused eyes met hers, sending her heart straight to the trampoline that apparently was now permanently installed in her chest. 'What that says about your level of taste, I don't know.' Kyran reached for the salt and ground some in, then stirred it through. 'Here,' he offered her the grinder. 'Put some in. You won't regret it.'

As happy as she was with the risotto, she did as she was told, then tried it again.

'Damn it. You're right.'

Kyran's suggestion had seen the flavours transform from fine to fantastic.

'I usually am.'

Again his brow furrowed. Surely not because of the food? Because his idea of adding salt to make it better had seen the recipe burst into life. No, Kenna pondered, this latest frown was to do with something else entirely. Something he'd been wrong about. Something she knew better than to enquire after. She wasn't going to rock the boat when they'd finally managed a few minutes in each other's presence without clashing.

'So what are we going to do about Sonia's grand plan?' Kyran set his fork down and sat back in his chair. 'I mean, it sounds like we're going to have to do as she says. God, I bet she's laughing her head off, wherever it is that she is, right now.'

Kenna choked on her food. Hastily, she brought her fist to her mouth to stop rice from spraying all over the table. 'You're not saying we should make Sonia's day and hook up?'

If the look of Kyran's face, which was turning a deeper shade of purple by the second was anything to go by, it was his turn to choke.

He shook his head violently. 'No. Nothing of the sort. What I meant was . . . ground rules. We're going to need even more of them if we're going to make this living arrangement work. Rules for work. Rules for home.'

Kenna felt her own cheeks heat up at her faux pas. Of course Kyran hadn't meant they were to get involved as Sonia had hoped they would. And it wasn't like he was going to hand over his half of the house to her, just as she had no intention of doing so to him. Kyran was right – ground rules would need to be set.

'You know, I didn't see myself becoming quite so rule-bound when I moved here, but I agree. We're going to need more rules if things are going to go smoothly. Mine are simple: I don't care which way the toilet seat is – up or down, I'm not bothered – but cleanliness in that area is a must, if you get my drift.'

'Absolutely,' Kyran nodded. 'And I'm house-trained, so there's no need to worry about that. I cook. I clean. I take care of myself.'

Kenna set her fork down and sat back in the chair, flummoxed. 'Well, so am I. So what more rules do we need? I mean, as long as we tidy up after ourselves it sounds like we'll be fine.'

'What more rules do we need?' Kyran crossed his arms over his broad chest. 'How about . . . you keep out of my business. We respect each other's space. We don't talk shop at home – assuming there's still a shop to talk about. At this rate I give it a month. If that. And if you bring someone home you don't make it too obvious . . . if you catch my drift.'

Kenna couldn't believe what she was hearing. Kyran was accusing her of being a screamer? Assuming she'd be bringing men home willy-nilly? Kenna matched Kyran's stance and crossed her arms over her own chest, then cast him her most unimpressed look. 'I could say the same for you.'

'You could, but you'd be wasting your breath. Relationships don't interest me.'

'You don't need to be in a relationship to bring someone home,' Kenna shot back.

'Maybe for some.'

The verbal eye-roll in 'some' threatened to send Kenna over the edge. Kyran Walsh really was an arse of the highest order.

'My gran must have been crazy if she thought I would have any interest in you.' Kenna mentally high-fived herself for keeping her tone even, despite wanting to hiss the words in Kyran's direction.

'Or I in you.' He shrugged like it was no big deal.

How could he be so cool? So uncaring? She'd just told him he was unwantable.

'Well. Good. That makes us both very much on the same page. Rules set. No shop talk. Keep out of each other's way. No bringing randoms or screamers or grunters home, and . . .' Kenna pushed herself up, grabbed her plate, went to the bin and scraped her barely touched meal into it. 'I'll cook for myself from here on out.'

Triumph puffing up her chest, Kenna set the plate in the sink, rinsed it, then placed it in the dishwasher, shutting the door with the gentlest snip so as to appear unconcerned, unbothered, unperturbed. Then, before he could send a zinging comeback her way, Kenna left the room, head held high, hoping her confident air gave Kyran the impression he'd not riled her.

Finding herself back in her grandmother's room, Kenna sat on the edge of the bed and stared out the window, not seeing the sea sparkling in the early evening sun, the butterflies dancing over the foxgloves, nor the grass – that needed mowing – fluttering in the breeze. A wave of tiredness hit her and she lay down, tucking her knees up and hugging them to her chest.

How she wished she could call her mother and talk things through with her, but she knew her mother's answer to Kenna's problems would be to come home, to return to her, which wasn't an option. How could Kenna ever find herself if she ran back to the person who just wanted to keep her safe? Finding her own place in this world meant digging in, showing grit, and not allowing the bumps along the way to feel like mountains.

Yawning, she felt her eyes grow heavy, and, rather than fighting it – suspecting she'd have her fair share of things to go up against in the coming weeks – she allowed sleep to overtake her.

Kenna's eyes fluttered open and her heart slammed against her chest as she was met with inky shapes that she couldn't discern. Closing her eyes once more she focused on breathing in then out, centring herself.

Breathe in. You're at your grandmother's.
Breathe out. You're in her room.
Breathe in. You're on her bed.
Breathe out. The bed that is yours now.
Breathe in. What the hell is that noise?

Pushing herself up onto her elbows, Kenna reached over to where she recalled the bedside table being and felt for the lamp. Finding it, she switched it on, blinking as she adjusted to the light, then turned her attention to what sounded like the gentle strum of a guitar.

Who'd be playing music at such an hour? Everything was so dark and quiet it surely had to be after midnight? A quick check of her mobile confirmed that it had just gone quarter past one. Far too late for some quirky village troubadour to be roaming about, or even for a local band to be practising.

Determined to find its source, Kenna rolled off the bed and crept towards her closed door. Pushing her ear up against it she could swear the strumming had become a hint louder. Which meant the instrument was being played outside by their front door, or from somewhere within the house.

Kenna tried to imagine Kyran playing; his large hand caressing the neck of the guitar, broad shoulders hunched in concentration. It didn't fit, but logically it was the only answer. Taking a deep breath in, she opened the door an inch, praying it wouldn't squeak, not wanting to alert the musician to her presence. When no noise from the door came, she continued to slowly but surely open it until she could fit through the space. Creeping down the hall, she followed the music, which became more in tune, more rhythmic, more pleasant to the ears the closer she got.

A light glowed from under Kyran's door, and through it came more of the music Kenna had heard, followed by low, gentle singing, with a huskiness that stirred something deep within her.

She couldn't catch the words, but felt their meaning. It was the sound of a person lost. Of someone who was wistful for times past. Who dreamed of a happier future. Of someone who yearned to know one's place. To be accepted.

Or maybe she was just projecting.

Backing away from Kyran's door, not wanting to be caught loitering, Kenna tiptoed back to her room, shut the door and leaned against it, trying to process what she'd just heard.

She'd not expected something so beautiful to come from Kyran. She'd gone to sleep seeing him as a man with a smirk on his lips, a twinkle in his eye, and a way of turning her heart into a trampoline park. A man she had no idea how to handle, how to get around, let alone how to understand.

Now? Perhaps she was looking for hope where there was none, but it seemed to Kenna that a man who could play and sing with such passion, whose voice touched her deep inside could be a man – given time as Marie and Sonia had suggested – that she could live and work with.

And if that was true, perhaps there was a chance she could make Dolphin's Cove the one place she had always dreamed of – home.

Chapter Five

The azure-coloured sky stretched, untouched by clouds, for as far as the eye could see, with just a hint of haze shadowing the horizon where it met the water. The sun, barely up, already held warmth, and the breeze was yet to kick up. All in all, it was a perfect day for fishing. And for keeping away from his new business partner cum flatmate.

Kyran shook his head as he wandered down the hill towards the wharf. He was going to have to find a way to feel more comfortable around Kenna, to stop being on edge, but it was a hard ask; she reminded him too much of the two women he'd loved. And lost.

In Kenna he could see Sonia's determination, her stubbornness, her dig-in-and-get-it-done nature. Then there was Kenna's positivity, her earnestness, her refusal to let his behaviour push her away. It reminded him somewhat . . . too much . . . of his first girlfriend. His fiancée. Ex-fiancée.

He pushed the thought away before he could let his mind plunge into the past, to the pain and heartache he refused to acknowledge, to feel.

Even now after all these years.

As he approached the shop, he couldn't deny the impact Kenna had already had on the place. In the twenty-four hours she'd been in Dolphin's Cove, she'd whipped Fishful Thinking into the kind of shape that was two hundred per cent better than when she'd found it. The windows gleamed, without a streak or dust spot to be seen. The corners were clear of cobwebs. And the spiders hadn't dared rebuild their homes overnight. Even through the last of the early morning gloom there appeared to be a brightness, a sense of renewal, to the store that hadn't been there two days ago.

Closing his hand over the door handle, a quiet sense of approval flooded him as he pushed it down and wasn't met with a locked door. Kenna had opened on time. Perhaps even early, considering he'd not heard her get up that morning.

Stepping in, he was met with a warm, friendly-sounding 'coming'.

Seconds later, Kenna appeared in the doorway that led to the storage area.

'Oh. It's just you.' Her customer-ready smile flattened out. 'In that case I'll go back to banging my head against the wall as I try and make sense of the shop's finances.'

Kyran shook his head. 'Oh no you don't. We've a customer booked in for a charter and I need you to put ice into the cool box, then help me bring out the rods and bait.'

'No point.'

Kenna backed into the room before he could stop her, forcing him to follow her in.

'What do you mean, there's no point?' Kyran couldn't believe the one eighty he was seeing. How could a person go from full steam ahead one day to a complete halt the next? Had Kenna decided his side of the business was a waste of time? Was that what the finances she was looking at had told her? Was she setting him free to do his own thing?

And if she was, would that be so bad?

'If you've changed your mind about keeping this place afloat that's fine, but tell me now so we can get it on the market and I can figure out my next move.' Even if that next move was to do as little as possible. Fish. Read. Play his guitar in the privacy of his room, while he wallowed in the memories conjured up by the music.

Kenna looked up from the book she was now hunched over. 'As if. You're not getting rid of me that easily. The customer cancelled. Said they got a better deal on a charter the village over. Same price, better boat. I had a look at the website of the bait shop you were telling me about yesterday. Place looks great. Clean on the inside. Welcoming. Functional website, too. Easy to navigate. We've got our work cut out for us if we're going to be as good as, if not better, than them.'

Kyran slumped against the wall. Tiredness overwhelmed him, and he dragged a hand over his eyes, wishing he could wake up to find this wasn't real life but a terrible nightmare, because at least you could escape a nightmare.

Kenna's head angled to the side, her lips pursed as a line appeared between her brows. 'Are you okay? You look like you're going to throw up. Or pass out. Hopefully the former rather than the latter. A bucket I can grab, but I refuse to throw myself on the floor mattress-style in order to give you a soft landing if you collapse.'

Kyran dropped his hand and focused on Kenna. 'You're safe. On both counts.'

'So what's got you looking so grey in the face? The lack of money, my sticking around, or the fact that your future is looking more and more uncertain, more and more out of your control?'

The steel in her voice made him straighten up and pay attention.

'Because if it's the latter, you've only got yourself to blame. There's exactly one person who can change your life. Your fortune. And that's you.'

Kenna's chest rose, daring him to deny the truth in her words.

Seconds later, her chest fell with a whoosh of air. Rolling her eyes, she folded her arms over her chest and straightened up. 'Okay, to be fair, while it is only you who can change your life, it will happen with a little help from me because, like I said, I'm sticking around and I am on a mission to save our business. Which is why I've decided to put an ad on our social media pages offering 10 per cent off everything, well, what little we have, in stock.'

'Our social media pages?' Kyran mirrored Kenna by crossing his own arms and widening his stance. 'What pages? Since when do we have pages? Sonia and I agreed no pages because she hated modern technology and I've better things to do than regularly update them, like actually work.'

'I don't remember me saying anything about you managing them,' Kenna shot back. 'And they're the pages I set up in the middle of the night while you were snoring your head off. Which, while we're here talking, you know there's help for that, right? Little thingymajiggies you put on your nose that widen the nasal passages and curb all that grunty snuffling you do?'

Kyran waved her idea away. 'I don't snore, and Fishful Thinking doesn't do social media.'

'Fishful Thinking does now.' Her chin tilted in defiance.

It was like seeing a youthful version of Sonia, but where Sonia was all ragged, cynical edges, Kenna was pure passion with a ton of fervour.

Enough to make him believe they could change things around?

'Kenna, I hate to break it to you, because I can see how much you believe in yourself and your ability to make things happen, but you're barking up the wrong tree. This place can't be saved.'

'It can't be if you continue with that sad sack donkey act.' Kenna let out a puff of exasperation, then released her hold on herself. 'Look, since nothing much is happening around here – as you've been so keen to impress upon me – why don't we take the day off? Go fishing? You can show me all the ins and outs so that I can sound knowledgeable when talking to customers. And maybe, while we're fishing, we can figure some business things out. Brainstorm, even.'

Kyran brought his hands up to his forehead and massaged his temples. Kenna was incorrigible, but she was also right. If she was set on trying to fix Fishful Thinking – of making lemonade out of lemons or broth out of fish heads – then she had to know what she was talking about, and bar asking Old Man Henry for a favour, he was the only person who could help her learn the ropes. And the rods. And the reels.

'I'm taking your silence as a yes.' Kenna clapped her hands excitedly. 'I'm so excited. I've always wondered if I was the seasick type. Now I get to find out!'

His gaze followed her as she half walked, half skipped her way round the shop. Minutes later she had rods, a cool box filled with ice and bait, and a big grin directed straight at him.

Something clenched deep in his gut as she gave him a thumbs up. Another time, another place, if he were another person, he could imagine liking Kenna. Wanting to get to know her. Wanting to embrace her enthusiasm.

Now it flashed at him like a warning sign. Telling him to keep away. To stay away.

Except he was about to spend hours fishing with her. And even if he tried to run away, or swim away, he had a feeling she'd catch him.

'How do you make it look so easy getting into this thing?'

Kyran couldn't help but notice how Kenna's joy had dampened somewhat in the last few minutes as she'd attempted to ease herself onto the boat, each time jerking back onto the wharf rather than just trusting that she could get in safely. 'I mean, you're a tall, strapping oaf of a man. You'd think the way you leaped into it you'd have tipped the thing over.'

'I'd be insulted if I wasn't the type to let insults roll off my oafish shoulders.' Kyran busied himself storing the rods under the seats and placing the cool box at the front of the boat. 'You just need to get in the first time and you'll be fine every time after that.'

'Is that your way of saying you aren't going to help me? Not even give me a hand? Literally?' Kenna's lips were pursed again, making them appear plumper than they already were.

He shook his head. Pushing away the thought of how her hand would feel in his. How soft it would be. How warm. How it would trust him to care for her. To not let her slip and fall. Get hurt.

Getting hurt? Hurting others? That was one of his specialities, along with making people want to leave him, which is why it was best he kept his distance from Kenna.

Guilt threaded its way through his mind as he watched her dip her foot a little towards the boat and then back up once again. The way Kenna was going, dithering back and forth, she *would* get hurt, and it would be all his fault for letting his pride, his pain, get in the way of doing what was right.

'Here.' He reached out to her, hating that she eyed his offer so distrustfully.

'Oh, so *now* you're going to help me?'

Kyran nodded. 'It's either that or we spend the next hundred years waiting for you to get the courage up to jump in.'

'Point taken.'

Kenna took his hand, her small fingers curling over his own, gripping them so hard he wondered how long it would be before he got feeling back.

'The trick is to board near the middle and step on slowly, then, once you've got a goodly amount of your weight on the boat, step into it proper. Once you've done it enough you'll be fine. It'll be like second nature.' Kyran knew he was babbling, but the words refused to stop. As if they knew by pouring forth they were distracting him from Kenna's touch, which, once you got past the death grip, was every bit as soft and warm as he'd thought it would be. 'In fact, you'll look back on today and wonder why you were so freaked out the first time.'

With one last distrustful look, Kenna's foot left the wharf in such a way that she began to lose her balance. Before he could overthink the situation, he reached out and took her by the waist, steadying her, while trying not to feel the heat of her skin radiating through her simple grey-marl T-shirt, or the way her waist had a defined, feminine curve. Or how his little finger was touching the flare of her bare hip.

'I would ask that the ground open up and swallow me whole, but we're hardly on solid ground, are we?' Kenna let out an embarrassed chuckle, then straightened up and shuffled carefully out of Kyran's hold, delicately extracting her hand from his.

Only then did he realise he still had hold of her. That he hadn't dropped her like a hot potato the moment he could have. Should have.

'Sit down. You'll feel more safe, more secure that way.' Kyran reached for a life jacket. 'Speaking of safe and secure, put this on.'

He grabbed his own life jacket and shrugged himself into it, buckling up with the ease of a person who'd done it a thousand times before.

Glancing up, he saw Kenna fumbling with the clips as she attempted to tighten them.

Any misguided pulse of attraction disappeared. *This* was who he was stuck running a fishing business with? A woman who couldn't even put on a life jacket? He sent a silent curse heavenward and hoped Sonia caught it.

Meddling old bat.

A rogue wave hit the boat sending it rocking, above him a seagull squawked.

Kyran shook his head. It was like Sonia had heard his grumping and found a way to tell him to settle down.

He glanced at Kenna to see her inching towards the seat, face as white as a sheet, buckles still hanging loosely.

'Here.' He found himself helping her sit down. 'Now, hold onto the side if it makes you feel more comfortable.'

Without a word, she did as she was told and he set to making sure her life jacket fitted properly so it would keep her safe should the worst happen.

As he did, the soft, innocently pungent scent of freesia greeted him, surrounded him, and he marvelled at how well it mixed with the tang in the air. Salt and sweet. A perfectly Kenna scent.

'Thank you.'

The words were a whisper, and barely audible over the cries of the gull that continued to circle overhead and the lapping of waves against the boat.

'I'm sorry that I'm so terrible at all this.'

Kenna's eyes were downcast, but a hidden gaze couldn't hide the red-hot shame on her cheeks.

He hooked his finger under her chin and gently tilted it up until her eyes met his. Locked. The shadow of humiliation was there, but was soon overtaken by an intensity Kyran couldn't begin to understand.

Or didn't want to.

Chose not to.

The dilation of pupils, which enriched the quality of her dark-emerald eyes, had nothing to do with . . . with anything.

Not the way his pulse had begun to race while touching her hip. Or how his heart had gone out to her when he saw her sunny nature hide behind a cloud of embarrassment. How for a split second in his mind's eye he'd seen his hand snaking around her waist, bringing her to him as he—

'You just got pooed on.' Kenna's lips trembled as she pressed them together, her shoulders shaking with tamped down laughter. 'And if you don't deal with it now it's going to dribble onto your forehead. Might reach your mouth if you're super slow about it.'

Could hot cheeks jump ship to another person? Because his were on fire, and the colour in Kenna's had settled back down.

'Getting pooed on? Perk of the job.' He moved away, fished out a tissue from his cargo shorts pocket and did his best to clean up the mess.

'Perk? Getting free fish to eat is a perk. Being pooed on is not.'

'And that's where you're wrong. Being pooed on is considered lucky. Must mean we're going to get quite the haul today.'

Her shoulders stilled and her lips turned downwards at the corners. 'I really don't know anything, do I?'

Kenna's tone was taut, and Kyran could all but feel the self-condemnation radiating off her.

Again the urge to go to her, to touch her, to reassure her overwhelmed him. But giving into it, letting a woman close, was not an option. Not again. Never again.

He untied the boat from its mooring rings, pulled the ropes in and circled them round into a tidy loop and tucked them away, then made his way to his safe space – the stern of the boat – and sat down. If he was captaining the boat, he'd be too busy, too content doing what he loved most to think about his sudden, unwanted and absolutely inexplicable attraction to Kenna.

The roar of the outboard motor, followed by its reassuring hum as they headed out into the bay served to settle the nest of nerves that twisted and turned low in his belly. He was in control, he was in a place where nothing and no one could hurt him. Not even the woman whose pallor had begun to turn a ghostly shade.

He caught her eye. 'Breathe,' he mouthed, then mimed a deep inhalation followed by a long exhalation.

Well, that was one thing at least – if she didn't have sea legs she wasn't likely to spend any more time on the boat, which meant he wouldn't have to worry about her being in his space any more than he already had to.

His boat would be his escape. As it always had been.

Minutes passed as they bounced over the small waves rippling the water, eventually coming to a stop in an area where Kyran could usually guarantee a fish or two would be hooked.

Turning off the engine, he pulled a rod out from under the seat and handed it to Kenna. 'There you go. Good luck.'

Kenna took it tentatively as if she was afraid it might bite. 'Great, er, thanks.' She sucked her bottom lip in, then released it with a small shrug. 'Exactly what am I meant to do with this in order to enhance the chance of fishing luck?'

'Bait it. Cast it. Sit and wait.' Kyran turned to his own rod and attached a bunch of juicy-looking ragworms to its hook. With the ease that came from years of practice, he cast the line out over the water, then sat down and closed his eyes, letting the gentle rocking of the boat lull him into an almost meditative state.

'Are you seriously saying that you expect me to put those worms on a hook? Will they bite?'

Kyran forced himself to keep in the sigh of irritation that bubbled up. 'They've been known to. Just keep your fingers away from their mouths.'

A moment of quiet passed, and he hoped that meant Kenna had figured out the bait situation.

'Nope. Sorry. Can't do it. You'll have to.'

Bugger being polite. This was his time, his boat, his serenity being intruded upon.

He let out the sigh, and added an extra huff at the end.

'There's no need to be so rude. I was just asking for help.'

Kyran didn't need to look at Kenna to know he'd upset her with his brusqueness, he could hear it in her voice.

He opened his eyes to see her staring at the bait like if she took her eyes away from it, it would use the opportunity to eat her alive.

'What's rude is insisting on going somewhere and then not wanting to do what you insisted you wanted to do.'

'I wanted to learn how to fish. That means I have to be taught. You're not teaching me.'

Kenna had a point. He hated that she had a point.

'Fine. I'll show you how to do one, but then you have to do the rest yourself. You wanted to learn the business, which means you need to be able to do the business.'

'In case you ever fall ill and need me to take people out fishing on your behalf?'

Kyran didn't bother to hide his laughter, which boomed out over the bay.

'Kenna, I am not letting you take groups of people out on my boat. This boat is my everything. She's all—' He caught himself before he let the truth slip out; that *Fishful Thinking Too* was the last thing he had left in his life that he truly loved.

Which is why he wasn't going to let Kenna anywhere near it. Being a passenger was one thing. Being in charge of the last facet of his life that he truly treasured? Never going to happen.

Kenna's shoulders squared and her chin lifted. 'I understand. It's your half of the business. You get to be territorial over it.'

Kyran didn't bother to correct her. It was safer she thought that than him denying it and being forced to open up about the pain caused from being left by his mum at an early age, his father later, then Jen, and finally, Sonia.

'In that case I guess I'll just have to work on making the bait shop the best it can be, so that if anything happens to you I'll still be able to keep myself afloat.'

'Good plan.' Kyran abandoned his spot and went to sit across from Kenna. 'It's never a good idea to rely on anyone else.' Taking hold of Kenna's hook, he held it up so it was in her line of sight, then placed the bait.

'You and Gran didn't rely on each other?' Kenna screwed her nose up as he offered her the hook and gave her an encouraging nod.

68

She paused for a long moment, then gingerly picked a worm up and, with shaking fingers, placed it next to its friend. A long, revolted shudder followed.

Kyran could feel his cheeks lift as a smile arose. 'We relied on each other to pull each other up when we were being idiots. Getting in our own way. That kind of thing.'

His cheeks stretched further as he recalled the yelling matches they'd had over the dinner table.

'You can't become an old, lonely recluse. That's my job. Get that hot bum of yours out there and meet someone who deserves you.'

'Like hell I will. The day I put myself out into the human-shaped meat market will be the day you get in touch with your daughter and tell her you're sorry.'

'I'd sooner eat a bucket of bait.'

And on and on they'd gone, in rowdy circles that were unwinnable. Him refusing to put his heart on the line. Her refusing to do the same. Pride getting in the way of both of them.

Until now. Sonia's pride, her inability to seek help until it was too late, had seen her stolen away from him. Now he was free to be as alone as he liked.

Except he wasn't alone. He was stuck with Sonia's granddaughter, who was currently attempting to stand up in the boat, causing it to rock from side to side.

'So I just bring the rod back and throw it forward, right?' Her gaze, full of determination, turned towards the horizon. 'Even I can do that.'

Kyran's heart rate picked up as a vision of Kenna overbalancing and toppling into the water clouded the reality before him.

'No. Stop. If you're going to learn to fish, you need to be able to cast a line properly.'

Pushing himself up, he placed his hand over Kenna's, stopping her just as she went to throw the rod back.

Prickles of discomfort pebbled their way over his bare skin as he grew conscious of her hand under his. The intimacy, the closeness, more than he'd felt in a very long time. He took a slow breath in, so Kenna wouldn't notice, and reminded himself that this was business, not pleasure, and that he didn't do pleasure, only business.

And it would do you well to remember that, his inner voice, sharp with fear, reminded him.

'You're likely to take an eye out – yours, mine, a customer's – if you cast like that. Here . . .' He took the rod off her, expertly flicked it out, then reeled it back in. 'There you go. Simple as that. Now, you give it a try.'

Kenna took the rod back, lifted it once more and brought it back with too much force, sending the line flying backwards.

A quiet curse word filled the small space between them.

Again Kyran was reminded of Sonia, who'd been fond of swearing. Although her words had come out louder, more forceful. She'd never cared who heard, and her cheeks certainly did not flame after the swearing had flowed. If anything she'd taken quiet pride in how her words could shock or offend. Bonus points if they did both.

'I suck at this.' Kenna clucked her tongue as she turned around and began reeling in the line. 'I should just give up.'

A harsh intake of breath followed, and she turned to face him.

'Not the shop. Just the fishing. I ought to stick to my strengths. Like, people. I'm good with people. And I have ideas. And I'm not afraid of hard work.'

Her words, while heartfelt, held a dejected tone, and Kyran's heart softened. Kenna was doing her best, and it wasn't like she'd been brought up here and had fishing and the sea and the ways of the ocean in her veins, the way so many others did. People who'd held a rod from the moment they could be trusted not to drop it off the wharf, or into the water.

'Don't say that. Don't let one bad experience put you off.' His heart sank as he realised what he was going to have to do to help her. Get close. Physically so. More than he was comfortable with.

If his hand upon hers could be so disturbing, what would his arms around her feel like?

'I'm going to have to invade your physical space though. Just for a bit. Not for long. As long as you don't mind. But if you do mind . . .' He held his hands up. 'Well, then I can't teach you, and I won't be offended.'

Wouldn't be offended? More like he'd be grateful for the rejection.

A tiny smile hit Kenna's lips. 'Do what you have to do. I won't take it the wrong way. You've made it clear that you're not . . .' The colour that had only just abated flared once more. 'Er, you've made it clear that you're not a creep. One to take advantage of a situation like this.'

'Okay. Great.' Kyran cleared his throat and prepared himself for contact. 'So, uh, you've reeled the line in. Great start. Now put this hand,' he tapped her left hand, 'at the base. Then this hand,' he indicated her right hand, 'on the shaft of the rod.'

Shaft? His own cheeks heated up. Could he have found a less . . . shaft-y word? Couldn't he have said 'the length'? He squeezed his eyes together. Nope. That would've been just as bad. Was there any word in the English dictionary that wouldn't have sounded rude?

If there was, he didn't have the literacy to find it.

71

He opened his eyes to see Kenna grinning at him.

'It's just a word. I know you weren't trying to be filthy.' She winked, then turned her attention to arranging her hands on the rod. 'Like this?'

'Not bad.' He took a long, slow breath in so as to make his rising nerves less apparent. 'But a bit more like this . . .' He widened his arms, longer than necessary to silently explain what his next actions would be, then on Kenna's nod brought them around her, and placed his hands over hers once more. 'A little more grip here.' He squeezed her left hand and felt her knuckles bulge as she followed his instruction. 'Pull this hand back a touch.' He clasped her hand and tugged it downwards. 'And you're ready to cast, like this. Work with me, okay?'

Kenna nodded, and for a moment Kyran was over-whelmed with her scent once more. This time paired with the salty smell of sweat from sitting under the warm sun. An intoxicating combination. One made up of hard work, determination, the ability to roll her sleeves up and make change happen despite the odds. To never give up, even when a man came along who refused to work alongside anyone he didn't know, didn't trust. Even if they'd given him no reason to think otherwise.

'Are you hoping the wind will change and keep us in the position for an eternity or are we going to throw this line out?'

Another smile stretched his face as he caught the impatience that tinged her joke. At this rate he'd have smiled more in the last two days than he had in the last year.

'It's your facial expression that stays the same if the wind changes, not your pose. And, no, I wasn't doing that. Just waiting for you to relax a little before we took the next step.'

He cringed at his choice of words. *The next step? Really?* The only step he was looking forward to taking was the one away from her. At least, that was what he was telling himself.

'Relax a little. Take a big breath in then blow it all out.'

Kenna followed his instruction, and just like that her shoulders dipped, her body slumped, and for a brief second she was pressed against him. Her body heat radiating through his T-shirt, her softness melded against the hardness of his muscles. The upper curve of her bottom pushed against his . . .

'Oh, shit. Sorry. Sorry for swearing. And for relaxing too much. And for getting too close than is permissible in a business relationship, and, oh hell, let's just send this thing flying, shall we?'

Before he could answer, before he could collect his thoughts, his emotions, his hormones, his arms were being thrust backwards then forwards and the line was sent arching over the water before the lure fell into its surface with a small plop and splash of water.

'Great. Done. Thank you.' Still holding the rod, Kenna ducked out from his grasp and settled on one of the boat's seats, her face turned towards the length of coastline, but unable to hide the spill of embarrassment that had the back of her neck burning like she'd been out in the sun for hours without sunscreen.

Kyran took a seat, grabbed his rod, and was grateful for the blessed silence that followed as they waited for a fish to take notice of their bait. Perhaps after this experience Kenna would be over any idea of fishing and would concentrate on the shop and her newly created social media pages, leaving him to do his thing – alone.

'You know, Kyran, I think I could get used to this fishing business. We should make this a regular thing.'

So much for alone. Kyran searched for a way to let Kenna down easy, to explain that he preferred to fish by himself when he wasn't out on a charter. That being out here on the water was his time, not his and her time.

No words floated up in order to let her down, and for reasons he couldn't begin to understand, or didn't want to understand, he wasn't entirely disappointed.

Chapter Six

'I'm not asking you to come to the pub with me. I'm telling you to.' Kenna hung her tangerine-coloured cross-body bag over her shoulder and gave Kyran a look that told him declining would be an unacceptable answer. 'Besides, I'm offering free beer as a thank-you for taking me out fishing. How could you say no?'

'Just like this: no.' Kyran shrugged. 'Easiest word to say. Besides, I know the publican. He always gives me my first beer free.'

'Geez, what did you do to get that honour?'

A shadow crossed over Kyran's face, then disappeared as quickly as it had arrived. 'Nothing much. We've just known each other pretty much for ever.'

'Well in that case you have to come with me and introduce me. Not just to the owner, but to everyone. I don't want to be some loser with no friends. I'll even buy you chips if you come.' Kenna pressed her hands together and gave him her best pleading look. 'So what do you say?'

Kyran closed his eyes for a long moment, his chest falling in a long, loud huff. 'You're not going to leave me alone until I agree, are you?'

Kenna nodded vigorously. 'Exactly. Look how well you know me already. Just do as I ask every now and then and we'll get along famously.'

Pulling her keys out of her bag, she went to the door and opened it. 'After you, good sir.'

With another shake of his head, this time with a hint of a smile accompanying it, Kyran walked through the shop's door and waited while Kenna locked up.

'I used to think Sonia would be the death of me. I'm transferring that dubious honour to you.' He set off away from the wharf and followed the curve of the bay towards the other end of the village, a short walk away, where a handful of shops, B&Bs and the pub huddled together.

'I bet she had her way with you more than I, though.' Kenna face-palmed herself, letting out an 'ow' as her hand met her forehead with more of a slap than intended.

'I thought we'd already gone over that – we weren't in that kind of relationship, and even if we had been, I have no intention of having my way with you. Or you with me, I imagine.'

Hearing the dry note of humour in his tone, Kenna relaxed. He wasn't angry at her misplaced words. If anything, he'd given her a polite out, and for that she was grateful.

'Absolutely. No desire to have my way with you. Or anyone, for that matter.'

'Not anyone?'

'Not a soul. I'm an all work all the time kind of woman these days. I mean, I've dated in the past, but nothing serious. Seems to me the moment you get involved with another person it only leads to trouble.' Or angry words. Recriminations. Being left. Followed by bitterness that lasts generations. In her case, from grandmother, to mother, to daughter. Not that she was bitter when it came to men, she just wasn't in a hurry to jump into anything with a man who could cheat on her like her grandmother had experienced, or up and leave when things weren't easy-breezy, as

76

her father had done to her mother when he'd discovered she was pregnant with Kenna.

Kyran strode ahead a few paces then turned to face her, matching her pace despite not being able to see where he was going. 'So you've never been in a proper relationship?'

Kenna shrugged in a way she hoped hid her surprise at Kyran asking such a personal question. 'Haven't. I mean, it's not like I've been a nun, or a saint or, if I'm going to be blunt, celibate. I've just never met anyone I could see the point in spending the rest of my life with. And . . .' She paused for a moment and wondered if honesty might be the best policy in this instance. If anything, it would see the topic steered away. 'If you want the absolute truth, I haven't had the best role models. Gran was left by my grandad for another woman, and that turned her into a hard woman. According to Mum, anyway. And Mum was left by my father the moment he discovered he had a baby on the way. Turned out he was there for a good time, not a long time. So you see . . .' She gave another shrug. 'The way I see it, I'm better off keeping away from relationships because all I've ever seen them do is cause pain.'

Kyran stopped short. 'Kenna Sanders, that is the most ridiculous thing I have ever heard in my life. The most ridiculous reason to choose to avoid relationships. To avoid falling in love.'

Kenna didn't bother to hide the shiver of anger that spiked at being told her reasons for avoiding relationships were invalid. 'Oh, really? And who are you to say that? Cupid? The great god of Love? What would you know about avoiding relationships for a good reason?'

'I know enough that once you've loved, really loved, and truly given a relationship a chance, that when that love leaves, you have a right to not want to give love a

77

second chance. But to earn that right, you need to have shouldered the pain. As far as I can see, you've not given love a chance to hurt you, let alone scar you, so what would you know of how bad it can feel to have it ripped away? You're simply the product of a cycle. One you're not even willing to try and break.'

Kyran shook his head – in disappointment or disgust, Kenna couldn't be sure – then spun round and continued marching towards the pub, not saying another word to her the whole way, leaving her to muse over his words.

Kyran had known love. Kyran had lost love. Now Kyran lived in a world of pain that saw him refuse to entertain the idea.

And he thought *she* was caught up in a cycle? He'd entrapped himself in his heartbreak. One, it occurred to Kenna, that he dealt with through music. Releasing his pain quietly in the privacy of his room late at night.

Had Sonia known? Or was the music new? Brought on by Sonia's death? Would she hear other music in the coming nights? Or was he so stuck on love lost that he only had the one song?

The scent of hops and fat from a fryer, as well as the happy chatter of punters, distracted Kenna from her thoughts as they walked up to the pub – a simple, squat building with whitewashed walls and a thatched roof, wooden shutters at its windows, and wine barrels overflowing with brilliant-red geraniums on either side of its open doors.

Kenna hung back, waiting for Kyran to take the initiative and go in first.

He stopped short of the doors and swung his arm out. 'Ladies first.'

'I'm not a lady,' Kenna shot back as shyness overwhelmed her.

This was her first time in the pub, a place that she imagined her grandmother had frequented regularly. Being a small village the people would already know who she was, or figure it out quickly, and would expect her . . . to what? Be like Sonia? To be bold and bolshy, with a devil may care attitude? Would they automatically dislike her in expecting her to be like the woman who'd driven people away with her tartness? Or would they give her a chance before judging her?

Kyran didn't budge. 'You might not call yourself a lady, but from my point of view you are and, besides, Sonia would have my guts for garters if I didn't use my manners.' Kyran hesitated. 'Not just on you, but in general.'

'Mum never mentioned that Gran was a stickler for manners. For rules, yes, but not manners.'

'Maybe her rules made more of an impression on your mother than her requirement for manners? And can you walk in already? All this hanging around has made me thirsty.' His hand twitched as he widened his eyes, silently indicating that if she didn't move he might well push her.

Kenna mentally braced herself for the curious glances and the inevitable questions. With a deep breath and a silent *you'll be fine,* she walked through the threshold into the bustling room.

'Walsh! Is that you? Get your skinny arse over here!'

Kenna followed the voice to a man standing behind the bar. An old-fashioned dark-navy captain's hat was sitting jauntily atop his head, at odds with the casual white polo shirt he was wearing. His hands were already busy, one holding a pint glass, the other pouring golden lager into it from a tap.

She turned to Kyran. 'Skinny arse?' she mouthed.

'He thinks it's funny. Has done since pretty much for ever.'

Again the shadow darkened his features, like the past hurt him to recall, even when remembering the creation of a long-held joke.

Kenna began working her way through the tables of customers towards the bar, intent on getting something to calm her nerves. The sooner they drank and ate, the sooner she could return home. To the cottage. To safety.

It was you who wanted to go to the pub, remember? You who dragged Kyran here? Suck it up, princess.

'And who do we have here?' The publican looked her up and down, then turned his attention to Kyran, brows lifting as he awaited an explanation.

'Sonia's granddaughter. Also my new colleague and flatmate.' Kyran smoothed out the slight crinkle on the drink mat in front of him. 'Always had to have the last word, did Sonia. Get her own way. Apparently that meant making sure I couldn't be left to my own devices.'

The publican chuckled. 'Well, from my perspective she's not wrong. Beer?' He began pouring before Kyran answered. 'And for Sonia's granddaughter?'

'Call me Kenna. Sonia's granddaughter's a bit of a mouthful.' Kenna offered a smile, and hoped it would be returned.

Her nerves settled as a warm, deep chuckle rumbled from the publican's body. 'Kenna it is. And I'm Jim, owner of said pub, and once upon a time nearly this lad's father-in-law, which is why you'll hear me give him all sorts of grief. I spent years preparing to be able to do so, and although it didn't come to pass . . .'

A similar-looking cloud as to that which had crossed Kyran's face moments before, passed Jim's.

'Well, I decided after our Jen left us, and our plans didn't quite go to plan, that there was no reason I couldn't

80

still treat him like family. On the rare occasion I see him.' Jim shot Kyran a look that was almost accusing, before turning his attention back to Kenna. 'Just as I'm sure he's treating you. Sonia being the closest thing to family that Kyran here has. But I'm sure he's told you that already.'

Kenna smiled weakly as she sensed the tension rolling off Kyran. His face was a stone wall, his body taut. Ready to run? Or to lash out?

Kenna's gaze went between the two men as a conversation she wasn't privy to ricocheted between them.

If she could've heard it she was sure it would've gone along the lines of . . .

'Did you have to say that?'

'Say what?'

'You know very well what.'

'She deserves to know what she's getting into.'

'A business. That's all.'

'Is that right?'

'Damn right, that's right.'

'Well then, there's no reason for her not to know the truth, is there?'

A benign smile tipped Jim's lips upwards as his brows raised once more.

Kyran's fists, which had curled tighter as time wore on, released, and his puffed-up chest sank.

Picking up his beer, Kyran turned to Kenna. 'What Jim's trying to explain is that I was once engaged to his daughter who . . .' Kyran pressed his lips together, his face turning even stonier.

'Who drowned while out swimming,' Jim filled in, before looking up to the ceiling and smiling sadly, softly, in such a way as to send love to his lost daughter.

'Oh.' Kenna rubbed her chest, her heart aching at Kyran and Jim's admission. 'I'm so sorry, I can't imagine how hard that must have been for you.' She turned to Jim. 'For all of you.'

'Thank you for your kind words. It was hard, but we've muddled along. Time doesn't make it easier not having Jen with us, but we get by. We have each other. We're lucky like that.'

Another meaningful glance was directed at Kyran, who returned the look with a blank face that gave nothing away.

'I can see you've a few lights that need replacing. Grab them for me and I'll get it sorted after work later this week.'

Jim waved Kyran's offer away. 'Don't worry about it. It's fine.'

'It's not fine. I can just see you getting up on a table, it tipping over and you hurting yourself, and that is one thing I don't need on my conscience.' Kyran turned from Jim to Kenna, instantly dismissing any further objections. 'I'll go get us a table.'

The statement was tossed over Kyran's shoulder as he waded into the crowd in a way that gave Kenna the impression that Kyran wouldn't care whether she joined him or not. That he regretted coming with her to the pub. That he'd be happier if he was left to his own devices.

Perhaps that was the problem? He'd been left to his own devices, his own thoughts, his own sadness too long? Built a wall three times higher than he was, and ten times thicker. Wrapped his pain up in a tough hide, only surrounding himself with people who wouldn't try to penetrate it. Like her grandmother and Marie. People who could see who he was underneath it all, but wouldn't push him too hard to change. To heal. Knowing to do so would only cause him to push them away, as he apparently had done to Jim.

82

'Don't mind him, Kenna. He's never been the same since Jen left us. Still helpful, still checking in on occasion, but distant in a way he never was. I imagine Sonia's passing's left him reeling as well. I mean, she wasn't just like extended family to him. She was the closest thing he had to—'

Jim straightened up, picked up a glass and shook his head like he was annoyed at himself. Because he'd nearly revealed even more about Kyran than Kyran would've been happy with?

She drummed her fingertips on the bar, resisting the temptation to press Jim for answers, knowing to do so would put him in an awkward position. Glancing over his shoulder at the line-up of wines in the fridge, Kenna decided to let the conversation lie. If Kyran wanted to talk to her about his past, it would have to come from his lips.

'Could I please get a glass of rosé, and a basket of chips, too?'

'Of course.' Jim's smile was small, but held a silent thank-you to her for letting him off the hook. 'I'll send two baskets over. The second's on the house. I know how much Kyran can eat.'

As she waited for Jim to pour the wine, Kenna leaned on the bar and took in the people sitting at the tables laughing and chatting in the way people who'd known each other for ever did. A community. Who had each other's backs. Who stood together through thick and thin.

The idea she'd toyed with of creating a festival of some sort suddenly felt less like an idea and more like a possibility. A way to reintegrate Fishful Thinking into the community.

'Jim, does Dolphin's Cove have much in the way of summer festivals?'

Jim unscrewed the cap from the bottle and began pouring her wine. 'Summer festivals? No. Not really. We do have

83

a Christmas market, but in summer we tend to go with the flow of things. It's generally busy enough with people heading to the beach that we don't need to drum up business.'

'Oh.' Kenna's heart sank. So much for that idea.

'Why? What were you thinking?' He set the bottle down and pushed the glass – fuller than it ought to have been, Kenna noted – towards her.

Kenna swiped her debit card, glad to not be able to see Jim's face as she blurted her proposal. 'Just that a fishing festival might be fun. Maybe with food stalls, games for the kids, that sort of thing. I'm working on tidying up Fishful Thinking, making it more welcoming, so perhaps I could tie a reopening in with it, if that wouldn't appear too self-serving?'

She held her breath, waiting for Jim to let her down gently, to tell her that the village didn't need anything of the sort; that they were fine as they were.

'You know, young Kenna? I think you might be the breath of fresh air this village needs. We've been doing things the same way for years now and it's time we changed things up. I say you run with that idea and if you need any help with permits or dealing with the council, you come to me. I know people and some of them owe me a favour, and I'm not afraid of pulling those strings when I need to.'

Kenna forced her eyes up to meet Jim, who was smiling widely and nodding.

Excitement bubbled low in her gut as she realised she had an ally in Jim. That her idea could become reality. 'Thanks, Jim. I'm sure I'll be able to manage it myself, but it's good to know you're there if I – we – need you.'

'It's the least I can do for the woman who managed to drag that hermit you came in with away from his boat and into the pub.'

84

With a wink and a shoo of Jim's hand, Kenna found herself leaving the bar and searching the crowd for said hermit.

She didn't have to look long. Even sitting down he towered above the other customers' heads, even without the help of his manbun, which gave him a good inch or two's extra height. She paused for a moment and took the sight of Kyran in, feeling safe to do so as his eyes were averted, staring into the middle distance, in the way of a person who was physically in the room, but mentally far, far away.

Thinking of Jen? Of Sonia? Of all he'd lost? Of how much he hated being stuck in the situation he found himself in? Wishing he could be rid of her?

Kenna tightened her grip on her wine glass and forced herself to power forward. She couldn't blame him for resenting their situation. He didn't ask for it. He'd been happy with the status quo. It was she, more than either of them, who was getting something out of it. So the least she could do was make her being part of Kyran's life worth his while – and that meant turning around the business. And maybe even, if he let her, bringing a spark of happiness back into his life.

She slid into the seat opposite and placed her glass on the table. 'I'd say "penny for your thoughts" but I don't know that you'd want my penny, let alone give me your thoughts.' She smiled as warmly as she could and continued speaking before he could come out with a terse reply. 'So I'm going to give you mine.'

She hauled in a deep breath and prepared for the worst: for Kyran to say her festival idea was stupid. To tell her it wouldn't work. To stand up and walk away without saying a word.

'I was thinking as a way to bring people back to the wharf, to the shop, to your business, that we could hold a fishing festival. It doesn't have to be anything too grand or over the top. A simple fishing competition. Food stalls. Music. Prizegiving. That kind of thing. Perhaps tie it in with showing off a freshly renovated Fishful Thinking. All things I could do with minimal input from others. "Others" being you. But if you wanted to help that'd be great, and much appreciated. I just don't want you feeling obliged or anything like that.' She picked up her drink and took a long sip, focusing on the pretty pink liquid that, through the glass, created a blurry Kyran, whose expression she couldn't quite read, which – considering the response she expected from him – she was grateful for.

Through her rose-tinged view she watched as Kyran stroked his beard. He picked up his pint and took a sip, then set it down again.

Sensing it was safe, that he wasn't about to tell her she was being ridiculous, or that he wasn't about to storm out leaving her looking foolish, Kenna set her own drink down, then placed her hands in her lap where they immediately intertwined, so tightly they threatened to cut off the circulation to her fingers.

'I could do birdwatching tours. It wouldn't be more than just a glorified jaunt around the bay in the boat, but it'd be something to draw the families in.'

Kenna couldn't believe her ears. Kyran didn't hate the idea? Kyran might even be on board with it? More than on board; actually interested in being part of it? Helping out?

'And maybe we could use that opportunity to drum up business for your side of things? The charters? Have leaflets printed that we hand out to all those who come to the festival and take a ride on your boat?' She untangled her fingers, then immediately crossed her index and middle fingers, hoping he'd like the idea. That he wouldn't see more business as an encroachment on the alone time, the hermit life that he apparently loved so much.

Kyran nodded, slow and steady. 'I like that idea, very much. Wouldn't have come up with it myself. Nice one, Kenna.'

Her cheeks heated at his compliment and she waved it away. 'It's nothing. I worked in a cafe back when Mum and I lived in Rotherham and they were always doing little promotions like that. Free mini muffin with your coffee. Buy a full English breakfast and your pot of tea's free. That sort of thing.'

'I still wouldn't have thought of it.' Kyran's hand clasped the pint, his eyes misted over in the faraway look he'd had before. 'Music, you said? What kind were you thinking?'

Kenna shrugged. 'No idea, to be honest. I don't know the musicians in the area. Even if there are any. And if there are, I have no idea who's good.' She paused a moment to see if Kyran would bring up his abilities, but when seconds passed without mention of it, Kenna continued, not wanting to let on that she'd heard him singing in case it embarrassed or irritated Kyran to have been overheard. 'I was going to ask Jim. Figured he'd be in the know, owning a pub and all.'

'Jim would be a good start. Did he mention he could help pull any strings with the council?'

'How did you know?'

Kyran laughed. Quiet, deep rumbling, filled with amusement. 'He loves to let people know that despite not being on the council, he pretty much runs things around here. Has done since as long as I can remember.'

'He seems to like you a lot.' Kenna pressed her lips together, kicking herself for bringing up what must have been a very sensitive, if not painful, subject for Kyran. 'I mean, of course he does. What's not to like?'

She closed her eyes as Kyran laughed, a little louder, and a touch more raucously this time.

Fingers, cool and damp at the tips from where a chilled pint glass had moments ago been, touched the back of her hand.

'The woman spins the kindest lies.'

Kenna went to jerk her hand away, but thought better of it. Better to put up with the strange fizzing she felt on her skin where Kyran's fingertips had touched, than show his comment had got to her.

She opened her eyes in the most chilled-out, unbothered fashion she could. 'I'm not lying. It seems that the people of this village think a lot of you. Marie at the cafe. Jim here. Old Man Henry down at the wharf.'

'But not you?'

'Well, we didn't get off to the best start, did we?'

Kyran nodded his acceptance of the truth.

'But I'm liking you right now. Quite a bit, actually. I mean look at us.' Kenna wagged her finger between the two of them. 'We're doing this. We're going to create a festival. You haven't even pooh-poohed it or anything.'

'I don't pooh-pooh things. I'm not an eighty-year-old woman. If I don't like something, I'm more likely to tell you it's a load of bollocks and it won't work.'

'Which you've not done,' Kenna asserted.

'Because it's a good idea.' Kyran set his glass down on the table and interlaced his fingers. 'And I'm glad you came up with it. It'll be good for our business.'

Tingles of warmth radiated from Kenna's heart, and spilled through her body.

Our business.

Kyran had described the business as theirs. It was a small act of acceptance, but she was willing to take it, run with it, and use it to fuel her as she cemented her place in Dolphin's Cove.

Hope surged through her as she saw her future unfold. As she saw herself accepted.

Kyran today.

The village in the coming weeks.

Her place, her home . . . for ever.

Chapter Seven

'What was I thinking deciding to refinish the counter? Has the wharf's rotting guts fish stench gone to my head? Or the fuel from the fishing boats? Or am I simply going insane?'

Kyran tried not to laugh as Kenna flopped dramatically on top of the half-sanded counter, eyes filled with woe and the corners of her lips turned down in defeat.

'I did tell you that I could find an electric sander if you really wanted one. You didn't have to decide that the sandpaper you found in the garden shed was all that was needed.'

Kenna wrinkled her nose at him and offered him a very Sonia-like scowl.

'I'll take that look to mean I'm right.'

Kenna straightened up and began sanding again with renewed vigour. 'Doing it by hand made sense at the time. I wanted to get started and didn't want to wait for you to faff around finding a sander. Time is of the essence if we're to pull this place together and organise a festival in a few weeks.'

Kyran set down the paint scraper he was using to remove the flaky paint from Fishful Thinking's outdoor sign. 'Speaking of. Have you reached out to anyone on the council yet? Who knows what permits we'll need, and, as much as I'd like to take Jim up on his idea to help us out, I think it's for the best that we do this ourselves. Who knows what information Jim has on those in council, and I don't like the idea of him blackmailing them into making this happen. Small villages have long memories and all that. Last thing we want is to get a bad name with the powers-that-be.'

Kenna's sanding slowed once more and the bloom of colour in her cheeks disappeared. 'Of course. I'm an idiot. I should be calling them and getting all that sorted, finding the right people to talk to, or figuring out what kind of permits or insurance or whatever it is we need, finding out if there's a fee to hold a festival. The last thing I ought to be doing is wasting my time sanding a counter that was working perfectly fine as a counter and could've gone un-sanded for some time yet.'

'Kenna.' Kyran, seeing that Kenna was about to implode due to stress, reached out and closed his hand over hers, keeping his focus on her face in the hope of not noticing any tingles or zips or zaps as skin-on-skin contact was made. 'I need you to breathe.'

'Okay.'

The word came out high and tight, like she could barely get the air he'd asked her to find.

'Tea?' He removed his hand and headed for the back-room, not needing to see her answer to know that tea was necessary. 'How do you take it?'

'Strong with a dash of milk.'

Kyran turned on the tap and let the water run into the kettle, before setting it back down on the bench and flicking the switch.

'Thank you.'

He looked over his shoulder to see Kenna hovering about the door, the colour in her cheeks starting to return.

'I freaked out for a second there, didn't I? I'm sorry. It's not something I usually do. Usually I know what I'm

91

doing, how I'm doing it, and nothing ruffles my feathers. The joys of working in cleaning crews and cafes, dealing with people my whole working life. Get in, keep your head down, work together to get everything done without mishap.'

'So what's changed?' Kyran grabbed two mugs from the cupboard under the sink, then took two teabags from the tin and dropped them in the mugs.

'I . . .' Kenna folded her arms over her chest, and hooked one leg over the other. 'I don't want to muck this up. This place feels like home and I want to do right by the people here.'

Kyran poured the boiled water into the mugs, then turned around and leaned against the bench. 'You make it sound like you expect to be chased out of here by torch-toting villagers if the festival flops?'

Kenna shrugged. 'Mum and I moved a lot, especially when I was younger. She called each new town or city "home", but it never felt much like it, and now that I'm back in my actual home – the place I was born – I want it to go well.'

'I can understand that.' Despite her openness, Kyran had a feeling he was missing something, like Kenna wasn't quite laying out all the cards on the table. 'Can I ask what stopped you from coming before now? You're an adult. You can make your own decisions.'

Kenna shook her head as she exhaled. 'Loyalty. Pure and simple. Possibly also fear. Mum didn't hold back about her opinion of Gran, and I was raised believing that if I came here I'd be found wanting. And it's not like I've ever done much with my life. Sure, I work hard, I'm reliable, but I'm not exactly someone you'd call amazing. I sure as heck didn't do what Gran did and raise a child on my own while working before opening up my own business back in a time when it was unheard of to do such things. I guess part of me was afraid she'd meet me and be disappointed with who I was or, more to the point, who I wasn't.'

'I see where you're coming from. And I can see why you came back when you did. It was the first time in your life that you felt you could.' Kyran took a teaspoon and began stirring the teabag round and pressing it against the sides of the mug to get the most flavour out of it. Grateful for an excuse not to look into the face of a woman who at that moment couldn't hide her vulnerability. So much so that even if she were to smile in order to try and hide her insecurities, it would still radiate off her. 'I guess I was lucky to live in the same town. Through thick and thin.'

'And it sounds like you had your fair share of both.'

Kyran shrugged in an attempt to make light of Kenna's words as he added milk to their tea. 'Yeah, well. Such is life. I aim for a nice steady average ordinary existence as much as I can these days. Here you go.' He passed the mug to Kenna. 'Shall we sit outside and take a break?'

Kenna took the tea with a wry smile. 'I think that's a great idea. If I look at that counter anytime soon, let alone the rest of the work the shop needs, I might really lose my head.'

'And we couldn't have that. That head is needed to talk to customers, the council and vendors.'

Picking up his mug, Kyran led them out to the front of Fishful Thinking, settled himself onto the ground, leaned against the wall and tipped his head to the sun, closing his eyes. 'Look, I know it's not my place to say this because I don't know the life your mother lived here, and I don't know who Sonia was back then, but I want you to know that she treated me well.'

Kyran kept his eyes closed, allowing the sun to fuel him, to give him the strength to do right by Sonia, even if it meant opening up in a way that felt uncomfortable.

'My dad took off when I was sixteen and left me to fend for myself.'

He caught a hitch in Kenna's breath, and knew the idea of a parent walking out on their child was shocking to her, a person who'd been close to her mother her whole life. Who'd known security and love.

'Turns out I wasn't great at being on my own back then, and Sonia noticed.' Kyran smiled as he remembered the day she'd turned up on his doorstep, taken him by the sleeve of his shirt, marched him to hers, then sat him down in front of a roast meal and told him if he liked what he ate he could stay. 'She insisted I come live with her. Even if I'd said no I don't think she'd have accepted that as the answer. She kept me in clothes and food, made sure I went to school, and never asked for a thing.'

'Not ever?'

Kyran shook his head. 'Never. So I started to work at Fishful Thinking as much as I could as a way of giving back to her, and then after Je—' And just like that, a lump appeared in his throat as it always did. Even after six years of not having Jen in his life, the sadness was still deep enough to cause him to choke up.

A gentle touch, one that showed caring and under-standing, fell upon his bare forearm. One he accepted, and was thankful for.

'Sonia helped you through your pain.' Kenna's tone was full of understanding.

Kyran nodded, unable to open his eyes, refusing to let Kenna see his hurt, even though he knew she felt it. 'Exactly. Then, after seeing how much time I was spending

94

out on the boat, Sonia came up with the idea for us to start the charter business. Her sneaky way to stop me from going too inwards.'

'She was a smart woman.'

The hand fell away, and part of Kyran missed it. Missed the weight of it that helped to ease the weight on his heart. Missed the heat of it against his skin, that warmed him more than the sun ever could.

'She was. And she had a big heart, even if she didn't always show it.'

Kyran swallowed, opened his eyes and made himself take a sip of tea, the action of doing something so normal bringing him back to the here and now. Nowhere near as comforting as Kenna's touch, but certainly safer.

'Thanks for opening up about you and Gran, Kyran. I know it can't have been easy.'

Kenna's voice was filled with compassion, but Kyran couldn't bring himself to look at her, afraid that if he saw pity in her eyes he'd get up, walk away and never come back, losing what little he had left in the world.

'I'll always wish I'd had a chance to get to know Gran, but knowing that she wasn't as bad as my mother believed her to be, experienced her to be, makes me feel like I know her a little better. And it only makes me want to get this place shipshape even more. Not just because I want to have a life here, but because I owe it to her. In leaving me my share of Fishful Thinking and the cottage, she gave me a lifeline, just as she gave you one all those years ago, and I'll not repay her by seeing all she worked for fail.'

Admiration stirred within Kyran as he turned to Kenna and saw her jawline tighten with determination as she nodded so slightly it was almost imperceptible. Like she'd made a promise to herself that failure was not an option.

Perhaps Old Man Henry had been right. There was more Sonia in Kenna than either of them knew.

'What?' Kenna wiped either side of her face, then brushed at her upper lip. 'Do I have a tea moustache?'

Kyran quickly shook his head and brought his mug up to his mouth to take a swallow, hoping its rim would hide the flush of heat hitting his cheeks at being caught so openly admiring Kenna.

'Oh good, because there's nothing quite so sexy as a woman with a glistening tea moustache.'

He chuckled at her dry remark, then dared glance her way once more only to catch Kenna looking at him, her eyes glittering with amusement, before she too looked away.

Their actions, their reactions, reminded him of two dogs circling, checking each other out, trying to figure out where they stood with each other.

Or like two people curious about each other. Liking what they see. Wanting to get to know each other better.

Kyran rolled his eyes at the teasing tone of his inner voice. It had been a long time since he'd been involved with another, but he was pretty sure that attraction didn't start with two people sniping at each other and having to make an effort to get along.

Not that he felt all that irritated with Kenna right now. If anything, he felt almost comfortable. Too comfortable?

Their gazes met once more, locking like magnets, and Kyran no longer heard the lapping of water against the wharf's poles, the sound of children playing down on the beach, or the cry of the gull that hovered above them like it was invested in their future. All he saw was Kenna. Her eyes filling with fire, a tendril of hair that had come free from her ponytail emphasising the curve of her cheek, her plump lips parting ever so slightly, and for a moment

96

he wanted all he saw. Her fire. Her sweetness. Her belief that everything would be okay so long as one didn't give up, hide or run.

He wanted *her*.

The realisation hit him hard in the gut, sending an emotional earthquake through him.

Wanting Kenna, wanting to be with Kenna, wasn't just a bad idea — it was the worst.

It was a path that led to no good. To heartache. To pain. A path he'd trodden down too many times. One he knew he didn't have the energy or the spirit to go down again.

Forcing himself to look away, Kyran did the only thing he could to keep himself safe. Pushing himself up, mug in hand, he headed inside, not once glancing at Kenna as he walked past her, terrified if he looked into her face, full of heart and hope, he'd fall victim to the burgeoning feelings he was determined to avoid.

Chapter Eight

Smoothing out the skirt of her dress, ensuring it was wrinkle-free and therefore giving her a respectable, business-like air, Kenna held out her hand, ready to greet the local councillor who'd kindly agreed to meet her so that they could go through what she needed to do in order to make the festival happen.

'Hi there, I'm Kenna Sanders. You must be Martin.'

'That I am. It's an absolute pleasure to meet you, my dear. An absolute pleasure. It's always nice to meet new blood.'

Kenna smiled, uncomfortable with the look Martin was giving her, like she was a juicy worm on a hook and he was a hungry fish.

'A pleasure to meet you, too, Martin. Shall we?' Waving him into Fishful Thinking, she glanced up at the clock and tried not to grind her teeth.

Kyran had promised he'd meet her at the shop five minutes before they were due to meet the councillor, but he was nowhere to be seen, and right now Kenna couldn't help but think his presence would be an asset. Not only because he was a local, but because Martin was having trouble keeping his eyes on her face, his gaze dropping in the direction of her chest every few seconds, and having a big, burly, scary-looking fisherman at her side would have made her feel less juicy worm-like.

'Can I make you a coffee, Martin?'

'No, thank you. No coffee needed. Despite my age, I think you'll find I've loads of energy. Positively brimming with it.'

Martin's gaze ran the length of her body in a way that confirmed Kenna's suspicions that he'd like to expend some of that energy on her.

Despite the prickles of disgust peppering her skin, she managed to keep her smile in place. Antagonising the man who held the key to ensuring her success would not do, but she didn't want to give him the impression that she was in any way interested in getting energetic with him, either.

'If not coffee, can I get you a glass of water? Something refreshing to enjoy while we wait for my business partner, who I'm sure is not far away . . .' She crossed her fingers behind her back, and prayed her lie would turn out to be the truth.

'No, let's just get things underway, shall we? No need to have outside interference.'

Outside interference? Kenna thought to remind Martin that her business partner was very much not outside interference, but kept her lips zipped shut.

'That's fine. Let's get down to business then, shall we?'

'Sounds great to me.' Martin winked.

Trying not to grimace, Kenna made her way around to the other side of the counter, deciding keeping distance between the two of them would be safest.

'So you've seen the outline of the event that Kyran and I put together. We're not trying to do anything too out of the box. We'd like to set up a small stage for entertainment, have food trucks come in and Jim's keen to have a drinks stall. Marie, the local cafe owner, would like to sell her famous pasties as well as other sweet treats. Other than that we'll be holding a fishing competition, offering

99

boat trips around the bay, and I plan to see if the school will put together some fun games for the kids to keep them entertained. All we need is the go-ahead from you.'

Under the counter she pushed her hands together in silent prayer, hoping with everything she had that Martin would see no reason to say no.

'I'd like to say yes, Kenna, I really would, but there's a problem that you've clearly not thought of. The problem is, you want to hold the festival on council land and for us to say yes to that we need at least three months' notice. Not only that, but you need to provide information including a risk assessment, how you'll deal with the toilet situation, the size of the crowd expected, first aid, insurance, traffic management . . . Need I go on?'

'Oh.' Kenna didn't bother to hide her disappointment. 'I didn't think of that. I mean, I knew we'd have to organise things like extra toilets and have someone on hand to do first aid, but I didn't think about traffic control or . . .'

'The fact that you're wanting to host this festival in just over two weeks' time when we ask for three months' notice?'

'Yes. That.' Kenna began gnawing at her thumbnail, wondering how she was going to let Kyran know how much of a mistake she'd made. How she'd wasted his time getting him to help her fix up the shop for a re-opening that would likely flop without a good reason for the locals to descend on the wharf. 'I guess I wasted your time coming here. I'm so sorry.'

'Talking to a constituent is never a waste of time. Especially one as lovely as you.'

Kenna managed to put a fresh smile on her face, while secretly wishing she could whop the lascivious git on the head for being so inappropriate.

'You know, Kenna,' Martin stroked his chin thoughtfully, 'I'm sure you and I could come to some kind of arrangement, if you're that desperate to hold the festival sooner rather than later. I'm sure I could, I don't know, backdate some papers? Scratch your back if you scratch mine?'

Sweat beaded the nape of Kenna's neck as nausea flooded her. There was no way she was scratching anybody's back, let alone a man who was old enough to be her father – who could well be her father for all she knew since she'd never met the man.

'Oh, that's kind of you, Martin, but I don't know that we need to be scratching backs to make this happen. There's always next year.' *Assuming the business manages to limp along until then.*

Martin began to round the counter, and Kenna followed suit. Taking a step backwards every time he took a step forwards, keeping him at a safe distance.

'I don't know, Kenna. You want something, quite a lot by the looks of it, and I'd love to help make it happen.'

Kenna spotted the rods lined up along the opposite end of the shop. Was there a chance she could duck around Martin, grab one and use it to fend him off should things come to that?

Backing away from him, plan in place, gratitude washed over her as, behind her, the doorbell jangled and – seconds later – Kyran was at her side.

'Sorry I'm late. Had to help Jim with those lights I saw were out at the pub the other night. Figured now seemed as good a time as any.'

The way his chest was heaving, Kenna could've sworn Kyran must've run over from the pub, but there wasn't a speckle of sweat to be seen on his forehead, and his composure suggested that he'd enjoyed a gentle stroll to the shop.

'Jim sends his regards, by the way, Martin. Says to say hello to your wife, too.'

Martin shoved his hands in his pockets, his expression turning sheepish. 'Er, that's great. When you next see Jim send him my regards as well.'

'Will do.' Kyran leaned against the counter. 'So what have I missed?'

An ache gripped the pit of Kenna's stomach as she summoned the words to tell Kyran the festival was dead in the water.

'Er, Martin was just saying that we needed to give three months' notice for the festival, and that because we didn't, we aren't able to hold it.'

'Oh, is that right?' Kyran's brows drew together briefly, then were replaced with a small smile. One that suggested Kyran knew something that neither Kenna nor Martin knew.

Was it something Jim had mentioned? Was he about to unload some information with which to blackmail Martin into turning a blind eye to their event?

The pain in Kenna's stomach intensified at the thought. As much as she wanted and needed the festival to happen, she and Kyran had both agreed blackmail was out of the question. Even if she'd already decided the man in front of her was a complete lech and needed to be pulled down a peg or seven thousand.

'Three months' notice, you say?' Kyran stroked his beard. 'But the wharf is private land, which means that we need to have the application in with ten working days to spare as it's classed as a temporary event.'

'Private land?'

The words came out of Kenna and Martin's mouths simultaneously, the two turning to each other. Martin with a look of dismay. Kenna returning his look with a smile that smacked of the hint of triumph she'd seen on Kyran's face moments before.

'Henry owns the wharf. All this land is his. I'd have thought, being our local councillor, that you'd have known that, Martin? Or, at the very least, done your due diligence before attending this meeting?'

Kyran's eyes glinted as he looked at Martin, and Kenna had the feeling there was more that he knew. Words that he didn't want to say but wanted to ensure were communicated man-to-man.

Martin reached into his trouser pocket, pulled out a brown and white plaid handkerchief and wiped it over his forehead, which had begun to gleam after Kyran's revelation.

'I must've missed that. My ward is rather large. These things happen. Possibly got it mixed up with the wharf the village over.'

'Possibly.' Kyran's tone was unbothered. That of a man who'd done his job in relaying the information Jim had given him.

'So what happens now?' Kenna turned a sweet smile on Martin. 'Can I go ahead and apply for the temporary event to happen?'

'Er, yes. Of course.' Martin shoved his handkerchief back in its pocket. 'Fill out the forms, submit them online along with the fee, and we'll take it from there.'

'And by "take it from there" I take it to mean you'll oversee the process to ensure nothing goes wrong?' Kenna fixed him with a determined look, one that she hoped echoed Kyran's vibe, that they were not to be messed with.

'Absolutely.' Martin strode to the door.

'Wonderful.' Kenna clapped her hands together. 'Thank you so much, Martin. Hugely appreciate all your help. Tell your wife we say hi and that we think you're doing a brilliant job.'

Kenna held back a laugh as Martin's face began to look distinctly pale. 'Yes, yes, I will. Well, good luck with the festival. Nice to see someone breathing life into the place.' With a nod, Martin was gone in a jangle of bells.

Joy swamped every cell in Kenna's body. It was happening. The festival wasn't over before it began. It was full steam ahead from here on in. All because of the man beside her.

Wrapping her arms around herself, half afraid she'd embarrass them both by throwing herself at Kyran in the kind of way that would involve hugs and kisses on both cheeks, and was in no way appropriate to do with a man you shared a business with, Kenna settled for bouncing up and down with excitement.

'How did you do that? You're a life saver. An event saver. I owe you all the beers in the world.'

'You owe me nothing.' Kyran shrugged off Kenna's gratitude, though his face brightened at her words. 'I simply popped into Jim's to sort out the broken lights, had a chat with him about the festival and told him that we were going to be talking to Martin, and Jim filled me in with some information that he thought we might need to know.'

'I thought we weren't going to blackmail him?' Kenna ceased bouncing and leaned against the counter, gripping its edge in case a fresh wave of happiness saw her wanting to lunge at Kyran and bring him in for a hug once more.

'We didn't. Sure, Jim let me know that Martin has a roving eye and that he'd once made the drunken mistake of trying to hit on Jim's wife, but we didn't say that, did we? We used facts about the wharf to get what we wanted. I just had the blackmail in my pocket as an absolute last-minute defence.'

'Ah, I see.' Kenna's respect for Kyran grew. He could've gone down the dirty route, ensuring Martin made the rest of their life simple when it came to anything council-related, but instead he'd chosen to take the higher ground. 'That explains why you and that slimy pillock had that feeling-filled but wordless conversation with your eyes.'

'Exactly. A man who likes power also likes to avoid marital strife. But I didn't want to put it out there that I knew his repulsive ways quite so obviously. Better he just assumes I know.'

'Indeed.' Kenna tried not to let the niggling irritation she felt that Kyran had kept the ownership of the wharf secret from her until now show. 'One more question. Why didn't you tell me that Old Man Henry owns the wharf? As far as I can see, it's kind of important information.'

Kyran ran his finger along the now fully sanded counter that was just needing Kenna to re-varnish it. 'I didn't tell you because I didn't know until today. I guess Jim knew I wasn't going to be comfortable airing Martin's dirty washing, so he let me in on that piece of information, even though I know he'd have felt bad doing so since Jim and Old Man Henry have known each other for ever.'

'Jim's a good man.' Kenna glanced outside just as Old Man Henry shuffled past, cigarette hanging out his mouth, rod in hand. 'And Old Man Henry is a sly old sea dog.'

'Sly and shy. According to Jim, he doesn't like people to know he owns the wharf or the buildings that he leases out, so he lets people think it's council land and just quietly keeps things ticking over. Even has a stipulation on the lease that the business owners say nothing about the owner. We could ask Marie who owns her place and she'd lie to our faces.'

Kenna pondered Kyran's words. 'What about this place? It's on wharf land, isn't it? How do we own it outright?'

Kyran shrugged. 'I didn't have time to ask. My guess from the way Old Man Henry talks about Sonia is that he had a sweet spot for her and that when the last owner left and she showed interest in taking it over, he offered it to her for sale, or she talked him into letting her buy it. I guess that's something we'll never know.'

'I guess you're right. Either way, it sounds like I owe Old Man Henry all the beers in the world, too.'

'Not that you can let on that you know.' Kyran wagged his finger. 'He'd be most put out if his secret got out.'

Kenna mimed zipping her lips. 'His secret's safe with me. And now that his secret has brought us a stroke of luck, we need to officially announce the festival.'

'What are you going to do? Walk about announcing it through some megaphone you've got stashed away?'

Kenna laughed, enjoying seeing the lighter side of Kyran. 'Come with me. I've something to show you.'

Taking Kyran's wrist in her hand, she dragged him to the back room, pulled her laptop out from her bag and fired up the social media site where she had the festival page ready to go live.

Clicking her fingers with impatience as she waited for the page to load, she turned to Kyran, curious as to the state of his arrival at the shop moments before, which still struck her as odd.

'Kyran, this might seem like an odd question, but did you run here from Jim's?'

A lopsided grin appeared on his face, and Kenna had to look back at the screen as her heart had a fresh attack of the bouncy trampolines.

'It was that obvious? After what Jim told me about Martin being a womaniser, I was worried you'd be eaten alive by the man. Probably amused half the village with my disjointed half-run half-walk getting here. Seems I had nothing to worry about though. You were fine when I got here, and you certainly held your own once you had the information you needed. I was impressed.'

Kenna tried not to squirm under Kyran's approving gaze, but knew she'd failed the moment her cheeks flared hot.

'*We* did well.' Twisting the screen to face Kyran, she held her breath as she prepared to make their plan a reality. 'So, now that we know we can do this, would you like to make it official?'

'I would be honoured.'

Kenna backed away, the glow of Kyran's approval becoming one of pleasure as she saw his cheeks rise high, matching the width of his smile. One she found herself enjoying more and more. One she'd hate to never see again. Another reason to make the festival a success, and to ensure the longevity of their business.

Happy at seeing him happy, she bumped her hip up against this.

'We're doing this.'

He bumped her hip back. 'We are.'

'No regrets?'

Kyran hit the button, making the social media page live for all to see. 'Only that you didn't come here sooner.'

Chapter Nine

'Kyran, how many fish are going to die during this festival? Are we going to be responsible for the overfishing of the area? Will this festival make the future generations of Dolphin's Cove hate us because when they go to fish there'll be nothing left for them to catch?'

Kyran shook his head as he applied a coat of white paint to the windowsill. The closer the festival got, the more nervous Kenna became; worries and questions and what-ifs spilling out whenever she had a moment to breathe. And no matter how many times he reassured her that everything would be okay, she still found more worries to voice. At least this latest concern he could easily deal with.

'Would you be happier if we were to do a catch and release competition using barbless hooks? Rather than weighing and measuring the fish, the person who catches a fish gets a ticket and then goes in the draw to win prizes? The more fish you catch and release, the more chances to win?'

'Can we do that? Is that a possibility? It's not too late to change the rules?'

'It's our festival, is it not? The rules are up to us, and if you don't want to see any fish harmed then there'll be no fish lost on my watch.'

'On your watch? You'll be gallivanting about the bay showing people the sights. Who'll be helping those who don't know how to release a fish? Old Man Henry?'

Twisting round, Kyran took in Kenna squatted down in front of the sign, eyes narrowed in concentration as she made an outline of a fish in turquoise blue. How she managed to concentrate and rattle out words at the rate she did, he didn't know, but it was another thing to add to the list of reasons he was beginning to like Kenna.

A list that was starting to feel dangerously long for a man who was determined to never let a woman under his skin ever again.

'Old Man Henry scares kids. It'll have to be you.'

'If it's me then who'll man the shop?' Kenna paused her painting. 'We can't just leave it open for people to come and go as they please.'

She had a point. But having Kenna out and about helping the locals would ensure they felt more comfortable coming into the shop in the future. With her warm smile and easy-going nature she was a million miles away from the snarls and sarcastic remarks of Sonia.

'That is true, but if you help with the fishing competition, it'll be a great way for people to get to know you.'

'That still doesn't solve the problem of who'll look after the shop. Also, I don't know how to do this whole catch and release thing. I'll end up killing more fish than I'll save.'

Kyran set his own paintbrush down on the tray he'd poured the white paint into. 'Is this the part where you decide you don't want to do the festival? That you've decided against it? Because all I'm hearing right now is excuses and all I'm seeing are roadblocks.'

'No . . . I'm just . . .' Kenna's head fell and she pressed the palms of her hands into her eyes. 'I'm just getting nervous. I want so badly for this to go right. To work for us.'

Kyran marvelled at how easy it was for Kenna to expose her true thoughts. To not be defensive and afraid of opening up. His heart ached at seeing her so unsure of herself, and part of him wanted to scoop her up and hold her tight. To tell her that everything would be okay and the festival would be a success, but the other part of him, the part that was guarded and controlled, demanded he keep his distance, reminding him that he'd lost or been left by all of the people who were meant to love him, and that allowing Kenna through his defences would only end in more pain.

Kenna let out a shuddering breath and palmed away what could only have been a tear.

Gritting his teeth, Kyran decided there was only one thing for it. While he couldn't allow himself to go to her, to comfort her, he could help Kenna the best way he knew how.

'I'll ask Jim's wife if she can look after the shop, and I don't see a world in which she'd say no, so that's that problem solved. As for the problem of you not knowing how to save fish from dying once caught, go get some bait and a bucket. I'll get the rods. We're going fishing.'

Dragging her palms towards her ears, wiping away any remaining tears, Kenna looked over at him, confusion rife in her bleary eyes. 'Fishing in your boat? What about customers? I mean, I know we don't have many, but what if one does happen to come along?'

'We'll fish off the wharf where we can keep an eye on the shop door. I'm going to teach you how to catch and release, because hiding or running from your fears won't fix them.'

Kyran inwardly cringed, feeling like a hypocrite for giving advice that he could well take for himself.

Kenna pushed herself up and placed her hands on her hips. 'I hate that you're right.'

'And I like that I am.' With an unapologetic shrug, Kyran went out the back to grab the rods, congratulating himself on finding a way to help Kenna while managing to keep his heart safe.

For now.

Ten minutes later, Kyran had started to think he'd made a grave mistake. He'd forgotten how companionable fishing could be. The two of them sitting side by side, lines in the water, the slap of water against the wharf's poles and the soft breeze lulling them into a state where easy, honest conversation could be made. What was worse was that he'd been the one to start the conversation that now wouldn't stop flowing.

'Are you missing your mum?'

Kenna bobbed her rod up and down, her face going blank for a split second, before her chest rose then fell. 'Yes, I miss her. A lot. She's all I've ever known. But because of that I'm enjoying having proper freedom. Not having to worry about her, or worry about her worrying about me. Does that sound terrible?' Kenna sunk her teeth into her lower lip, her face grimacing at her own honesty.

'It sounds normal.' Kyran tried to reassure her, but could see his words did little as her teeth continued to graze her lower lip. It was clear Kenna and her mother had a deep bond, and that the separation between the two was taking its toll.

Kenna leaned out over the wharf and eyed the water like she hoped doing so would see a fish leap upon her hook. 'What about you? Do you talk much with your mum?'

The question tightened Kyran's throat. Something he was grateful for. He didn't like talking about his childhood. All it contained was abandonment and pain. It had been hard enough opening up to Kenna about how he'd come to live with Sonia, but talking about the first person to ever abandon him was too much. To this day he couldn't understand how a mother could leave a child so young, and anytime he dared to question why his mother had left him, all he could come up with was that he hadn't been what she wanted. That he wasn't good enough. Not that he'd ever voiced that belief to anyone. Not that he ever would.

'I'll take your silence as a no.'

Kyran nodded, feeling it was safer to keep his reactions simple than risk saying anything that could lead to more questions.

'What about your dad? Did he get in touch after he left?' Kenna glanced out over the bay, her eyes brightening. 'Though why anyone would go somewhere that's not here I don't know. I think Dolphin's Cove is perfect. I only wish my mother could see that.'

Grateful for the segue, Kyran jumped on the chance to not talk about his past. He'd told Kenna as much as he felt comfortable with already; anything further would need time and trust before it was willing to come out.

'Does she really despise this place that much?'

A seagull squawked above him and Kyran glanced up to see it hovering over them, its gaze zeroed in like it cared what Kenna had to say.

Kenna's eyes narrowed as she pondered his question. 'I want to say yes, but in truth I think that so much bad happened here, between my father walking out on her, and my grandmother and her not seeing eye to eye, that when she thinks of Dolphin's Cove all she can feel is pain. I think that's why she was so against me coming here.' A disappointed sigh left Kenna's lips. 'We've barely talked since I left. And when we have it's been all polite person surface level stuff or her trying to convince me to return to Leeds. It's like she doesn't want to know about my life here.'

'Because she doesn't see the possibilities that you do? Can't see why you'd go to a place she was unhappy in?'

A soft 'huh' left Kenna's lips. 'I think you've hit the nail on the head. To me, Dolphin's Cove is filled with possibilities. At least it is when I'm not having a meltdown about all the things that could go wrong in my life.' She fixed Kyran with a soft smile that threatened to send all his stoic resolve that he wouldn't get emotionally involved with Kenna fleeing into the ether. 'Thanks for saving me back there. For suggesting this. For not letting me get in my own way.'

'It's nothing, really. Least I could do.'

'It was more than the least. You could've just ignored me and left me to deal with my issues.' Kenna reached over and touched the back of his hand, sending a zap of electricity up his arm and down his spine, followed by a ripple of goosebumps over his skin. 'Cold?' Her head tipped to the side, her eyebrows angling together in surprise. 'It feels warm enough to me.'

'Must've been a rogue wind.' Kyran mentally face-palmed himself as the white lie came out sounding every bit as weak as it ought to have. 'Or tiredness. I'm not the best sleeper.'

'That I understand. I'm a bit of a night owl myself.' Kenna's gaze intensified like she was debating telling him something, opening up some more. 'Oh!' Her line strained, and she quickly removed her hand from his and grabbed the rod. 'Oh! Oh! Oh! I've got one!'

Grateful for the interruption, Kyran flushed with pride as Kenna expertly reeled in the fish the way he'd taught her to during their fishing expedition on the boat.

'Congratulations. Now, watch me,' he instructed as he dunked his hands in the bucket of sea water knowing he had to work quickly in order to give Kenna the confidence to try releasing a fish for herself, and then for others at the festival. 'Fish don't like dry hands, so it's best to make sure yours are wet before handling.'

'So we'll need buckets filled with sea water dotted around the fishing spots on the day of the festival.'

'Exactly.' Reaching out, Kyran caught the wriggling fish. 'When catching it you want to avoid holding it by the gills, try and hold it by the fins here. Then . . .' He ran his hand down the line to where the hook was embedded in the fish's lip. 'From here the hook should slip out the way it went in, like this.' Kyran breathed a sigh of relief as the hook easily came away. 'Then it's time to let the fish go. Goodbye, my fishy friend. Safe travels.'

With a flip of its tail, the fish disappeared into the depths.

'You made it look so easy.' Kenna added fresh bait to her hook and cast out once more. 'Is it that easy?'

'With a bit of practice it is, which is why we're going to be practising this every day from now until the day of the festival. If you can pick up the basics of fishing as well as you have, I have every confidence that you'll be a catch and releasing pro in no time.'

Kenna's small frown remained. 'What if one dies? Or if I can't remove the hook in time?'

'The goal is to save as many fish lives as possible, isn't it?'

Kenna nodded.

'Well, sometimes you have to break a few eggs to make an omelette.'

Kenna groaned. 'That is a terrible saying. Couldn't you have said, sometimes you have to have a few fish dinners in order to save an ocean?'

'I don't know that that one's much better.'

Kyran's heart quickened as Kenna fixed him with her 'whatever' stare. Her cheeks becoming more pink the longer they held each other's gaze. Silently daring the other to look away first. To relent. To give in. To admit the other was right. Or that they both were. That together they made a wonderful team. Could perhaps be some other kind of wonderful if one of them would just gave an inch.

Kyran let out a slow sigh of relief as Kenna's pocket beeped, breaking the moment.

'That'll be my phone.' She patted her pocket, the colour in her cheeks fading along with the tension between them. 'Check it. I won't be insulted.'

Pulling it out, her eyes scanned the screen, then she sighed.

'Someone you'd rather not hear from?'

'No. Just a case of speak of the devil. It's my mother checking in.'

Kyran could see Kenna's internal struggle; the part of her that loved her mother and wanted to do right by her warring with the part that was searching for freedom, for her own place in the world. Surely the two could co-exist?

'Call her, Kenna. Make things right. Don't let your moving get in the way of your relationship with her. Take it from me, not having your parents around is hard. If you have a chance to heal things, then you should. Time doesn't always make things easier.'

Kenna put the phone down, lifted her rod and jiggled it up and down. 'I'm going to have to, aren't I?'

'Well, you wouldn't want history repeating, would you?' Kyran turned his attention to his own rod, knowing once again that his words were another piece of advice he would do well to pay attention to. But, unlike Kenna, he'd been left and he'd lost too many times now to ever allow it to happen again. He was better off keeping himself to himself, rather than giving his heart to another. Even if a small belief, buried deep down, told him that the person sitting next to him could be the person to heal that very heart.

'Oh!'

Kenna's voice, full of excitement, broke through his thoughts.

'I've got another one!'

'Well, you know what to do, so do it.'

Kyran shuffled to the side, as much to give Kenna space to try her hand at releasing the fish as to give himself space, to evacuate the danger zone that had that rebellious part of him wanting to reach out to help her, to touch her, to become closer. Because even if he could admit that yes, he liked Kenna, and yes, he had the feeling there was something between them, there was no way he could allow himself to go there.

Not again. Not ever.

Chapter Ten

'Thanks for the chat, Mum.' Kenna looked out at the sea sparkling in the distance, and wished her mother could see it. Wished she was here in the garden, sitting in the chair opposite, sharing stories about the day that had been. Instead she was far away, sitting in the flat they'd shared, tired after a long day working as a receptionist, no doubt getting ready to reheat leftovers for dinner.

'Anytime, Kenna. And I'm glad things are working out. Really. I miss you.'

'I miss you, too.' Kenna paused, unsure how her mother would feel if she were to ask her to visit. Afraid to ask in case it created a new rift in their relationship.

'My love, is it still as beautiful as I remember?'

Tears arose unexpectedly, prickling the back of Kenna's eyes as she heard the wistful tone in her mother's voice.

'Oh, Mum. It's beyond beautiful. The air is so fresh, and the sky and the sea changes every day.'

'The same as ever then.'

'I guess so.' Kenna waited for her mother to say she'd come visit. That they could reunite not just by phone but in real life, but no offer came. Just a long, lingering silence, broken by the sound of Kyran yelling to the empty cottage that he'd arrived home. 'Well, I guess I'd better go. Talk soon?'

'Of course. Talk soon.'

Setting her mobile down, Kenna tried to ignore the disappointment that gnawed at her, hating that while Kyran's suggestion to get in touch with her mother had gone some of the way to remedying the rift between them, it still felt like there was distance between the two. The kind that no amount of phone calls could fix. That only holding each other in a long, warm hug could heal.

Blinking away the tears that had sprung forth, she lifted her arms, interlaced her fingers, flipped her hands over so her palms were facing the sky and pulled herself up tall, deciding that if she couldn't fix her relationship with her mother right now, it was better to focus on the final details of the festival.

Currently top of the list? Finding a musician to play.

Jim had come through with a list of bands he'd used in the past, but they were all missing the key ingredient – the willingness to play for their very modest budget. With the festival a week away, and not seeing any easy way to make some extra money to pay for a band, Kenna was fast feeling like she was running out of options.

'Thought I'd find you out here.'

She glanced up to see Kyran looming over her – his customary beer in hand and a glass of Sauvignon Blanc for her. It amazed Kenna how easily, once they'd gotten over their initial issues, they'd settled into a routine of catching up over a drink on the patio at the end of the day. Some days it felt almost as if they'd known each other for ever. Their conversation flowed freely – so long as it was about work, Sonia, village life, the festival. She'd figured after her attempts to find out more about his family life, that it was better not to get too personal with Kyran. To do so would only see fresh barriers erected. He'd open up when he was ready.

She smiled up at him, loving that the smile was returned. 'Where else would I be? A girl has got to enjoy the quiet moments, and the sun, while she can.'

He passed her the wine glass. 'Cheers to that.'

They clinked, then Kyran sat in the chair opposite, stretching his long legs out in front of him, and resting one arm on the table.

In these moments, Kenna could see beyond his strong, wild, manly looks to the person he could be if he wasn't so guarded. That first swallow of beer would see his muscled limbs go heavy, then his brow would relax, his lips would kick up just a hint, and the intensity behind his eyes – that reminded her of a big cat constantly waiting for a bigger predator to take it on – would fall away, leaving a man who had all the appeal of a big, cuddly teddy bear.

'So what's causing you to look so un-Kenna like?' His head tipped to the side, his eyes narrowing as he gazed at her, like he couldn't figure out what was wrong.

'Un-Kenna like? I have a "me" look?' Surprise tightened Kenna's gut. She'd not thought that Kyran had been inspecting her so closely. Yes, he looked at her, as you would look at someone who you lived and worked with – passing glances, polite attention, and on occasion in a way that if it had been anyone else but Kyran, she might have thought there was a flicker of romantic interest – but she'd never caught him staring at her, taking her in. Peeling back her layers with his eyes.

Which meant he must've done so when she wasn't looking.

A zap of something that felt like pleasure but surely couldn't have been, because there was no reason to find the thought of Kyran taking the time to truly see her, to be interested in her, as pleasurable, zigged and zagged its way through her stomach.

'You're an open book, Kenna. It's not hard to pick up your thoughts or feelings.'

And just like that, the tingles disappeared. So much for Kyran being interested in her. She was simply easy to read.

'And here I was, thinking you'd been ogling me when I wasn't looking,' she joked, hoping to ease her embarrassment at jumping to crazy conclusions. 'And the look you were seeing was that of a woman pondering a problem.'

Kyran's head angled to one side as his brows drew together, forming a crevice between them. 'What kind of problem?'

Kenna took a sip of her wine, glad to be back on solid festival-talk-only ground. 'The lack of music problem. I can't find a band willing to play for—'

'So little it might as well be free?'

Kenna grimaced and nodded. 'Exactly.'

An image of a guitar sitting to the side of a bed rose in her mind. Kyran's guitar. One she'd glimpsed on her post-work shower missions, when she'd scuttled between her bedroom and the bathroom wrapped only in a towel, not wanting to get dressed in a steamy room or get caught all but naked by Kyran. The very guitar that she'd found herself listening out for at night, Kyran's gentle strumming along with his quiet, soulful singing comforting her, helping her drift off to sleep.

The man had talent. He could play. He could sing. Some would say he was the perfect solution for the pickle she found herself in.

'Does a festival really need music? Could we do without it?' Kyran shook his head and waved his hand before she could state the obvious. 'Ignore those daft questions. Of course a festival needs music. Would borrowing a PA and playing music off a laptop do the job? Or maybe we could put feelers out and see if one of the local kids is a bedroom DJ just aching to play to a crowd?'

'I guess we could.' Kenna drummed her fingers on the patio table's top and wondered if mentioning the guitar would be seen by Kyran as her intruding on his space. Not that she'd been intruding. It wasn't her fault he left his door open and that she had to walk by it multiple times a day. 'But I just think live music makes an event that much cheerier. I mean, even if it was just a person playing a guitar.'

Kenna let the suggestion hang in the air, hoping Kyran would take it, run with it and solve all her problems without her having to ask. Enquire. Or beg.

Kyran stroked his beard thoughtfully. Clearly, to Kenna's chagrin, not taking the bait.

'Maybe we could put a sign up in the pub? Or at the cafe? That might pull a latent musician out of the woodwork?'

Kenna stifled a groan. Was he being this obtuse on purpose? Surely he could see what she was angling at.

'I mean, we could, I guess. I'm sure Marie and Jim wouldn't mind. My concern would be that the quality of musicians who'd come forward wouldn't be that great. And I don't fancy the time it would take to audition them. There must be someone, somewhere in the village who can play a guitar and sing decently enough that we can approach?' Kenna paused, giving Kyran a chance to click as to who she was talking about and offer his services up.

'If there is, I can't think of them,' Kyran shrugged. 'I guess we'll have to go down the audition route. If you're too busy I'm more than happy to take that on, and I've got no problem telling people that they're not right for the festival if they sound like a croaky cat or play like they've never had a lesson in their life.' He took another sip of his beer and let out a deep sigh of satisfaction. 'Problem almost solved. I'll put together a couple of signs and drop them into Marie and Jim.'

Kenna sucked in a long breath, then blew out the irritation. Her plan to go gently in broaching the subject of Kyran being the one to play at the festival wasn't working. Farthest thing from it. Which meant she was going to have to do the one thing she didn't want to do and straight up ask Kyran to play.

Lowering her lashes, she pretended to focus on the condensation dribbling down her wine glass. Surreptitiously, she lifted her gaze, just to make sure Kyran wasn't having her on. Playing with her. Knowing exactly what she wanted but refusing to give it to her, just to see if he could get a rise out of her.

His demeanour was relaxed as he slowly circled the beer glass round and round. His shoulders had the droopy look of a man in true chill-out mode, and there was no twitch or kick up of teasing lips to be seen.

There was no duplicity here. No winding her up. Kyran simply didn't see himself as being the person to play at the festival, even though, if what she'd heard was anything to go by, he was their best bet.

Folding her arms across her chest, Kenna rallied the courage she didn't feel to ask him to play and braced herself for his reply, knowing instinctively that his music was for his ears only and he'd see her asking as an intrusion of his privacy. An intrusion on the deal they'd made to keep out of each other's personal lives.

'You've got a guitar, right?'

Kyran's shoulders hitched up so quickly Kenna was surprised they hadn't hit his earlobes.

'You've been in my room? Prying? Snooping?' His brows drew together.

Kenna could almost see thunderclouds appearing out of nowhere, rotating menacingly over his head. She swallowed hard, and prepared herself to keep going with her line of enquiry. It was too late to back out now, and the last thing she wanted was Kyran walking away believing she'd intruded into his life, when all she'd done was pass his room with no intention of going in there, ever.

She shook her head. 'No. Not at all. It's simply in clear view of sight whenever I come out of the bathroom. I swear I've not been snooping. Snooping's not my style.'

Kyran's shoulders didn't so much inch as millimetre down, but his brows remained fused together, and his eyes were still narrowed in suspicion.

Kenna knew, without a doubt, she was going to have to beg. *Damnit.*

'Also, in the spirit of honesty, I've heard you playing and singing late at night.'

'With your ear pressed to my bedroom door, I take it?'

His demeaning tone saw the last of her nerves at talking to him scuttle away. Who did he think he was, imagining that she spent her nights hanging around his bedroom door?

'Did you not hear the bit about how I'm not a snoop, Kyran Walsh? I can promise you that the last thing I do is spend my precious evening hours lingering in the hallway, listening to your dulcet tones. I have no interest in what you do at night. My interest in you is purely professional – as we *both* agreed our interest in each other would be – so the only reason I thought to ask you to play at the festival was because what I've heard echoing down the hall through my bedroom door, where I'm very much

123

tucked up in bed minding my own business, is pleasant to my tired ears. You can play. You can sing. We need a musician who can do both, and who's willing to do both for a small payment for the *benefit* of *our* business.'

Kenna tightened her grip on herself as she pressed as far back into the chair as she could go, waiting for the storm that was sure to be unleashed after her tirade, while refusing to look like she was afraid of what was to come.

Silence stretched long, uncomfortably so, between them as Kyran eyeballed her, his lips showing no sign of moving. Of saying yes or no.

Kenna refused to be the one to break, to give in, to say sorry, or take her request back, because this wasn't about her. This was about the business they were trying to revive. About creating an event that would get them into the good graces of the community. This was bigger than either of them, and if Kyran wanted to say no, he could. But it had to be his decision, it had to be on him. She was doing her best for the business, and she expected him to step up as she had.

'Impossible woman.' The muttered words were paired with an exasperated sigh. 'And they say the apple doesn't fall far from the tree.'

'Is that a yes?' Kenna leaned forward in her chair, her arms unfolding, her hands coming together, fingers tangling in a silent show of hope.

'It's a no.'

'No?' Kenna sat back in surprise, unable to comprehend his answer. 'Are you sure?'

'That's what I said.'

She closed her eyes, her brain unable to comprehend his answer. 'But you have the talent. The ability. And you'd be free on the day.'

124

'I'm doing the birdwatching tours, remember? So I'm hardly free.'

Kenna waved his excuse away. 'We could find someone else to do tours of the bay. It's not like there's a shortage of sailors around here. It has to be you, Kyran. You're the person I – we – need to save the festival from becoming a complete and utter failure. You'd inject life into it. Give it atmosphere. I know you would. Please, Kyran.' She stretched her steepled hands out, hating that she was going down the pleading track, but not knowing what else to do to persuade him to change his mind. 'I'm at a complete loss. I've exhausted all my options, and I can't trust that we'll find the right kind of talent in time by putting up a few posters at the cafe and pub.'

She searched Kyran's face, hoping to see signs of a shifting in his perspective, if not a hint that he was about to give in and say yes.

His spine remained rigid. His jaw unyielding.

She sat back in her chair with a huff. 'Fine then. The very least you can do if you insist on being so stubborn about playing is to tell me why you won't sing at the festival? Is it stage fright? Are you afraid of what the locals might say if they heard you? Because, based on what I've heard, I know that they would only say good things, because you really are very good.'

Kyran lifted his shoulders in a 'so what?' manner. 'I know I am, but I don't intend on changing my position on singing in public anytime soon. Or ever.'

Kenna went to push once more, to tell him that if he knew he was talented it was wrong to hide it in their time of need, but bit the words back. The shadow that every so often darkened his eyes, shrouded his whole self, had returned, which meant if she continued to prod him, he'd only retreat further, which could see the decent relationship they'd cobbled together fall apart.

'If you're trying to figure out how to get me to budge, you need to stop. There will be no budging from me. My mind is made up.' Kyran folded his arms over his chest; a physical block that served to emphasise his verbal one.

'Understood.' Kenna gave a brisk nod. 'Even though I still don't understand why you won't. If I had your talent I'd be at the pub every Friday night singing up a storm.'

'Well that's you, isn't it?' Kyran loosened his hold on himself, but didn't relax his arms completely. 'You're the personable one out of this duo. I'm the guy at the back of the room.'

'Just watching the world go by. Not participating. Not adding to anything. Happy to let things go to hell rather than step up.'

Kenna closed her eyes, wishing she could take the words back. But it was too late, they were out there now, which meant at any point she'd hear the scrape of chair on paver, followed by the sound of angry footsteps walking away.

When no sound came, she opened her eyes to see Kyran casting a speculative look in her direction. His eyes zeroing in on her. Sizing her up. Like he was considering opening up to her, but wanted to ascertain for himself that she was worthy of his confidence. Of his trust.

'What is the worst thing that's ever happened to you, Kenna? Caused you the most hurt?'

A shiver rippled over Kenna's arms, despite the warmth of the sun on her skin. He wanted her to open up first? Needed her to before he could?

She tried to swallow as she considered her answer, but found she couldn't. Her throat had gone desert dry. Was she afraid to be honest with Kyran? Afraid that he would find her hurts pitiful compared to his?

It was clear Kyran's pain was greater than hers in the way he conducted himself. In the way he kept so many at a distance. Which perhaps meant they weren't all that different from each other. The biggest difference being that where Kyran pushed people away, Kenna had naturally felt separate from others. Felt empty on the inside because she'd never lived anywhere that felt like home. The bustling cities and towns that her mother had settled in never giving Kenna the connections that a close-knit community could bring. One where family roots stretched deep in the ground, anchoring you. Making you feel safe, secure.

'You'll think I'm stupid if I tell you.' She stood and went to the brazier, which she'd set earlier with paper and wood, ready to light when a hint of chill hit the air. Now, with the chill coming from deep within her, felt like as good a time as any to ignite it.

Slipping her hand into her shorts pocket, Kenna pulled out the matches, struck one and lit the small pyre. The heat flared, and Kenna found herself wishing its warmth could melt the steel lump that had formed in her gut at the thought of Kyran mocking her pain, of the festival failing, of her one chance at creating a proper home disappearing. 'Especially after . . .' She shook her head, not wanting to drag Kyran's past into the now any more than she already had.

'Especially after what I've experienced? With Jen dying?'

Despite the heat from the fire, Kenna shivered at the harsh way Kyran had described his fiancée's passing. 'Here I was, trying to be sensitive.'

'I've had six years to process it.'

127

'Processing isn't the same as healing.' Kenna, instantly regretting her observation, turned to face Kyran. 'I'm sorry. It wasn't my place to say that. You may well have healed. It's not like I've known you all that long. Or like I know you at all. We work together. We live together. But you're still a mystery to me.'

'A mystery? Me?' Kyran's lips quirked to one side. 'I've always thought I was a very simple person to figure out.'

Despite the serious turn their conversation had taken, Kenna found herself chuckling. 'Oh, you're about as simple as a Rubik's Cube.'

Kyran followed her laugh with one of his own – low, deep, amused but also held back. The kind of laugh a person gave when they were bemused, but not planning on giving anything away.

'You know, Kenna, there are tutorials on the internet that can teach you how to solve a Rubik's Cube.' He came to stand beside her, his back to the brazier, his gaze firmly on her. Not darting away, even for a second.

Had Kyran grown taller in the last few minutes? Had his shoulders become wider? Had his presence become even more commanding? More masculine? Kenna breathed in, only to catch his heady scent – salt and soap, tinged with sweat. The aroma of a man who spent his life outdoors, who worked hard, who was honest, true, loyal. Passionate.

Passionate? Kenna looked away and faced the fire once more; considered leaping into it. For some mad reason it felt the safer, less dangerous, option.

She forced a smile and aimed for a joking tone. Anything to lighten the frisson of something she was too afraid to think too much about that had sprung up between them.

'Are there internet tutorials on how to solve a Kyran?'

'Don't know. Never looked. Why? Do you want to solve me?' He inched closer and hip-bumped her.

Kenna waited for Kyran to move back, but he stayed put, just inches away from her, forcing her to tilt her head back in order to properly see him. To gauge his thoughts. His feelings. His intentions.

His eyes bored into hers, his lips relaxed, parted. His brows rose ever so slightly. A silent invitation. To kiss him? Was he daring her? Or simply trying to put her off finding out more about him? Finding out why he wouldn't play at the festival? Or how deeply he was wounded underneath all that gruffness? A show of flirtation to distract?

Bingo.

It was a cheap move on his part, one she was grateful to have seen through before doing anything stupid.

'Don't think being cute with me is going to distract me from finding out why you won't play music anymore,' she retorted, making a show of moving to the other side of the brazier. 'And don't think I'm going to tell you about my pain until you share yours.'

Kyran took a step back, his expression blank, any flirt or fun gone. 'Your pain is easy to see, Kenna. It's obvious in the way that you made your way to the village the moment you heard you were the benefactor of Sonia's shop. Obvious in the way you chose to power on with freshening up the shop even though the business was showing all the signs of going under. Obvious in the way that you've decided to create a festival out of thin air, while befriending anyone and everyone who crosses your path. Your pain is that you need to feel safe, to feel at home. Which tells me that you never have, and that you've not had the opportunity to try and do so until now, and even now you're not sure you'll succeed, which is why you're so scared of the festival failing. That *you* will fail. Because if you can't make your life in Dolphin's Cove work, you believe you'll drift for the rest of your life.'

Kenna's throat felt like it had become more concave with every judgement Kyran had made. Every *correct* judgement. If he was a Rubik's Cube, she was a two-piece jigsaw puzzle. Easy to put together. Easy to pull apart.

'That's not true.' The words were pushed out whispered and harsh.

'Isn't it?' His brows rose.

Kenna struggled to find the words to lie, but none came. She couldn't fib in the face of obvious truth. She looked into the fire, watched as the flames burned bright, red and orange on the outside, but their heart a deep blue.

The hottest part has an icy-looking heart.

The words came to her, reminding her of the man in front of her, whose mask of impassivity had slipped, revealing a triumphant expression. Kyran had won. He'd made it so Kenna would back off. Or so he thought.

She willed her spine straight, searched for a spark to ignite within her. She wasn't letting Kyran get one over her, even if that meant fighting fire with fire.

'How could you be so cruel?' She kept her hands straight at her side, refusing to let her fingers curl, to show her anger, her frustration. 'Why go in for the kill if you already know the answer to the question you posed to me? Why not let it be? Can't you begin to imagine what it would feel like if I began to probe into your life rather than just ask and hope for an honest answer? If I were to put it out there that I believe you're afraid of letting people get properly close, which is why you've all but locked yourself away? That Sonia's death has only caused you more pain because she was one of the last people you could be comfortable with because she let you be? Just like Marie lets you be? Whereas Jim, who I can see cares deeply for you, you keep at an arm's length because he has the power to crack your heart open and make you feel again?'

With every word, every sentence, Kyran's demeanour morphed from one of triumph to dead stillness. His eyes became neutral. Not moving up or down, or to the side. His lips devoid of upward curves or quirks to the side.

She'd got him. Found his hurt spot and needled it as he'd needled hers.

So why didn't she feel better? Why did the rush of success not course through her as it had done to Kyran? Why did she only feel worse?

'I don't know what causes you to be who you are, Kyran.' She backed away from her accusations, hating herself for even going there. 'All I know is that I'm sorry I asked you to help with the festival. I'm sorry I tried to get to know you better. I'm sorry to have opened up to you at all.'

The pain in her chest that had bloomed, brighter, harsher, pushed its way up, and Kenna knew if she didn't leave now tears would fall. And she wouldn't let Kyran see her cry. Not now. Not ever. She'd not give him the satisfaction.

'Enjoy the rest of your beer. I'm going to bed. The early bird sells the worms and all that, so I wouldn't want to be late.'

Forcing herself to walk, not run, she left Kyran standing by the fire, arms wrapped around himself, eyes trained on the flames. Flames that she suspected could burn brighter than the sun but they still wouldn't warm, let alone melt, his frozen heart.

Chapter Eleven

How long could a man simultaneously wonder what had just happened while berating himself for being the one to make it happen?

An eternity. That was the conclusion Kyran had come to. He rocked back and forth on his feet, staring at the dying embers in the brazier that were valiantly trying to stay alight, but each burning out, one after the other. Soon they'd be as dark as his heart. Or as dark as his heart was meant to be. Right now the ache he felt in the centre of his chest belonged to a heart that was still capable of feeling something. A lot of something. In this case, guilt.

He shook his head violently, trying to clear his thoughts, to make sense of what had just happened.

Kenna had been prying. Determined to find out what caused his refusal to play at the festival, and he'd been equally determined not to talk about it with her because the memories attached to his playing were too much to bear, and talking about them would have been more painful than being flayed alive.

How could he explain to Kenna that he used to play every Saturday night at the pub when Jen was alive, and that the gigs while for the punters, had felt – for Kyran – like they were directed at Jen, the woman who'd championed his playing and insisted he share his talents.

Jim had asked him to continue to play after Jen had passed, but with her gone so had his love of performing, of entertaining. Of anything. All he'd wanted to do was to be alone, out at sea, with his maudlin thoughts and broken heart.

But did that mean he had to stay that way? Emotionally arrested? Afraid to take a step towards a different future? Was he destined to live in the past? Stay stuck there? And was he willing to hurt Kenna, who'd never done a thing to him, in order to maintain his stasis?

Kyran mentally kicked himself once more for his behaviour. He wasn't a bad person, not really. Not at heart. Just determined to not get hurt ever again. And when Kenna had continued to badger him, looking past his absolute 'no', searching for the reasons behind it, he didn't know any other way to get her off his back other than to direct her line of questioning elsewhere, which had only ended up in rockier territory.

First, with his stupid idea to flirt with her in order to deter her, which had resulted in abject failure, then by pointing out with deadly precision her weak points. Her need for security, her determination to secure it, and what would inevitably happen, how she would feel if she were to make a mess of everything.

His words had the effect he'd been looking for. Kenna had stormed away and left him alone, just like he wanted.

Except in the hour that he'd remained outside, he'd not once felt a sense of success at pushing her away. If anything he'd felt worse with every passing minute, his stomach remaining clenched, his chest muscles tense.

He'd attempted to breathe in and out slowly, hoping to relax, but all he'd found was wave after wave of fresh guilt that demanded he fix his mistake. That he apologise. Make things right.

Because the last thing he wanted to do was push Kenna away?

He toyed with the idea, turning it over in his mind. He didn't hate having her around. If he was honest, the more they got to know each other, the more he was glad she was here. Conversation with her was easy. She was funny; even making him laugh on the odd occasion. She certainly made him relax.

He couldn't remember the last time he'd happily sat in the garden, breathing in the scent from the flowers, drinking a beer, night after night.

Living.

Not just existing.

Was he willing to drive someone who made him feel like that out of his life?

With a sigh, knowing the answer, Kyran went to head towards the cottage to make peace, to apologise, but stopped himself as he drew up to the back door. It was too soon. He'd been too harsh. Kenna would need time to get her thoughts and feelings together. The apology would have to come at a time that suited her, not him.

Which meant he had to get away from the cottage, because he didn't know that he could hold his tongue that long.

Striding around the cottage and down the garden path, he found himself heading towards the village, following a path he'd gone down more times than he could ever count, which allowed his brain to try and find the right words to apologise to Kenna, without fear that he'd take a misstep, trip over and hurt himself.

He had to be clear in his apology. Not muddled. Definitely not convoluted. It had to sound sincere. It had to come from the heart. Anything less and Kenna wouldn't believe him and they'd be back at square one.

Surprise stopped him in his tracks. He'd thought his feet were carrying him to the wharf, to his boat, to the one place where he could be alone, except he found himself standing outside the pub. The lights from inside flooded the street in gold, the chatter and laughter of people with more than a few drinks in them spilled out, along with the tinny sound of generic pop music played through a cheap sound system.

How many times had Kyran told Jim to update the sound system? At least once a week when he used to regularly frequent the pub. Each time, Jim had laughed and said that as long as he had Kyran available to play there was no need. Except Kyran hadn't played there for years, and Jim still had the same shoddy stereo.

It was almost as if, after all this time, Jim still held out hope that Kyran would one day pick up his guitar, stroll on in, take a seat on the small stage in the corner of the room and begin strumming.

The door opened and two customers, a young man and woman arm-in-arm, all but rolled out of the pub. Their smiles were so wide it was a wonder their faces didn't crack; their eyes only for each other.

Kyran rubbed the crevice he could feel creasing the area between his brows. What was he doing here? And what were the chances of escaping without being noticed?

'Kyran, my boy!'

Zero, it seemed.

'Get in here. I've got a beer with your name on it.'

Knowing backing away was not a possibility, Kyran drew in a deep breath, fixed a pleasant smile to his face and weaved his way through the tables to the bar where Jim was already setting down a pint of Kyran's favourite pale ale on the mat.

'So what have we done to deserve the honour of your presence?'

Kyran slid onto a stool and accepted the beer with a nod of thank you. 'Just needed to get out, get some air.'

Some space. Not that he'd say that to Jim. Doing so would be as good as laying all his worries out on the table – or bar. That, and he didn't want to admit the surge of uncomfortable feelings he'd just experienced – realising that another woman had somehow managed to get under his skin – to the man who was as good as his father-in-law, if not the closest thing to an actual father he had.

Jim picked up a damp rag and began wiping down the bar, even though it was spotlessly clean. 'Young Kenna giving you grief?' His brows rose as he fixed Kyran with a curious look. 'Wanting you to not leave things lying about? Put the toilet seat down? That sort of thing?'

Kyran repressed a snort at the idea of Kenna being the tidy one. For all her proclamations of being house-trained, he was always finding shoes shucked off in odd spots around the house, cardigans draped over furniture, and the woman hadn't yet managed to learn that rinsing a dish wasn't the same as rinsing a dish and then stacking it in the dishwasher. Not that he wanted her to do that. The few times she had decided to place a dish in the dish-washer, he'd spent double the amount of time rearranging everything into an orderly manner.

'I'll take that as a no?'

Kyran took a sip of his beer then set the glass down as gently as he could so as not to give away the turmoil that lay in his gut, in his heart. 'Take it however you want it.'

A gruff 'humph' met his ears.

'So you've got feelings for her then?' Jim picked up his ever-present glass of beer and took a sip. 'Because it

136

would be understandable if you do. She seems like a good person. Hardworking, determined. And, if I may say so without sounding like an old dinosaur, not bad on the eye, either.'

A flush hit Kyran's cheeks as an image of Kenna, eyes dancing, pink lips smiling as she greeted a customer, came to mind. Not bad on the eye was an understatement. She had a natural beauty that could've been intimidating if it wasn't combined with a down-to-earth charm.

Rubbing the back of his neck, he tipped his head back, averting his gaze from Jim, while hoping the answer to Jim's question would materialise from the ceiling. All he found were specks of dirt and the odd indent that may or may not have been created by exuberantly corked bottles of bubbles. Dirt, indents, but no answers were to be found on the ceiling, not when – deep down – he knew the truth could be found in his heart.

Kenna had wriggled her way under his skin, and he didn't know that he could find a way to hook her out. Or that he wanted to hook her out at all.

Everything about her – from her give anything a go ways, to her refusal to let the business fall apart, to even the way she left the little sockettes she wore with her trainers about the house – intrigued him. Compelled him.

Compromised him.

'Don't think the ceiling's going to answer for you, lad. It's not usually the talking type.'

Kyran refocused his attention on Jim, and decided it would be best to try and avoid the topic of Kenna alto-gether. It was one thing to have a chat about women problems with an old friend, but another thing to do so with an old friend who was the father of the only woman you'd ever been in love with. 'You're chatty tonight. Is that to hide the sound of your terrible sound system? Remind me to help you shop for a new one, okay?'

Jim shrugged unapologetically. 'The sound system is fine, and it's not often one of my favourite people comes to visit. It's given me a second wind. And don't think you can distract me from my original question. I'm like a dog with a bone when I catch wind of a meaty topic.'

Despite thinking himself too old to squirm, Kyran found himself tapping the bar, while jiggling his foot to a tune only he could hear. 'The problem with you publican types is that you see too much.'

'Only when we want to. Only when we care enough that we bother to look.' Jim turned around, grabbed a packet of salt and vinegar crisps, ripped the bag open and placed it between them. 'And, believe it or not, I do care.'

Kyran helped himself to a crisp. 'I know. I've drunk enough of your free beer to know.'

'My caring could have cost me a bloody fortune over the years. I should be grateful you've kept your distance as much as you have. Except I'm not, because I've missed you.' Jim shook his head, fondness deepening the lines that creased the sides of his eyes. 'So, are you going to tell me what's going on?'

Kyran turned the crisp left, then right, taking in the ridges, the tiny brown blemishes, the small chip taken from its side. If it wasn't a metaphor for his life, for him, he didn't know what was. What was once a potato – simple, basic, easy to understand, knew its place in the world – had been forced by events outside of its control to become something else entirely. Something not quite so simple, some would say an acquired taste.

He popped it into his mouth and relished the crunch of it, the salt that coated his tongue, the vinegar that made his eyes water. He loved a basic potato in all its forms – mashed, baked, roasted – but he had plenty of time for salt and vinegar crisps. And while he knew, like the crisps, he too was an acquired taste, the people who did make time for him, who understood him, were the people he was happy to have in his life.

How do you think Kenna feels about salt and vinegar crisps?

Ignoring the little voice in his head, Kyran swallowed and prepared himself to do the one thing he struggled to do – voice his true feelings.

'You know I love Jen, right?'

'Love?' Jim placed his forearms on the bar, interlocked his fingers and leaned forward. 'Not loved?'

'*Love*.' Kyran placed as much emphasis on the word as he could, wanting Jim to know that his feelings for his daughter had never died, even after all these years. 'She was my everything. She saved me from myself. She made me a better person.'

Jim's eyes narrowed in sympathy. 'You're being hard on yourself, son. I knew you before you two got together, and you were always a good lad. Quiet, insular, but I never heard a bad word said against you.'

'If by quiet and insular you mean sullen and moody, then you'd be right. And the reason no one said a bad word about me was because I kept myself to myself.'

'As someone from your background would do. It's not like you've had a lot of reasons to trust many people, what with your mum leaving you when you were a toddler, and your father taking off, leaving you the way he did. Sixteen years old and being expected to fend for yourself.' Jim clucked his tongue while shaking his head disapprovingly. 'You did well to turn out as great as you did. Many wouldn't have.'

'Many didn't have a Sonia to take them in, a Marie to mother hen them, a Jen to love them, and a Jim to keep an eye on them.' Kyran propped his arms onto the bar, mirroring Jim's stance. 'I was lucky. Simple as that.'

'You give Lady Luck too much credit.'

Kyran shrugged off Jim's comment. 'Well, that's how I felt. How I still feel. Except now I have no Jen, and no Sonia.'

'But you have me. And Marie. And now you have Kenna.'

'Who I never asked for. Or wanted.'

'I hear past tense in that "wanted", does that mean you want her now?' Jim leaned in closer, his eyes searching Kyran's, like he was looking for a lie, or perhaps just the honest truth.

'Would it be wrong if a part of me – a very small part of me – did want her?' Kyran inhaled deeply in an attempt to still his pulse, which had ramped up with his admission. 'Would it be disrespectful to Jen?'

'Son, this is a touchy subject for me to broach. But, um, since Jen passed have you not . . . you know . . .'

Kyran had never seen Jim at a loss for words. It was a rare and disconcerting sight.

'You and the ladies . . . I've not seen you . . .'

Understanding dawned over Kyran. Poor Jim wanted to know if he'd all but entered a monastery since Jen's death. The answer to that was easy.

'Have I not been with anyone since Jen? No. Not at all. No dating. No hand-holding. No kissing. No . . . er . . .' It was Kyran's turn to not find the right word. 'No *anything*.'

Jim shook his head slowly, his shoulders further slumped. 'Son, it's been six years. Too long for a man to wallow in grief. To not hope for more. To not even try to find happiness, or at the very least a little fun, with someone else.'

'But I didn't want more. I wanted Jen. She was my everything.' Irritation rose in Kyran's heart as he heard himself speak, as he realised he'd relegated her to the past. 'She *is* my everything.'

'But she's dead, son. She's not coming back.' Jim's eyes closed. Goosebumps peppered his big, strong-looking forearms. 'I wish she could. I've wished more times than I can count that she would. But she's not walking through that door. She's not sitting at any of these stools. She's not laughing at my failed attempts to sew a button on a shirt, or bemoaning her mother's inability to keep a houseplant alive. She's gone.'

The annoyance that needled Kyran morphed into anger, fuelled by Jim's truth. 'But that doesn't mean she has to be gone in here.' He pressed his clenched fist to his heart. 'That doesn't mean I have to let her go. To forget her.'

Jim opened his eyes, then reached out and closed his hand over Kyran's fist. 'No one's asking you to, son. What I'm saying is that it's okay to hold her close, to treasure the love you shared, but there's nothing wrong with allowing new love in. With embracing new love. With letting life go on as life should. I know it's a lot to consider, especially when grief runs as deep as it does for us, but just think about it, okay? Maybe give you and Kenna a chance before you dismiss something that could be special.'

Removing his hand from Kyran's, Jim went to serve a customer, leaving Kyran alone with his beer and the thoughts he'd been ignoring for far too long.

He ran his finger through the puddle that had formed around the base of the glass, then swiped his wet finger on the bar mat, before picking up his glass and taking a long drink, hoping the coolness of the beer and its anaesthetic qualities would calm the disquiet buzzing in his head.

How could Jim suggest it was time to move on from Jen? How could he be so callous as to expect Kyran to find the same depth of love with another person? To laugh as freely as he'd laughed with Jen over everything and nothing – a neighbourhood cat turning on a dog that was chasing it and taking a swipe that sent the dog home howling, the sight of a toddler's eyes widening in wonder at their first lick of ice cream, the way Old Man Henry routinely shook his head at the gulls that circled over the wharf then, a second later, tossed them the crust from his sandwich. How could Jim expect Kyran to want to be as tactile with another person as he had been with Jen – walking hand in hand everywhere, hugging for no other reason than the love they felt was so overwhelming they needed to share it with each other, spending hours talking about their future, how their life would look at thirty, forty, fifty and beyond.

Kyran's stomach turned at the mere thought of experiencing that kind of intimacy with another person. With giving that much again, risking his heart all over again.

He glanced up to see Jim standing in front of him once more.

'If you gnaw that upper lip much harder, you'll find yourself lipless by the end of the night.'

Kyran released his lip. 'Didn't know I was even doing it.'

'You never do when you're deep in thought.' He picked up his glass, drank half of what was left in one swallow, then wiped his mouth with the back of his hand. 'If I know you, you're worrying over my words. Wondering how the father of the girl you loved could give you his blessing to move on.'

'Something like that.' Kyran hated how surly he sounded. Like the teen boy he'd once been, intent on keeping everyone at a distance. 'It doesn't seem right. Feel right.'

'Seeing you mope around for the last six years is what's not right. I voiced my concerns to Sonia once, and she said to give you time, but it seems that for once in her life she was wrong. Time's not helping you because you've been intent on remaining stuck in the past.'

Kyran tried to find a shot to fire back in Jim's direction. Wished he could accuse Jim of being stuck in the past as well, of not moving on, of being just as bad as he was, but he couldn't. He knew Jim had done his best to nurture his life since Jen's passing – everything from updating the bar's decor every few years, to ensuring he and his wife took trips to sunnier climes together during the depths of winter when the village was so quiet you could hear a pin drop and opening the bar was a waste of time and profit. Yes, he carried the weathered look of a man who knew heartache, but he also carried the pride of a man who hadn't let pain beat him into submission.

Whereas, Kyran wondered, how did he look to outsiders? How did others, even those nearest and dearest, view him?

Like a man whose legs were encased in concrete. Along with his heart.

Anger reared once more, not at Jim, but at himself.

'Ah, there. I see it.'

Jim leaned over so he was at Kyran's eye level. Kyran forced himself to meet his gaze, to not shy away at what he saw in it – triumph.

'A spark. A knowing. Some might say hope.'

Kyran rolled his eyes. 'You've been reading too many self-help books.'

Jim straightened up with a laugh. 'Blame the missus. That's been her way of moving through the waves of pain that wash over her. She experienced tsunamis at the start, now it's just the odd rogue wave. She came to the conclusion she had to go with the flow, let the pain in, but also not hold it too tight, allow it to ebb away. She's a wise woman.'

'So building a dam to keep the pain in isn't the right thing to do?' Kyran's heart lightened at his small joke. Perhaps admitting to how he'd been dealing with Jen's death was the first step to truly moving on.

'Probably not. Dams have been known to break. Especially when someone comes along and aims a sledge-hammer in their direction.'

'I wouldn't call Kenna a sledgehammer.'

Jim's face lit up as the delight in his eyes spread down into his cheekbones, followed by his lips, lifting the corners of them high. 'I like it when I'm right.'

'Oh, shush.' Kyran flicked his hand in Jim's direction, knowing Jim would pay no heed to his action. 'It was just a slip of the tongue.'

'I could say something much cruder right now but, being a gentleman at heart, I won't. You really need to think before you speak.'

Kyran scrunched his face up in revulsion. 'You were almost my father-in-law, remember? You can't say things like that.'

'I'm also the owner of a pub. I've heard and said far worse.'

Kyran offered a full body shudder in reply then, with a grin, drank the rest of his beer. 'Well, if anything, it matches the rest of this evening. Unexpected.'

Unexpected feelings. Unexpected desires. Unexpected realisations.

Unexpected actions to come?

He set his glass down with a firm thump. It was too soon to think about taking action – of any kind. Not when he didn't know how Kenna felt. Not when he wasn't even entirely sure how he felt. Not when the most important thing he had to do right now was to apologise to Kenna, and only then, should she forgive him, could he test the waters and see if the attraction he felt towards her had any depth.

'Another?' Jim picked up the glass and held it under the tap, his hand hovered at the handle.

Kyran shook his head. 'No, it's time I headed home. There's more work to be done at the shop in preparation for the festival.'

'Fair enough. Just remember to be kind to yourself, okay, son?'

Kyran slid off the stool and gave Jim his best 'what are you on?' look. 'Too many self-help books, Jim.'

With another smile, one that was far more real than the one he'd walked in with, Kyran waved, then made his way out of the pub. Stepping into the cool night air, he breathed in the tangy sea scent and began the walk home, feeling lighter with each step, feeling more hopeful than he had in far too many years.

Chapter Twelve

As the tip of her pinky finger's nail investigated the corner of her eye, Kenna pondered the irony of the gunk that settled in it being called sleep, when it seemed to gather in greater multitudes the less sleep you had, as she'd experienced last night after she'd left Kyran by the brazier.

What had she been thinking, believing he could open up? That the moment things looked to be deepening between them he'd not push her away? She'd been a fool.

No more, she decided as she dug the last of the crust out and flicked it into the small rubbish bin she kept behind the counter. From now on she would treat Kyran as he was: her business partner. No more. No less.

With an inward sigh of acceptance, Kenna turned her attention to the customer browsing the small stand of sun hats and T-shirts she'd set up the previous week, after coming to an agreement with a local screen printer to sell on their behalf for a small cut of the profits. It wasn't the greatest business win ever, but as far as Kenna was concerned it was a start. It grew the offerings in the shop while making the place look more successful simply by having something to offer. Experience working behind the counter in a failing corner shop had taught her the less you had on the shelves, the less likely people were to buy from you. Best of all, by coming to the arrangement she was supporting a local, showing locals that Fishful

Thinking wanted to be part of the community, and once the festival proved to be a raging success, so would the business.

She hoped. She crossed her fingers quickly, then uncrossed them as she put on her sunniest smile.

'Morning!' She clenched her teeth as she realised how overly exuberant she'd sounded. Pulling herself back from sounding like she was insane – which perhaps she was, given she was neck-deep in festival organisation and heart-deep in 'what's going on with my flatmate/business partner' sludge – she moderated her tone to something resembling normal. 'Can I help you with anything?'

The customer turned to her with a polite smile, and Kenna took a small step back. The smile, even in its well-mannered 'leave me alone'-ness was stunning. Even, white, perfectly spaced teeth. Lips that were perfectly symmetrical. Surrounding them was a face that was attractive, to say the least. Clear blue eyes, a good mop of blond hair, skin that looked almost airbrushed . . . Kenna cursed herself for not dotting the hormonal breakout that had appeared on her chin with concealer before leaving the house.

Once upon a time she would have said the man standing in front of her was 'her type'. The kind that she knew would be a classic case of here for a good time, not for a long time. The no-strings safe type. Now? Despite the beautiful smile and the pretty face? She searched her body for signs of attraction. No heart hammering. No fizzy veins. No head fog that tied her tongue in knots.

Strange. Still, she straightened her shoulders and widened her smile. She wasn't here to meet her match, or if not her match then discover the potential of an evening's fun – she was here to work. And by the look of his immaculate polo shirt, wrinkleless knee-length shorts and expensive-looking brown leather sandals, he could afford to splash out a little. Or a lot. Which made him perfect customer material.

'Might I interest you in this?' She picked out a T-shirt from the rack and immediately regretted her choice. With bright-orange fabric sporting 'behove the cove' and a cartoon dolphin flipping out of the overly bright blue sea on it, it was in no way suitable for the man standing before her. 'Not this.' She shoved it back on the rack and chose a simple navy blue cap with 'Dolphin's Cove' written in basic font in the lower left-hand corner. 'This. A nice memento of your stay. Not too, er, ostentatious.'

'Unlike the atrocity you nearly offered me just now?' His polite smile widened into a proper grin. 'I wouldn't even give that to my brother as a joke gift.'

Taking the cap off her, he placed it on his head and took a look in the small mirror she'd set up to the side of the display.

'Can't say I blame you,' Kenna agreed. 'I wouldn't give it to my brother either. If I had one. Or my worst enemy.' She clapped her hand over her mouth. 'I really shouldn't say that about the T-shirt, being that it's my job to sell the thing.'

'"Thing" is an excellent description.' He took the cap and handed it to her. 'I'll take it. And how do you know I'm not local? Do I look like a sea shunner?'

Kenna took in his evenly tanned arms and the sun-lightened streaks in his hair, then laughed. 'Perhaps. I'd put the hair down to a talented stylist, and the tan down to an at-home sunbed.' She grinned to show she was teasing.

He passed his money card over with a sigh. 'Is it that obvious? Note to self: lay off the sunbed, but the stylist stays.' His eyes crinkled as he smiled. 'But you're only half right. I do enjoy a spot of fishing here and there, but

I'm not married to the sea. The hair and tan's down to working on a flower farm over the way.'

Kenna returned his smile. 'Ah, so I was right, you're not local.'

'Correct,' he nodded. 'It's my day off, so I thought I may as well take myself on an adventure.'

Kenna passed his card back. 'Well, it's a touch quiet today, so I can't see you doing much adventuring around these parts, but if you are looking for something to do in the future, you should come down this Saturday. We're holding a fishing festival.'

'Which would be great if I was a better fisherman. I'm more of a picker than a hooker.' He grimaced. 'That sounded better in my head.'

Kenna laughed and waved his comment away. 'You're fine, and you don't need to be an expert at fishing to enjoy the festival. There'll be music.' *Hopefully*. 'Food trucks. The local school is holding egg and spoon races, sack races, that kind of thing.'

'I'm too old to race children. It'd be cruel.'

'There's an adult category.' Kenna looked up as the doorbell tinkled to see Kyran hovering about the door.

The face full of thunder she'd seen yesterday had disappeared. If anything he looked at peace. Had he realised how awful he'd been and come to apologise? Giving him a quick wave, she turned her attention back to the customer.

'Well I do like adult things, especially fun adult things. So perhaps I'll make the effort to come back.' He slid his card back into its slot in his wallet. 'Will you be there?'

'Of course. I'm organising it.' She glanced over at Kyran. His mellow – for Kyran – demeanour had disappeared, replaced by a glower. Because she'd said she was organising the festival and not including him? 'Actually, *we* – my business partner over there,' she indicated to the shop door, 'and I are organising it. You should definitely come. It'll be a fun time.'

'In that case, if you're there and it's going to be fun, I'll make the effort. See you then.' With a nod and a smile that promised a lot more than just a brief 'hi, how are you' the next time they met, he turned and left the store, nodding at a now murderous-looking Kyran on his way out.

'Flirting with the customers? Is that your latest grand plan to make more money? Is this equal opportunity flirting? Will you be extra friendly to every person that comes in, say Old Man Henry? Or are you saving the big smiles and the invitations to events only for the good-looking man types?'

Kenna couldn't believe what she was hearing. Kyran was accusing her of flirting in order to make money? Yes, she'd found the customer attractive, but she hadn't been attracted to him, and, even if she had, she was too professional to pick up a date at work.

Anger roiling in her veins, she gripped the edge of the counter and hoped Kyran was grateful for its existence as it was the only thing keeping her from marching up to him and sticking a finger in his chest repeatedly until he apologised for being a rude arse.

'At least I was doing something to make this business grow. What have you done today? I don't see any fishing charters in the calendar. I haven't seen you do a thing to rattle up more business. And I bet all the fish in the sea that you've not changed your mind about singing at the festival.'

His face remained mutinous as he crossed his arms across his chest, but the snarl lifting his lips had settled a little.

A sign she'd gotten to him? Gotten through to him? Good.

Kenna waited for the excuses to come from his mouth, but Kyran continued to stare at her, his face now devoid of emotion.

Glancing down, she saw her knuckles had begun to bulge as her hold on the counter tightened with every passing, silent second.

Do not speak first. It's his turn.

She held his gaze. And held her breath. Death was preferable to being the one to break. To speak first. To offer up an apology when he was the one to throw the first insult.

Kyran's arms dropped to his sides and his chest, puffed up with indignation, fell. 'I've been a humpback whale-sized arse, haven't I?'

Kenna shrugged, trying not to let her surprise at his admission show. 'I've not seen a humpback whale's arse, so I can't be sure. But I do know that you've been an arse. A Kyran-sized one.'

'I'm sorry.' Kyran dipped his head so she couldn't see his eyes, see what was going through his mind. 'You got to me yesterday. Made me think of things, feel things, that I would prefer to keep pushed down.'

The remains of her irritation fled. God, he was so broken. So shut off. How hard it must be to live with a mind and a heart that bolted down.

Despite the current tension between herself and her mother, Kenna had always had someone right there, in her space, ready to support her should she need it. And Kenna had been open to that. Welcoming of it. Grateful for her mother's constancy in her life. Kyran though? He had people around him who wanted to be there for him, but he kept them at a distance, refused to let them in.

But maybe, just maybe, given time and patience, she could be the one to get through to him? To let him know that she could be trusted with his feelings. That she wouldn't hurt him.

'Talking things out isn't the worst thing, Kyran. Some people – people with big, fancy degrees – even say it's a good thing.'

Kyran glanced up, his gaze heavy with defeat. 'I guess I'm not much of a talker.'

Kenna pursed her lips and raised her brows. 'Really? I'd never have guessed.'

And just like that, her dry joke broke through the invisible barricade between them. Kyran's face softened, and she felt her grip on the counter ease off.

If heart-to-hearts weren't going to fix things between them, perhaps the tactic she needed to employ was a little humour mixed with honesty.

'I wasn't joking about you being a Rubik's Cube, Kyran Walsh. You really are a complete mystery to me. We've lived and worked together for a good couple of weeks now and despite us spending time together, most of it really nice time, I still don't feel like I know you any more than I did the day we met.'

His eyes widened just enough to register surprise. 'Really? I feel like I'm as open with you as I am with anyone else.' His gaze darted to the left then returned to her. 'Which, I guess, means I've not been very open with you at all. Which is how you don't know that I've done this . . .' He held his hand up, revealing a sheaf of paper. 'I made these and printed them out.'

He offered them up to Kenna for her to view. On them was the Fishful Thinking logo, with a picture of a boat and an offer of 15 per cent off weekday charters.

'You did this?'

Kyran's cheeks flushed. 'I did. I know they're not amazing. I'm no computer whizz, but I've seen all the effort you've put into this place and wanted to show you I was just as invested. Is it a terrible idea?'

His vulnerability touched Kenna. Kyran might never be open enough to talk about his feelings, but that didn't mean he couldn't be open with his actions.

'They're perfect.'

'Phew.' Kyran wiped imaginary sweat off his brow. 'So, do you want to come to Marie's with me to drop them off? While we're there I'll buy you a coffee as an apology for last night. And for being so rude just now. I know you weren't flirting to get business. I was just being . . .'

His lips twitched like he was trying to find the right words but failing.

'You were just being protective?' Of her? Of the business? Kenna wasn't about to ask, because she knew pressing Kyran would only result in him pulling back.

'Protective. Something like that.'

Jittery panic at the idea of shutting the shop for even fifteen minutes, of potentially losing business, filled Kenna, but she pushed the fear away, knowing that if the business was going to survive in the long run, it was more important that she get on with her business partner, and that meant not ignoring the olive branch he was offering.

'Coffee it is.'

She grabbed the keys and met Kyran at the door, where he was holding it open for her. His lips were curved into a soft smile, his cheeks flushed a soft pink, and for a moment his eyes shone with what looked like pride. Like he'd taken a big step. Done something he'd not done in a long time.

Asking his business partner out for coffee? Asking a *girl* out for coffee?

Was this more than an olive branch? Was this some kind of date? Or at least the precursor to a proper, officially asked out one?

Surely not? But what if it was?

She entertained the idea as she pushed the keys into her shorts pocket. The thought of dating Kyran causing her heart to fizz like it was carbonated, her body to prickle all over in a delicious way.

Kenna turned to Kyran, who was now rocking back and forth on his heels in a very unstoic Kyran way. In a way a man might if he *had* just asked someone on a pre-date.

And if that was the case, if his small gesture could become a great one, there was only one thing left to do.

'To the cafe,' she declared.

And no one was more surprised than she when Kyran nodded, then offered her his arm.

Chapter Thirteen

What are you doing?

Kyran glanced down at Kenna's arm, companionably interlocked with his, and was thankful that he'd chosen an old-fashioned method of escorting a woman to a destination rather than the far more intimate hand-holding, which would have caused Kenna's hand to become clammy with his sweat if the dampness currently encasing his palms was anything to go by.

Are you off your rocker?

He shook his head, grateful Kenna was a head shorter than him and staring forward so she couldn't see how miffed he was by his behaviour.

Breathed in too much sea air?

Maybe. He wasn't sure. When he'd stepped into the store his plan had been to apologise, to make small talk, to show Kenna he was willing to step up and do his best by the business, and to use his flyers as a way to take the smallest step towards getting to know her better, and in doing so hopefully finding out if the feelings that were growing inside him had any substance at all, or if they were caused by over half a decade of keeping well out of the way of any woman who he might find attractive or be attracted to.

Which had been easy enough to do until he'd been forced into a living and working situation with a woman who ticked both the 'attractive' and 'attracted' boxes.

Thanks, Sonia.

He tipped his head as a seagull squawked above him, like it had heard his sarcastic thought and felt the need to berate him for it. Sonia in gull form. He inwardly chuckled at the thought.

Sonia had always been in control; some would say controlling. Despite leaving him to his own devices when it came to the business, in the last few years she'd often bluntly suggested that it was time he started dating, put himself out there, gave if not love then lust a chance. Told him that he was too young and handsome to be a recluse, that there was only room for one bitter old recluse in the village, and that was her.

Each time he'd laugh and tell her she was hardly old, not with her quick mind and snappy tongue that could run rings around people half her age, or the feisty spirit that dared those around her to tell her she couldn't do something simply so she could prove them wrong.

When her constant pushing and prodding at him to get out and meet someone became too much, he'd often distracted her with a challenge. Watching her build a tree hut for the kids across the road, whose parents were too busy working to do so themselves, had been a joy – and had kept her out of his hair for a good two weeks. And seeing her training to prove she could get herself fit enough to pass the police fitness test, after laughing at the village constable's hobbling run while chasing down a teenage shoplifter carrying three bags of crisps in one hand and a bunch of chocolate bars in the other, had seen her too buggered to harass him for a good week.

What a glorious week that had been.

Kyran slowly exhaled as sadness settled over him. How he missed her.

'You okay?' Kenna tipped her head up to him. Concern drawing her brows together. 'It felt just now like, this will sound stupid, but like a cloud passed over you. It made me shiver.'

And this was how Kenna differed from Sonia. She had an empathy that Sonia never had. There were no sharp edges, no curt words. Determination, passion, a readiness to dig in – yes. But her kindness set the two apart.

They reached the cafe and Kyran pulled the door open, unhooked his arm from Kenna's and nodded. 'After you.'

As she entered, the concern etched into her face didn't budge, and he had the feeling that she wasn't going to let the shiver of gloom she'd previously felt go without a conversation. Or a fight. Which was where their conversations inevitably ended up.

Not this time, Kyran vowed. He'd do his best to curb his tongue, to unblock the barriers he instinctively created when dealing with people he didn't know that well. Hell, his defences went up around people he knew very well. It was an instinct borne of years of rejection, or fear of rejection. An instinct he had to rid himself of if there was any chance of discovering whether their relationship could become more than that of just colleagues and housemates.

'Kyran! Kenna!' Marie rushed into the room, her oven mitt-clad hands holding a tray of golden pasties. 'To what do I deserve the honour of seeing you both at the same time?' Without waiting for an answer she turned her back on them and began efficiently filling the pie warmer. 'Has the shop burned down?' She glanced over her shoulder and winked. 'Just joking. I haven't heard any fire sirens.'

Kenna went to the table by the window and settled into a chair. 'No fire sirens. No fire. Not much business, I'm afraid.'

'Speaking of. We're here to drop off some flyers, if that's okay?' Kyran set the flyers down on the counter, then took in the array of food arranged in the cabinet.

Marie slid the warmer shut, put the tray and tongs down and removed the mitts. 'Of course you can leave the flyers here. And I'm sorry business isn't booming, but it'll get better. I'm sure of it. People are really excited about this weekend's festival. The amount of smack talk I've heard from the local families has been . . . well . . . amusing.'

'Smack talk?' Kyran picked up a plate and began filling it with sausage rolls. He pointed his finger at a chocolate coconut-covered cake-like creation. 'Er, what's this?'

'Lamington. Sponge cake, dipped in chocolate icing, rolled in coconut. I discovered them when I holidayed in Australia and have always wanted to make them. What with all the new exciting things going on in the village, I thought now was better than never. Why put off 'til tomorrow what you can do today, and all that jazz.'

'They sound disgusting.' Kyran screwed up his nose.

'They sound amazing,' Kenna called out. 'Get me one, please, Kyran. Along with a latte.'

'I live and work with a crazy person.' The words came out before he had a chance to self-edit. So much for not starting a fight. Here he was, not minutes into what was meant to be good-quality, argument-free time spent with Kenna, not a date – at least that's what he was telling himself – and he'd already managed to insult her. Get her hackles up. Give her every reason to stand up and walk out.

'Takes one to know one,' retorted Kenna with a snort.

'Feel free to laugh louder, Kenna.' Marie rang up Kyran's food. 'That old stick-in-the-mud needs to be laughed at once in a while.'

158

'Stick-in-the-mud? Me?' Kyran pressed his palm over his chest and widened his eyes. 'I'm anything but. I'm sunshine and light and all that. And I'd also like a latte, please.'

'Not your usual flat white?'

'I said latte, didn't I?'

'First latte you've had ever. Are you trying to impress Kenna with your cosmopolitan ways?' Marie's lips quirked to the side.

'Not at all. Just in the mood for a change.'

'For the first time ever,' Marie shot back. 'Have you been body-snatched overnight?' Marie took his money, plated up their food and set it on the counter, then moved to the coffee machine.

'You know, Marie, considering all this grief you give me, I don't know why I come here.' Kyran picked up the plates of food and wrinkled his nose at Marie before grinning at her.

He knew exactly why he came to Marie's. She was the closest thing he had to a friend in the village, and had been since they were little. While never best friends, because Kyran had kept himself to himself for as long as he could remember, she'd taken it upon herself to take care of him in what little ways she could – or he'd allow. Like offering him something from her school lunchbox when she noticed his eyes hungrily taking in other kids' food when his father had, yet again, forgotten to pack his lunch. Then, when Kyran had grown old enough to pack his own, she'd gone out of her way to include him in conversation at school. It must've, Kyran imagined, been harder than pulling teeth with plastic tweezers, but Marie had never given up on him. And when Jen had passed she'd been the first to turn up on Sonia's doorstep with a lasagne in hand along with a card saying if he needed to talk she was there.

And while he'd never taken Marie up on her offer to open up about Jen, he'd made sure to support her cafe when she'd taken over it from the previous owner, made sure to make small talk when he popped in, small talk that progressed into good-natured teasing, and eventually a proper friendship that Kyran felt if not safe, then comfortable, in.

'Go. Sit.' Marie flapped her hand at the table. 'I'll bring over your *latte,* you fancy man, you.'

Kyran scrunched his nose up and glared at her once more for good measure, then turned to see Kenna fanning herself, her cheeks red, and eyes watering with unshed tears of laughter.

'I'm glad you find Marie's teasing amusing.'

Kenna continued to fan her face. 'Oh, more than you know. You're so serious about everything, and everyone seems to tiptoe around you in fear of – I don't know – setting you off or having you push them away, that it's glorious to see someone not just stand up to you but take the mickey out of you. And are you sure you want a latte? It did sound like you're more of a flat white kind of guy.'

'A barista once told me a latte is no different from a flat white,' Kyran paused before continuing on with the story, 'after they gave me a latte when I'd ordered a flat white, and I'd decided to question it, because . . .' His cheeks heated up. 'I do prefer a flat white. That's my go-to.'

'Your only. Usually.' Marie set the latte bowls down. 'And the barista lied to you. There is definitely a difference. They were just too lazy to make a fresh coffee. Cheeky sods.'

'Agreed.' Kenna wrapped her hands around the bowl. 'I'd have been fired from the last cafe I worked at if I'd been caught saying that.'

'I'd have fired myself.' Marie sniffed the air. 'Ooh, that's the banana loaf five minutes away from burning. I'll leave you two to it.'

Kyran watched as Marie hurried back to the kitchen.

'You and Marie, did you two ever? You know?'

He turned back to Kenna to see her brows raised, her head nodding like a toy dog you find on a car's dashboard.

'Me? Marie? Like that?' He shook his head so violently he saw stars. 'Friends. That's all. She prefers her boyfriends to have something called a good personality, which is something you know as well as I do that I couldn't give her. I'm an acquired taste. A bit like that coconutty, chocolate thing you're going to eat, I suspect.'

Kenna's eyes narrowed and he could almost see the set of scales in her mind weighing up whether to continue the line of romantic enquiry, or if it was safer to leave that topic of conversation alone. Part of him wished she would take the latter route, but he also knew that if he was going to let things deepen between them, he was going to have to be honest. Open.

'Truth be told, there's been no once since Jen.' Despite the casual tone he'd delivered the news with, Kyran's gut clenched. It wasn't that he was embarrassed to have not been with anyone else, but for some stupid reason he cared about Kenna's opinion of this fact.

Would she see him as less of a man?

Did it make him look like the walking wounded?

Was it a turn-off?

The lamington Kenna had picked up hovered in front of her mouth as she stared at him with unabashed shock. 'Never. Ever. No one. Not a soul since? Not even a one-off one- night stand type of thing? A kiss behind the pub?' She grimaced. 'Not that you'd kiss behind the pub. It's a little too . . .'

'Too close to home?'

'Exactly. I mean. Never. Wow.' She stuffed half the lamington into her mouth, placed the rest on the plate and began to chew, her eyes as large as the bowls Marie had served their lattes in.

'Thish ish. Really. Good.' She pointed to the lamington and flashed him the thumbs up. 'Can't. Believe. It.'

'Your gran would have a heart attack at you talking with your mouth full. And what part can't you believe? How good that . . . lami–whatever thing . . . is? Or that I've kept myself to myself?' Kyran took a sip of his latte, then waggled his index finger in Kenna's direction. 'And do you know that you've now got yourself a coconut moustache?'

Kenna groaned and swiped at her face, managing to make a mess of the table as little white bits of desiccated coconut fell from around her mouth.

Eyeing the mess she'd made, Kenna began swiping the coconut into her cupped hand before depositing it on a serviette. 'Better?' She offered her face up for Kyran's inspection.

'Marginally.' Before he could stop himself, before he knew what he was doing, he reached over, cupped her chin in his hand – while trying not to marvel at how perfectly the curve of her chin and the line of his palm married, how right they felt together – and brushed away the remaining bits of coconut she'd missed.

His thumb caught the edge of her upper lip. Its ridge surprisingly firm compared to the softness of the skin that lay below.

Move your thumb away.

His body paid no attention to his mind's command, and continued to follow the rise and fall of Kenna's lip, before settling on her cheek.

Her lips parted, and Kyran braced himself for Kenna to find the words that would give him the bollocking he deserved for being so forward. Or as forward as he'd been in years with a woman.

Certainly the most intimate.

It was one thing to have hooked his arm and escorted Kenna here. A show of chivalry. A peace offering after his ridiculous flash of jealousy at seeing her so friendly with another man. But to touch her, to caress a part of her that was saved only for a few – or so he assumed – that wasn't just crossing a boundary, that was taking a flying leap over it.

And yet his hand was still there. Still cupping. Magnetic in its touch. Energetic in the way his hand had grown hot, sending a sizzle of electricity running down his arm, heating his blood, whisking his heart into a frenzied patter, awakening another area – one that had not been forgotten but, on the by and large, ignored for a long time.

Too long.

'All gone now?'

Kenna's words were so quiet Kyran found himself leaning forward to hear them.

Bolting back, Kenna's chair tipped, and her knees hit the underside of the table sending the bowls of coffee, the sausage rolls, and what was left of the lamington flying.

Kyran whipped his hand back, realising Kenna had thought he meant to kiss her when he leaned in.

'Oh god. Kenna. I'm so sorry. I wasn't going to . . .' Seeing the mess on the table, Kyran began gathering the bowls and saucers. 'I mean, I wouldn't. Business partners. Flatmates. That's all. Keeping out of each other's lives. Like we agreed.' He stood and called out to Marie. 'Marie, tea towel, cloth, something. Please.'

He cringed at how pathetic he sounded. How flustered. How out of control.

This was not him. This was not who he was. Kyran Walsh kept his emotions tight. He didn't get swept up in romance. Or soft lips. Or pondering and wonderings of what-if.

He leaned down to pick up the coconut-covered treat that had been the root cause of all the commotion, and was met with an 'ow' followed a sharp pain to his forehead.

Clutching his head, he scuffled away and looked up to see Kenna clasping her eye, tears streaming down her face.

'What the hell is going on in here?'

He forced his gaze away from Kenna's pain to see Marie, hands on hips, towering over them, her forehead corrugated in dismay.

'I leave you two alone for five minutes and you trash the place? And beat each other up? Honestly.' She tutted, thrust a tea towel in Kyran's direction, picked up the dishes Kyran had stacked, walked them to the kitchen, then returned seconds later with a damp cloth. 'Here.' She threw it at Kyran. 'Wipe down the table.' She turned to address Kenna. 'Do you need an ice pack?'

Kenna nodded. 'Please.'

Ten seconds later, Marie was back with a bag of frozen peas and passed them to Kenna.

'It's all I have, but it'll do the trick. Kyran, why is your bum still on the floor? Clean that mess up like I told you.'

Kyran gingerly touched the spot on his forehead where Kenna had collided with it. Sure enough, an egg was forming underneath.

'And don't play the damsel in distress. I know for a fact that your noggin can handle much tougher cracks.' Marie squatted down by Kenna, lifted the edge of the pea bag and peered at the area around her eye. 'I don't think there's going to be a bruise. Good thing, that. Wouldn't be the best look for the festival if the organisers were to look like they've been going ten rounds with each other.' Marie straightened up and exhaled loudly. 'Right, I'm heading back to the kitchen. When I get back I expect to see you both in your chairs and,' she waggled her index finger in quick circles, 'for whatever's going on between you two to be sorted.'

Kyran saluted her, grateful that she'd chosen not to enquire what 'this thing' might have been. 'Ay ay, captain.'

'That's enough cheek from you, young man.' Grimacing at Kyran, then winking at Kenna, Marie strode away, tutting as she went.

Kyran closed his eyes as his head began to pound. So much for having a tough noggin.

'She's going to make an excellent parent one day.' Kenna shook her head in admiration. 'Her kids are going to be the best behaved around.'

Kyran pushed himself up, went to Kenna and offered her his hand.

She glanced at it wearily, then clasped it, letting him pull her up.

Stepping away before she got it in her head that he was about to force himself upon her, he nodded. 'She's a natural mum. I can't think of a time in my life when she hasn't been there for me. Well, as much as I'd let her be.' His ears perked up at Marie's off-key whistling, and he smiled, knowing she was doing her best to mind her own business, and making sure they knew she was doing so.

'And why does she always mum you?'

Kyran shrugged. There was being open to giving he and Kenna a chance to get to know each other, to see if there was anything more to the weird way his heart flip-flopped whenever she turned her full beam smile on him, and then there was telling her his life story, which he was in no way ready to do. 'It's just Marie's way. She's a caring person, much like a lot of the villagers here.'

Kenna slumped into her chair, her hand still clutching the bag of frozen peas to her head. 'Wow, you and my gran must've done a number on the village to have them back away from you, from the business, the way they did.'

Turning his chair round, Kyran straddled it and wrapped his arms around its back. 'I guess we weren't the most approachable people. The old-timers didn't mind. If anything they preferred the way we kept ourselves to ourselves and left them to get what they wanted without a hard sell – or any kind of sell. Unfortunately the problem with the old-timers is . . .' Kyran lifted his finger to the sky.

'I see. They are a passing clientele.'

'To put it nicely. Unfortunately our way of dealing with customers didn't go down so well with the young families who were wanting to introduce fishing to the next generation but wanted it to be a fun experience for them. I had no patience for the way they'd leap about the boat, and Sonia hated the way the kids touched every single thing in the store and messed the place up. The number of times a little kid left that shop in tears after a sharp word from her.' Kyran shook his head at the memory of one little kid who'd howled so loudly he'd taken pity on him, gone to Marie's and brought him back a slice of chocolate cake. Not that his cake apology had done any good. He'd never seen that family in the shop ever again. 'I guess Sonia and I were our own worst enemies.'

Kenna grabbed the cloth and began sopping up the spilled coffee. 'Not any more though, right?'

'That's my job. You're the sitting wounded, remember?' He reached over to grab the cloth from Kenna. Tingles sparked his fingertips as his hand met hers. Warm and comforting in a way that made him want to cover her hand with his. To flip it over. Trail his fingers over her palm, to caress her fingers with the tips of his own. To create not just sparks but a burning fire. To take their burgeoning friendship further . . .

Kenna relinquished the cloth with a small frown. 'You don't have to do that. I'm quite capable of holding peas to my eye and cleaning up mess at the same time.'

He tugged the cloth away. 'I know you're capable, but we're partners, remember?' He scrunched the cloth under his hand. Partners? Next thing you know he'd be on bended knee offering up a shiny bauble of his everlasting affection. 'Business partners,' he amended.

A slow, sweet smile spread on Kenna's face. 'I know what you meant, and thank you.'

'For what? I haven't even begun to clean up the mess we made. Marie's going to have my guts for garters if she comes out here and it's not done.'

Kenna's hand fell upon his and gave it a squeeze. 'Thank you for giving us a chance. And by "us", I mean you and me.'

Kyran's heart caught in his chest as a lump made its home in his throat. A current of emotion overtook him. Tears prickled at the back of his eyes, and burned the inside of his nose. He blinked them away then inhaled deeply, desperate to reassert control over himself.

Kenna pushed her chair back and stood. 'I'm going to return the peas to Marie. While I do that, you clean this up. Then shall we head back to the shop and hammer out the last-minute details of the festival? I've decided to play music through a sound system, but it'd be good if you could help me put together a playlist.'

He nodded, not trusting himself to speak. Unable to put the maelstrom of feelings that swirled in his heart, in his mind, in his gut, into words.

Was he finally, after all these years, healing by letting another person in? By allowing himself to be less insular, part of the community, part of something greater than the four walls he'd built around himself?

And would he be brave enough to keep going? To further deconstruct the barriers he'd created? To move on once and for all to a future that wasn't constricted by the past?

A future that might feature a long-haired brunette who'd been forced into his life?

Kenna re-entered the room, and just like that, it felt like the space was brighter, warmer.

Like he had found home.

Chapter Fourteen

'Where do you want us to park?'

'Could you get that food truck to move? I don't want its crêpe scent to mingle with the scent of my paella.'

'Do you know where the sacks for the sack race are meant to go?'

Kenna covered her ears as the squeal of the PA blasted over the wharf. She tossed a glare in its general direction, glad to be far enough away that poor old Jim, who Kyran had roped into setting up the sound system, didn't sense or see her irritation.

Three hours of anxious sleep, hours spent awake worrying about the festival, topped off with far too much coffee courtesy of Marie, had her stress strings drawn ping-tight. One more silly question, one more petty complaint, one more irritation and she'd be heading to the end of the wharf and jumping into the sea. And god help the person who tried to save her.

Something tugged at her T-shirt and Kenna spun round, ready to train her irritation on the source of said tugging.

Guilt flooded her heart, cooling her annoyance, at the sight of a pair of luminous, tear-filled brown eyes staring up at her.

She crouched down so she was at eye-level with the youngster. 'Are you okay?'

'I lost my dada,' whispered the wee boy. 'And Mama said if you lose your parent you should go and find another mama.'

Kenna glanced down at her outfit – a plain black T-shirt paired with navy-blue shorts and black canvas shoes. Chosen for simplicity, for not having to worry if she spilt anything on it while carrying out the day's duties, she could see how she might be mistaken for a mother – even if there was no child attached to her.

'Your mama is very smart. Here, shall we find a tall spot and see if we can find your dada?'

With the trust that only the innocent had, the little boy placed his hand in hers and she directed them towards the makeshift stage. Climbing the few steps, she hoisted him onto her shoulders.

'There you go. Can you see your daddy?'

'Dada!'

It wasn't hard for Kenna to spot 'Dada'. A man with the same large brown eyes and matching head of dark, bouncy curls came running towards them, relief making his eyes even larger.

'Will, thank goodness.' He ran up the stairs, swooped the small boy off Kenna's shoulders, hugged him tight, then turned his attention to Kenna. 'Thank you. Truly. His mother, my wife, would've killed me had I lost him . . . or worse.'

Worse. The thought hadn't even occurred to Kenna. She'd created a family fun day by the sea, by the wharf. Places where children could run off, get lost . . . or worse. Much worse. Imagines of frantic caregivers looking for children who'd fallen prey to 'worse' jostled for room in her overloaded mind.

'Well, I'm glad I could help.' She smiled weakly. Too weakly judging by the fresh look of concern on the man's face.

He leaned in, inspecting her. 'Are you okay? You've gone a bit peaky?'

'Fine. Fine. Just . . . er . . . fine.' If only 'fine' meant a jackhammer hadn't started up in her head, or that a whirlpool of nerves hadn't taken residence in stomach.

'Is everything okay here?'

Kenna had never been so relieved to see Kyran, even if he had that same odd look on his face as he had the day she found him talking to the cap-buying customer.

Something akin to jealousy, but most definitely not. Sure, they'd had a few moments where they'd stared at each other a touch too long, seconds where some odd energy, that felt not unlike attraction, sprang up between them. Then there had been the whole weird cafe scene – starting with being escorted to the cafe like she was on a date and finishing with, not just an odd energy, but the straight up bolts of electricity she'd experienced when Kyran's thumb had brushed the length of her lip. But those moments of connection – what kind of connection she didn't want to consider for fear she was wrong, that she'd make a misstep in verbalising feelings and see the foundation of connection they were slowly building tumble down – didn't, or shouldn't, have added up to jealousy or possessiveness of any kind on Kyran's part.

She rubbed her eyes as weariness threatened to overwhelm her. Straightening up, she sucked in a lungful of salty air. *Pull yourself together, woman. It's barely the beginning of the day. You've got six more hours ahead of you. At least.*

'Everything's fine. My son managed to evade me and this young woman here took great care of him. Honestly, what might've happened to him if she hadn't gotten to him.' The man shook his head, instinctively hugging his son tighter to him.

Kenna didn't have to be looking straight at Kyran to know he was thinking what she'd been thinking. Didn't have to be a psychologist to know that his reaction to the possibilities the day could bring would be ten times worse than hers.

She wasn't the one who'd lost the love of their life to the sea.

Lightly, she touched the man's forearm, hoping to add greater weight to her act of reassurance. 'He was fine. Honestly. He's a very good and smart boy. He knew to find a mum if he got lost.'

'Just like Mama said so.'

The boy gave his father the cutest 'duh' look that Kenna had to press her lips together to stop a laugh bubbling out.

'Well, in that case, since you were so good and paid attention to what your mummy said, shall we get an ice cream?'

'Sounds like a great idea,' Kenna agreed. 'The ice cream stand's next to the popcorn stand.' She took hold of the little boy's hand and gave it a wiggle. 'Stay close to your dad, okay?'

A solemn nod later and the two were on their way, hands holding each other tight.

Kenna turned to Kyran and placed her hands on her hips, ready to defend her honour. 'Were you about to accuse me of flirting with a man in front of his son?'

His cheeks pinked up in response.

'Really?' She huffed her disapproval. 'Is there a reason I can't just talk to a man without you assuming I'm about to jump their bones?'

'If I said it was because I'm an idiot, would you accept that as a reason and an apology?' He jammed his hands into his short pockets and rocked back and forth.

Kenna dropped her hands and steadied Kyran, feeling seasick despite being on solid ground. 'I'd take it as an *excuse*, and also as an apology.'

'That's fine by me. So, what's got you looking so ill?'

'Same thing that had you looking so worried a second ago. Kids. Water. What can happen if they slip away from parents and get to said water.' A full body shiver rocked her body. 'If that happens . . .'

Kyran's firm, large hands gripped her upper arms, steadying her emotionally. Anchoring her to reality.

'It won't happen. That kid running off was an anomaly. People around here are careful. And the kids around here grow up being told to be careful, and being taught how to be careful. We've only ever had one drowning in my living memory.'

Kenna's heart plummeted straight to the bottom of her stomach. Despite Kyran's hold on her, the world went sideways.

Jen. His fiancée. Of all the people the sea could take, it had been her.

'Oh.' Kenna closed her eyes and attempted to centre herself. 'I'm sorry.'

'There's no reason for you to be sorry. You had nothing to do with what happened.' Despite his light tone, his eyes narrowed, and his brows drew together. 'And it was a long time ago, right? At some point we have to move on from our pain. Or at least do our best to make it hurt less?'

To Kenna's ears it sounded like Kyran was trying to convince himself rather than her, but his honesty, his openness, his attempt at a change of heart, took her by surprise. Was his saying those words out loud proof that he was willing to try and move on? Move forward with his life?

With you? Kenna refused to pay attention to the voice of hope that had risen from nowhere. Kyran's moving on had nothing to do with her. At least not in the potentially romantic way the voice in her head had indicated.

'Kenna, open your eyes. You can't run today with them closed, and the booking schedule I set up to take people out on the boat is already nearly full, so I can't be your guide dog for the day, even if I wanted to.'

Kyran's curt tone put paid to any wistful wonderings. His interest in moving on was for his benefit only. It had nothing to do with her entering his life, professionally or otherwise.

'Right. Of course. Well, thank you for setting me straight. I guess I'll go and check on the stallholders, make sure Jim's wife is okay holding fort at the shop, then officially open the festival.'

'Excellent idea.'

Kenna stuck her tongue out at Kyran's retreating back.

A buzzing in her pocket a minute later alerted her to a text message. Pulling it out she was surprised to see Kyran's name on the screen.

K, You've got this. I promise. Just be you and it'll be fine.

Kenna reread the text in disbelief. Kyran was being supportive? More than that, he'd seen her worry and wanted to help ease it in a way that suggested he cared not about the business, but her?

It was a sign from the universe, Kenna decided. The festival would be a raging success. The people would come, they'd eat, they'd play the games they'd organised, pop into the shop, see why they should recommend a fishing charter with Kyran to any visitors who might come to Dolphin's Cove, then walk away filled with feelings of warmth towards the owners of Fishful Thinking. Putting Fishful Thinking top of mind when they needed any fishing gear.

Job done. Success sorted.

Squaring her shoulders, she made to march up the stage's steps, her confidence faltering as she passed a family group.

'This sucks,' a surly teen complained to his parents. 'There's nothing here.'

'Can we go home? I promised a friend we'd game today.'

Nothing? Kenna tried not to be insulted. There was popcorn and ice cream, candy floss and tacos, paella and crêpes. Marie had set up a pasty stall, and Jim had a drinks stand. There were games planned. Kyran's boat tours. The fishing competition would provide literally hours of entertainment. What more did the kids want?

The answer was obvious: a proper sense of atmosphere. Music. Not the clean styles of music produced in a studio and piped through a sound system, but the live kind, which may not have been perfect, but had soul.

She bit down on her lip, gnawing at it as she tried to find a solution. Short of getting up there herself and playing the spoons terribly, while singing even more terribly, there was no way to fix the problem she'd foreseen from the start.

Unless . . .

Spotting Kyran talking to Old Man Henry at the edge of the wharf, she raced over and pulled him away with a polite, 'I'm sorry, it's important.'

Yanking him toward Fishful Thinking, Kenna worked through how best to tell Kyran that the festival was destined to be a failure. That despite the food, the games, the outings he'd be taking on, people were already bored. That it was unsavable. That their attempt at creating a buzz in the community was a flop, and while he'd survive it because he'd lived in Dolphin's Cove for ever and kept himself to himself most of the time and no one would care, the villagers would remember her involvement and she'd be a community outcast for the rest of ever.

'Are you okay, Kenna? I can all but see the steam coming out of your ears.'

'Oh, shush.'

Kenna continued propelling him away, only stopping once they'd reached the shop and were out of earshot of both the festival-goers and the customers browsing inside.

Her plan to calmly explain the failure didn't translate to real life and she found herself pacing back and forth, the words tumbling from her mouth.

'Kyran, this festival isn't working. Big time. It's only just started and already people are complaining. Not to me. Oh no, not to me, but to those around me. And because they don't know who I am, they're not holding back.' She looked down to see her hands flapping madly. Stuffing them in the back pockets of her shorts, she forced herself to stand still. 'We have to do something. Anything. I was thinking a talent show. Maybe we could get kids to show off their gymnastic skills? Or Marie could lend us some spoons and someone could play us a song? I thought about doing it, except I can't. We need proper entertainment. A talent show would provide that, and it would include members of the community, which could only be a good thing, right?'

'A talent show would only humiliate a bunch of people when faced with the realisation they had little to no actual talent. This isn't a big town or a bustling city, Kenna. We don't have much in the way of facilities that breed talent. And the people here are humble, hardworking types. Not flashy. We don't even have that one quirky person who walks around to the beat of their own drum like all good villages are supposedly meant to have. In all my life, I've never seen or heard anyone do anything that could be considered properly entertaining.'

Kenna looked at Fishful Thinking. The fresh paint job, clean windows and jaunty blue-and-yellow-painted sign that she and Kyran had spent hours working on failing to spark happiness within her. Not when she'd done all she could, and all she could sense ahead was failure.

'So that's it? Game over? Festival over? We just let it die a sad, depressing death? Watch as people trudge home with disappointed – or worse, annoyed – looks on their faces?' She resumed her pacing. Giving up, giving in, was not an option. She hadn't come this far, worked this hard to let her dream, her hope, her future fall over. 'No, there must be a way to breathe life into this.'

Kyran glanced over towards the crowd, hoping to see a sign that Kenna was overreacting, that the festival was going well.

The slow trail of people leaving showed him a story he didn't want to hear. To know.

Kenna was right. The festival hadn't even got off the ground and it was already crashing, and burning. He knew what the villagers were like: kind, yes. But to a point. Something like this would be nattered about over the tea cups and pint glasses for years. And, again, Kenna was right in her assessment of how they'd be affected: he'd be fine. She would be the one they'd see as being responsible for the lack of promised fun. They knew him well enough to know he would've been forced into creating a festival, that it was the newcomer who had the bright idea but had failed to ignite that spark.

He turned his attention back to Kenna who'd begun pacing again, her hands at her side scrunching and unscrunching as her lips moved wordlessly.

She was in a state, and he was the only person who could help her. But was he brave enough? Strong enough?

Oh, for Pete's sake, man. You're six foot three, broad as they come, and a grown adult. Pull yourself together.

177

So much for wanting to tip-toe into healing. He was being shoved in the deep end.

He only hoped it would be worth it.

But, first, he had to stop Kenna wearing out the soles of her shoes.

Stepping in front of her, he forced her to come to an abrupt halt.

'What? What is it?' Her eyes were wide with hope. 'Have you figured out what to do? Could we pull off a talent show? Have you thought of a few people you could convince to go up on stage?'

'Yes and no. Look, there's something I have to do. I'll be back in fifteen.' He went to leave, afraid if he didn't take action there and then he'd chicken out of his grand plan.

Quick footsteps saw Kenna in front of him, walking backwards, paying no heed to what might be in her way.

'You're abandoning me? Just like that? To do what? Hide from the carnage? Leave me to deal with this sad excuse of a festival? I can't believe you'd do that. All this talk of us being partners, of working together, it was just that, wasn't it? All talk.'

Kyran caught her hand and held it tight in his. 'Like I said, just give me fifteen. I promise I won't let you down.'

'Yeah right,' Kenna muttered under her breath as Kyran turned and jogged away.

You've got this. The three words rotated through his mind as he powered up the hill to the cottage, gathered the few items he needed, and then jogged back down.

As he drew nearer, he could see the crowd had further dwindled. To the side of the stage sat a dejected-looking Kenna. Her knees were drawn up to her chest, her hands wrapped around her legs, her lips turned down in a frown.

Hopefully not for too much longer.

Striding through the crowd, ignoring those around him nudging each other and pointing, paying no attention to the buzz of excitement that followed him, he strode onto the stage, lifted the microphone high enough on its stand that it was by his lips, hung his guitar around his neck and prepared himself to do the one thing he'd swore he'd never do again.

'Good afternoon, Dolphin's Cove!' He grimaced as a squeal of feedback flew out over the wharf. Seeing a few members of the public clap their hands over their ears, he took a small step back from the microphone and forced himself to continue. 'Thank you for coming to the first annual Dolphin's Cove Fishing Festival.'

Out of the corner of his eye he could see Kenna mouth 'first annual', her face a perfect storm of shocked, horrified and hopeful.

'Sorry for the delay in starting. Being our first event we wanted everything to be absolutely perfect, and that meant making a few tweaks to the day. One of those tweaks being me.'

'Great start, mate,' called out a random voice.

Ignoring the jibe, hearing that it was said in amusement rather than cruelty, Kyran took a deep breath and continued on.

'The fishing competition is ready to start. We're keeping things simple this year with a ticket given for every fish caught and released, and prizes will be drawn from there.'

'That's Henry out of the running. I've yet to see him catch a thing.'

Kyran grinned as Old Man Henry waved a fist at the local who'd dared to deny his fishing prowess.

'As Fishful Thinking is the sponsor of the festival, Kenna and I have provided extra rods for those who don't have

179

their own, and we've provided the bait for those who need it too. Prizes will be for vouchers to Coffee, Tea and Sea, as well as to the pub, and a fishing trip with yours truly for up to five people, snacks and beverages included.'

A cheer went up from the crowd and Kyran could see those who'd started to leave filter back, their interest in the event renewed. The jitters that had sent his heart racing and the blood in his veins hurtling settled. Another quick glance at Kenna saw the colour had returned to her cheeks, and her shoulders were no longer in danger of touching the ethereal lines of clouds that stretched over the sky above them.

Everything was going to be okay.

'The wonderful Kenna here will be in charge of registrations. So follow her to the end of the wharf.' He gave Kenna an encouraging nod, and was bemused to see her cheeks had further reddened. Was it his use of 'wonderful'? Or the embarrassment of having attention drawn to her causing her to flush?

Probably the latter, preferably the former. The idea that Kenna found his calling her wonderful sent his own flush of pleasure through him. Compliments from people you don't care about barely skimmed a person's emotional surface, but from someone you had feelings for? They could make a burly man's knees turn into jellyfish, or a determined woman's cheeks go the colour of ripe raspberries.

'Around you, you'll find a delicious range of food and beverages to keep your stomachs full as you fish, or to give you energy when you take each other on in the egg and spoon, and sack races. While you're here, we'd love it if you'd pop into Fishful Thinking and check out our new look. We've all sorts of plans for the store in the coming weeks and months and can't wait to be of service to you.'

Claps of approval met his ears, giving him the courage he needed not to go on with his opening spiel, but to take to the stage the way he'd once done. The people here had his back even after all this time. They wouldn't let him get egg on his face, or mock his efforts. They were a community, *his* community.

The realisation hit him straight in the solar plexus, almost knocking him backward.

All these years he'd shunned the people who were now looking up at him, smiling in his direction, encouraging him with subtle nods of their heads to go on. All these years the support he'd needed but denied had been right there in front of him, just waiting for him to accept it.

And here he was – accepting it. Because of Kenna. Because he didn't want to let her down. Because he knew how important being part of this community was to her. Because he wanted her to be happy.

He wanted her to stay.

In Dolphin's Cove.

With him.

For ever.

And that meant not letting her down. Never giving her a reason to leave. And he wouldn't.

From this moment on, he was going to be 100 per cent present and active in the business. He would stop blocking her attempts at getting to know him; if anything he'd embrace them. Because he wanted her to be with him, to care about him, to flush at his compliments, to not just link arms, but to hold hands.

Because he *liked* her. More than liked her.

He took hold of the microphone stand, afraid that his knees – which had indeed turned to jelly – would fail him at any second.

Focus. He coughed into his shoulder, and reminded himself why he was on the stage, what he had to do, and who he had to do it for.

The community.

Kenna.

Himself.

'Henry will be taking the tours of the bay in my boat.' He caught Old Man Henry giving him the two-finger salute and stifled a laugh. It'd cost him a good ear-bashing later, but needs must, and Old Man Henry was the only person he trusted with *Fishful Thinking Too*. 'Because I have my own job to do.' He strummed the guitar. Revelling in the whoops and hollers that rose from the crowd.

A surge of adrenaline raced through him, as it always had when he'd taken to the stage, and he thanked the small part of himself that had refused to let him put the guitar down for ever, that had insisted he play at night to his audience of none.

Or, in more recent times, of one.

He turned to Kenna and mouthed 'thank you' to her. Had she not asked, had she not pushed, had she not told him he was wasting his talent by not playing, he wouldn't have been up here now, doing the one thing he'd ever loved, second and third only to loving Jen and Sonia.

Kenna's smile was so sweet, her eyes so full of pride, he almost forgot to keep playing, but in true Kenna-style she flicked her hand impatiently towards his audience before trotting down the stage's steps towards the end of the wharf.

What a woman.

An impatient squawk caught his attention. Kyran glanced up to see a gull circling ominously, its beady eyes on him as it cawed once more. Telling him to get a move on. To stop faffing about.

Grinning up at the bird, he acknowledged its presence with a nod, and launched into his first song, thinking it was better to sing than be shat on.

Chapter Fifteen

If a person had told Kenna a year ago, even a month ago, when she'd first arrived in Dolphin's Cove, that she would one day become a pro at detaching flapping fish from hooks, she'd have laughed and called them crazy. Turns out the crazy one would have been her for doubting she could even do such a thing.

With Kyran's tutorage, followed by three solid hours of unhooking them by hand, only using long-nosed pliers when it was absolutely necessary before releasing the fish back to their home, she felt confident in saying her bait and release game was strong. Her belief in herself further backed up when Old Man Henry, whilst on a break from bay tours, had told her he'd yet to see any of her fishy friends belly up in the drink.

'All good here?'

Baiting a hook for one of the youngsters, she turned to see something, or should that be some*one* else she'd never have believed she'd come to enjoy: Kyran. In all his tall, broad-shouldered, handsome-faced, manbunned and full-faced beard glory.

He'd been popping up beside her every time he took a break from singing; checking on her, bringing her food and drinks, making sure she had everything she needed. And with each visit she'd felt something in him change. Shift. The glower that she'd come to believe was permanently etched upon his brow had disappeared. The heaviness of his step replaced by a jaunty spring. She'd even seen him high-five a little girl who'd caught a sprat.

Was this the true Kyran she was seeing? The Kyran he'd once been before tragedy had stolen his joy and kept it under lock and key, unless he was with those he trusted . . . until today?

'Kenna?' He touched her arm, a quizzical look upon his face.

God, she must've looked a right twit staring at him without answering.

Less pondering, more talking, Kenna.

'Sorry. Was off with the fairies for a second there. Must be all the sea air paired with a big day.' She made a show of pulling out her mobile and checking the time. 'Not long to go now. Just the prize-giving, and then we can pack up and . . .' She shrugged, unsure quite what the plan was once all was said and done. Part of her wanted nothing more than to head home and sleep for as many hours as her body and mind would allow, the other was in the mood to celebrate what surely had been a success.

A big enough success to save the business? Only time would tell.

'After this, do you think you'll have enough energy left in you to have a drink at Jim's with me?' Kyran's nose twitched, like he'd caught a whiff of something bad. 'Perhaps after we have a shower?'

We? Kenna pressed her trembling lips together, not wanting to laugh at Kyran's faux pas when he'd been so thoughtful, so kind towards her all day. Not after he'd saved the festival from being a flop.

'I mean . . . you have a shower. Then me. Alone. Certainly not together.' He shuffled from one foot to the

185

other. 'You know what I mean. After playing music all day I'm a bit ripe, and that's putting it mildly.'

Kenna brought her hands up to her face, cupped them and breathed in. The whiff of salt and the briny scent of fresh fish filled her nostrils. She'd smelled better. Summer sun, saving fish, and stress-sweating did not make for an enticing aromatic mix.

'Don't worry.' She grinned up at Kyran. 'I do know what you mean. And a drink, after a shower, sounds good. My shout.'

'Your shout?' His head angled to the side. 'What have I done to deserve you shouting?'

'I think it's more of a case of what haven't you done.'

Her gaze was meant to be pointed, but when it met Kyran's soft, sweet one, something changed inside her. Melted. The past irritations between the two of them evaporated, leaving two people who'd learned to work together, learned to trust each other, who had each other's backs and only wanted the best for the other. No longer just business partners, but friends.

Kyran's little finger hooked around hers, sending a firestorm of desire flashing through Kenna. Her heart halted in her chest, the world around her blurred as she looked into his deep, dark eyes and could see her feelings reflected back at her.

Not business partners. Not friends. Something else. Something bigger than she could've believed, or hoped for.

She squeezed Kyran's finger and inched closer, unable to stop, not caring what those around her would think, just wanting to be close to him, to feel him, to know him . . .

A thin screech filled the air, followed by the fumbled thump-thumps of someone turning on a microphone haphazardly.

186

The magic that had sprung up between them fizzled out, and with small smiles that spoke of later, they turned to see Jim on the stage, his face beet red, his knees visibly shaking even from where Kyran and Kenna stood.

'He gets terrible stage fright,' Kyran whispered in a confiding tone. 'Says he's a one-to-one kind of guy, rather than a crowd type. Back in the day, when I played at the pub, he'd go white as a ghost before introducing me to the audience. I ended up telling him not to bother because I was afraid he'd vomit all over the equipment. So if he's up there, it must be important. Perhaps we'd better move closer in case we're needed.'

'Good plan.' Kenna twisted around and checked that those who'd continued fishing after the competition ended were fine without her, then followed Kyran into the crowd that had gathered to the stage to hear Jim's announcement.

'I think we can all agree that today has been one for the books. Even the weather came to the party.'

The crowd chuckled appreciatively at Jim's small joke and his knees appeared to firm a little under the weight of his nerves.

'I wanted to say a few words before the event ends, in order to give credit where credit's due. I think we can all agree that Dolphin's Cove was in need of a shake-up. As small as we are, we'd settled into our daily lives, perhaps too much. Gone inward. Forgotten that what makes a community isn't the place you live in, but the people who live in it – and the better those people get along, the more we invest in each other, the greater, the stronger a community becomes.'

'So much for stage fright,' murmured Kenna as she took in the faces of those she'd seen but yet to properly meet. Their faces were upturned, bodies leaning towards the stage. 'He's got everyone under his spell.'

'The man could've run this town, this whole area, in an official capacity had he been brave enough to campaign.'

'From what you've told me, I'd say he does anyway.'

Kyran nodded sagely. 'This is true.'

An irritated 'ahem' met Kenna's ears. With a grin she mimed zipping her lips and turned her attention back to the stage.

'The Dolphin's Cove Fishing Festival would never have happened without our newest resident.'

Kenna's heart rate ratcheted up. Much like Jim, she preferred person-on-person communication. Her stomach turned at the thought of getting up on the stage and facing the people who she'd been so close to failing.

'Kenna, come on up here, and bring that business partner of yours as well.'

Flames of embarrassment licked over her body as she forced herself to walk through the crowd that parted, making her trip up to the stage easier than she'd have liked. Running the opposite way being her preferred method of dealing with the situation. It was one thing to want to be part of a community, another thing entirely to have the spotlight thrust upon her.

'You'll be fine.'

Kyran's hand surrounded hers, then squeezed, his thumb running over her knuckles, soothing, encouraging.

'Here they are. Hurry up so I can be relieved from this horrible position I've put myself in.'

Kyran's hand stayed firmly in place as they climbed the stairs and made their way to Jim. Up close, Kenna could see beads of sweat peppering his forehead, some trickling down, getting caught in the maze of lines that gave his face its warm, open character.

Turning back to the crowd, Jim swept his arm out in a flourish. 'These are the two people who not only conceived of but created this wonderful community event. Kenna and Kyran, the owners of our very own bait shop and fishing charter, Fishful Thinking. Let's give them a round of applause and show them our appreciation for all their hard work.'

Without hesitation, the villagers went wild. Hooting and hollering, clapping and whistling.

Kenna's heart expanded, so much so she was afraid it might explode. This was more than she could've hoped for. She'd wanted, *yearned*, to be part of a community. To be recognised as someone who belonged, and here it was happening before her eyes. She looked up at Kyran whose face – what you could see of it beneath all that beard – had gone lobster red, but even his embarrassment couldn't hide his joy. His lips were stretched wide, even though his head hung in humbleness.

After what felt like an eternity – the most glorious, heartwarming of eternities – the noise died down.

'So,' Jim continued, 'the next time you need bait or a rod, a life jacket or cool bag . . .'

Pushing her nerves to the side, Kenna stepped forward and leaned into the microphone. 'Whatever your fishing needs . . .'

'Indeed.' Jim winked. 'Forego the online shopping, ignore the bait shops down the line, and shop local. Show your appreciation for Kenna and Kyran as they've showed their love for our community today.'

Unceremoniously, Jim shoved the microphone in Kenna's direction and scurried off the stage, wiping the sweat off his face with a handkerchief as he went.

Kenna closed her eyes for a moment, stilled her racing mind, her overwhelmed emotions and reminded herself that she had a job to do.

Opening her eyes, she tightened her grip on the microphone so as not to let it slip through her sweaty palms and faced the audience.

This is your home, these people will one day be like family, treat them as such.

'Friends, before we move on to the prizegiving, I'd like to just take a minute to say a huge thank-you on behalf of Kyran and myself.'

A comforting weight fell upon her shoulders, and she didn't have to look to know it was Kyran's arm wrapped around her shoulders, silently supporting her. Proving in his own, quiet way that he wouldn't let her fall. Wouldn't let her – or the business – fail.

'It's been a pleasure getting to know so many of you today. The way you've embraced the event, the way you've welcomed me into your community.' Her hand fell upon her heart as she saw smiles widen. 'It means more to me than you'll ever know. Now,' she turned to Marie, who had arrived at the side of the stage, holding the vouchers and a basket of tickets, 'shall we announce the winners of the fishing competition?'

The roar of approval that met her ears was all the answer she needed.

And all the proof she required that she was where she was meant to be. Finally.

'You look proud of yourself.'

Kenna waited for a barb to follow Kyran's words. Expected him to turn 'proud' into 'smug'.

She angled her head to get a better look at him as they trudged up the hill towards the cottage. Towards home. His head was tilted, facing her, his eyes luminous. Looking as proud of her as she felt of herself.

No barbs. No barriers.

Something had transformed within Kyran, and it made him beautiful. Inside, as well as out.

'That's because I am.' She unlatched the gate and made her way down the garden path, taking a moment to appreciate the hollyhocks nodding in the breeze, the Cornish daisies that were slowly but surely taking over every inch of the garden, and the bees that meandered from flower to flower. 'I was so afraid that we wouldn't be able to pull this off, that it was all going to go wrong. The fact that it went so right . . .' Kenna shook her head, part of her still in disbelief at how successful the event had been. Pulling her house key out of her bag, she pushed it into the lock. As always it slipped in without protest, and she knew it would turn just as easily. Kind of like how she and Kyran had worked together that day. A perfect team. A perfect match? An unexpected shiver prickled over her.

Kyran's change of temperament. His acts of kindness. The hand-holding. The shoulder-hugging. His actions had felt heavy with meaning earlier in the day, filled with promise. But now, in the soft light of the early evening sun, where the world held a haze that stretched all the way out, thickening at the horizon where the sea met the sky, Kenna couldn't help but wonder if she'd imagined it all. And even if she hadn't, would going there with Kyran, entering into a relationship that was more than business partners or friends be stepping into dangerous territory? Especially when they had so much to lose if things went wrong between them – their business, their livelihoods, their home.

'It really did go right, didn't it? I'd say it was perfect.'

Kenna pushed the door open and turned to Kyran. 'Perfect if you ignore my freak-out at the beginning.'

'Even that was perfect. It forced me to take my head out of my arse and do something I should've done a long time ago.'

Kenna leaned against the doorway. 'You played beautifully. The crowd loved you.'

'I'm not talking about playing music. I mean, yes, I should've done that years ago, but I'm talking about being part of the community. Opening myself up to a life much bigger than the one I'd pushed myself into.'

Honesty. Kenna added it to the list of ways Kyran had changed. He was being honest about his feelings. His actions. His past.

He took her hand in his and tugged her towards him, his eyes not leaving her face as his other hand cupped her cheek. Little by little, his face, his lips moved closer, and she took the moment to study him, unabashed, unafraid. Knowing he wouldn't mind.

Weathered from a life spent outdoors on the sea, the lines of his face were strong yet comforting. The angles mellowed by the curve of his cheeks, his lips. She closed her eyes and embraced the feel of his touch. His thumb pad rough against the smoothness of her skin. His touch firm but tender. Making her feel like she belonged, like she was wanted, like she was . . . .

Loved.

Shock brought Kenna to her senses. Her eyes flew open and she jerked backwards.

This was madness. To think that Kyran's touch could make her feel loved. To believe it held the power of love. Yes, he'd changed, but a person didn't go from putting up with someone, barely tolerating their presence, to having big, romantic feelings in the blink of an eye. Or in the time it took to run a festival. And she couldn't afford to put her life on the line, one she was just getting together for a moment of passion.

'I just smelled myself.' She blurted by way of explanation. 'You deserve better than to smell me.'

Forcing herself to ignore the look of confusion, followed by hurt that flashed through his eyes, Kenna turned away from Kyran and made herself walk as calmly towards her room as possible, not wanting to give a hint of the turmoil that swirled in her heart, in her head. She didn't want to dive into anything with him on a whim. If there truly was something beautiful blossoming between them, it had to be done carefully. It had to be done right.

'You shower first. I'll be having a quick lie-down before we head to the pub.' She sent a soft smile his way, hoping it would reassure Kyran that her actions were all about her feelings and nothing to do with him.

Safely inside, Kenna shut the door, belly-flopped onto the bed and groaned as loudly as she dared into her duvet, then ground her forehead as far into her bed as the mattress would allow and let out a growl of frustration.

Why had she pushed Kyran away like that? They were two adults. They could kiss if they wanted to. No harm, no foul.

Or a lot of harm, and a lot of foul.

She closed her eyes, acknowledging the truth. Her pushing Kyran away had been an act of self-preservation. Life preservation. All she'd ever wanted was to feel like she'd found her home, and after today she was beginning to feel she had. The locals had been warm, bordering on friendly, as she helped them with their rods, showing them how to cast out as Kyran had taught her, thanking her when she dealt with the fish they caught, telling her they'd see her around and to not be a stranger if they crossed paths.

And kissing Kyran could've – would have – ruined those tentative steps to being part of something bigger.

One kiss might lead to ecstasy, but the two of them turning on each other would lead to agony.

One kiss might lead to ecstasy, followed by happily ever after. Ever think of that?

But could it? She followed the trail of breadcrumbs the little voice inside her heart – because there was no way her head would be coming up with such an insane thought – had left, and tried to imagine a life where she and Kyran lived and worked not just as colleagues, or as friends, but as a couple.

Days spent checking in on each other as they ran their halves of the business.

Coffee and lamingtons at Marie's.

A quiet drink at Jim's after work.

Followed by dinner cooked by Kyran.

A night cap outside while watching the sun set in the warmer months. Hot chocolate by the fire in the sitting room during the cooler ones.

Kenna pushed herself up into a cross-legged position on her bed. So not that much different to how life looked now.

But with kisses.

And hugs. And bedroom antics.

And no more running to and from the bathroom so he doesn't see you half naked, because he'd be allowed to see you fully naked.

Er, that would be just 'naked', she corrected her inner voice.

Whatever, came the airy reply.

Rolling her eyes at herself, she let out a soft 'ha' of a laugh. She was going barmy. Chatting to herself the way she was. Still, the nutty part of her that insisted she think about what a relationship with Kyran could look like, had a good point.

It was a nice life she'd envisioned. Better than nice. It was bliss. Yes, there'd be ups and downs, but they'd get through it. Easily. After all, they'd managed to get through being forced to live and work together without tearing each other apart. If anything, they'd built each other up.

So . . .

A squeak came from down the hall. The bathroom door. Kenna had been meaning to oil its hinges for an age, but had been too busy or too tired to bother. A good thing because now she knew exactly what she needed to do, and there was no time like the present.

Springing off her bed, she pulled open the door and bounded into the hallway to find exactly who she was looking for looking exactly how she thought he would look fresh from the shower.

Droplets of water clung to the smattering of hair on his chest. Others created small rivulets of water that slowly made their way over his taut stomach, that showed the hint of a six-pack, towards his v-line, that all but pointed her gaze down to the towel slung low around his hips.

Eyes up. Lust later, romance first.

Dragging her gaze away, while clutching her hands at her side where surely, *surely* they'd be safe from the urge coursing through her, begging her to slip her fingers over the edge of the towel and drag Kyran towards her.

One look at his face, taut with want, his eyes filled with fire, and she knew she was lost. Game over. Any restraint she'd attempted to show was scampering down the hallway, out the garden path to who knows where.

Who cares where.

The deep-brown eyes she'd looked into so often burned darker than ever with a passion that saw her heart jump up to her throat, blocking any attempt at verbal communication.

His hair hung in damp waves, framing his face. She'd never seen it out before and it only added to his raw, effortless masculinity.

Unable to stop herself, unable to think straight, to consider consequences for one second longer, she reached out and curled a lock around her finger before releasing it, then running a finger down the line of his beard.

Lusher than it looked, and softer than she'd expected, she brought her other hand up and placed her palms on either side of his face, relishing the way the heat emanating from his skin warmed hers. Gave her the confidence to move closer. To make her intentions clear.

'If we do this . . .'

Kyran's voice was thick, rasping, like he was trying as hard to control himself as she was. Like he was afraid speaking would break the spell that surrounded them.

'We could lose everything.' Kenna finished his sentence.

'Or gain everything.' Kyran angled his head down so his lips were only inches from her.

She inhaled quickly, surprised not only at his honesty but how his train of thought had been so similar to hers, how it chased away the last of her hesitation, cut the last strings of logical thought that threatened to have her back away.

Standing on tiptoe she pressed her lips to his, brushing against them, slowly back and forth. The smallest movement, but one that elicited the softest of moans from Kyran. Finding the centre of his lips once more, she took them against her own, and held them still. Giving him a chance to back away, to change his mind.

Please don't change your mind.

His answer apparent as his arms circled her waist, before pulling her hard up against him. The oblong of age-roughened material knotted around his hips did little to hide his desire, and only served to heighten Kenna's own. Opening her mouth, allowing access, the salt and sour from a day spent drinking coffee and eating handfuls of crisps met Kyran's minty-freshness. An intoxicating combination that further heightened her need to feel every part of him. Their tongues met, sliding and slipping around each other, probing, demanding. Answering the questions they'd been asking themselves.

What did they feel?

Should they do this?

Would opening up to each other be a mistake?

The answers: attraction, absolutely, never.

Pushing her hands into his hair, Kenna brought Kyran closer still. Wanting him more than she'd ever wanted a man before.

Wanting to know him. To feel her way into his soul, to see what no one else could see. Or had been allowed to see.

His lips left hers and it was her turn to moan as feather-light kisses peppered the length of her neck, sending goose-bumps skittering over her body. Kenna's breath hitched in her throat as all gentleness was dispensed with and Kyran nuzzled into the spot where her neck and shoulder met. The electrical storm that had been brewing sparked over her body. Her pulse a frenzy, her heart racing, her mind unable to think straight to barely think at all – one thought on repeat: I need you.

Her hands fell from his hair to stroke the length of his back. Muscles corded and flexed underneath her touch as she skirted the width of his towel. The temptation to untuck hitting her full force. The desire to know if he was a work of art in every area, overwhelming.

Walking her backwards until she hit the wall, Kyran worked his way up to her mouth once more, his hands sliding over the curve of her breasts, past her waist to her hips. She pushed up against him, wanting to be lifted, demanding to be closer.

The tinny ring of a mobile phone split the air, breaking the two apart.

Kyran took a step back, his hand going to his lips, his eyes wide with wonder. 'That'll, ah, be Jim. Wondering where we are. I mentioned we'd be going in for a drink.'

'Jim. Of course.' Kenna searched his face for signs of regret. Of guilt caused by kissing someone who was not Jim's daughter. Relief washed through her as his hand dropped from in front of his mouth to reveal the smallest, but sweetest of smiles. 'I guess we should go. Can't keep him waiting. He'll wonder what happened to us.'

'I wonder what would've happened to us had he not called.' Kenna bit her lip, surprised at how forward she was being.

Kyran's brows rose. 'I don't know about you, but I think something wondrous would've happened. Out of this world. An event for the books. Much like the festival. But better.'

Kenna giggled at his show of silliness. She liked this side of Kyran. Relaxed, teasing, flirty. Barrier-free. 'Are we actually agreeing on something?'

'I guess it had to happen one day.'

'I'm glad it was this we agreed upon.'

He tugged her towards him once more and laid a long, lingering kiss upon her lips that threatened to turn her knees to marshmallow once more. At least they'd match her heart, which felt as warm and gooey as a marshmallow toasted over a roaring fire.

The roaring fire being the passion Kyran had brought forth in her.

Reluctantly she broke the kiss and forced herself to pull away. 'I could do that all night. I want to do that all night. But I'm still stinky and Jim's going to want to hear back from you or he'll send out a search party. And I'm not sure I'm ready for the town to see us like this.'

A crease appeared between Kyran's brows. 'Yeah, sure. Of course. I understand. Nobody likes to be the topic of village gossip. I'll get dressed and meet you in fifteen? Can you be ready that quickly?'

'I can be ready in ten. The sooner we head to the pub, the sooner we can come home and . . .' Kenna pressed her lips together as she reminded herself it was okay to be open with Kyran, that what had happened just now in the hallway of the little cottage they shared wasn't a one-off. Something that felt that good, that right, couldn't be. 'We can come home and be more wondrous with each other.' With a wink she walked past him into the bathroom and shut the door.

Leaning against it she hugged herself, then pinched the inner flesh of her arm.

Was this a dream?

The dull pain she'd created said no.

This was it.

She had a home. She had a job, a business, someone who she could share her life with.

She belonged.

Finally.

Chapter Sixteen

'To Kyran and Kenna.' From behind the safety of the pub's bar, his 'safe space' as he'd once explained it to Kyran, Jim's voice boomed over the sea of patrons as he raised his pint glass in yet another toast, which were coming more often and more exuberantly with every quarter of an hour or so that passed. 'To bringing life back to Dolphin's Cove.'

A sea of glasses rose to meet his. 'To Kyran and Kenna!'

Kyran forced himself to look up and smile at the villagers who'd come together to make the most of their day. The last few hours had been some of the most uncomfortable of his life. Nearly as bad as the time immediately after Jen had passed, when he hadn't been able to move a few feet down the street without being stopped and offered sympathetic looks and condolences, or open the cottage door without finding some sort of meal packed up and waiting for him. The only difference was this time he was being shouted beers and being clapped on the back or his hand clasped and shook. The attention, either way, sat with him equally uncomfortably.

Underneath the table, Kenna's hand found his knee and squeezed as it had every time a fresh wave of praise had been sent their way.

He raised his glass high in silent thanks and marvelled at how his world had changed so hugely in the space of a month. How the woman beside him had resuscitated his life, given him a reason to want to be more, to do better. To communicate. To connect.

To move on.

He shook his head as another fresh glass of beer and a glass of fizz was placed in front of them. At the rate they were being shouted, he and Kenna wouldn't be so much walking home as crawling home.

'More?' Kenna swayed a little in her seat. 'Can this be the last one? Maybe set up some sort of "for future drinks" system? At this rate I'm going to be ninety per cent Prosecco. I have work tomorrow, you know? We both do.'

Kyran went to place his hand on Kenna's shoulder in support, but stopped himself. She'd made it clear back at the cottage that she wasn't ready for word to get out about them – not that there was much 'them' to talk about, yet – and he had to respect that, even if part of him had felt a stab of rejection. Had wondered if she wanted to keep things below board in case their relationship sputtered and died. Wanted to save face in the place he could see was quickly becoming home for her. Just like she'd always wanted.

Was she afraid if things broke down between them, and she was accused of further hurting poor, broken Kyran, that she'd be chased out of the village? That she'd lose everything she'd worked so hard to build?

He circled his glass round in thought, then berated himself for thinking such things of Kenna. She wasn't like his father. Kenna wouldn't just up and leave him if things went wrong between them; she'd find a way to work things out. To make it so they could still live and work together without issue. She wasn't like Sonia either. She wouldn't keep secrets from him and hurt him that way, the way Sonia had by not revealing her cancer diagnosis until

201

it was too late. No, he was reading too much into things. Letting years of fear fog the truth: that Kenna wanted to be with him. She'd seen through the emotional walls of concrete he'd created, scrambled over the barbed wire of his words and ways, and survived every attempt he'd made to push her away.

She hadn't just gotten under his skin, she'd settled in there, and he couldn't imagine a day without her in his sphere. A day that didn't see her glancing up at him while setting stock out on the shelves, a twinkle appearing in her eye before telling him he had bird poo on his ear, or hair or shoulder. Or a night where he could appreciate the way her lips curved around a forkful of whatever he'd made for dinner, before tilting up in appreciation. Or the moments when she was getting ready to tell him what's what, hands on hips; her spine would straighten and her chin would tilt in defiance before it even needed to.

The latest addition to the ways he'd come to love Kenna? The way a soft 'uh' emerged from the back of her throat when he pushed up against her and claimed her soft skin under his lips.

The ways you've come to what about Kenna?

Kyran picked up his beer and took a long drink, finishing half of it in one go. Love? Like. He *liked* Kenna. It was too early for love. Too early to consider such feelings. Too soon in their situation to attach such a deep feeling; to open himself to fresh hurt should it all go wrong.

'Don't know that Kyran's finished drinking for the night, the way he slugged that beer back just now. Or maybe it just got a little hot in here for the lad?' Jim picked up their empty glasses, his gaze settling upon the table, right where Kenna's hand was still caressing Kyran's knee; her thumb was moving back and forth in languid strokes.

Who knew the man had x-ray vision? More like the vision of a man who'd seen it all.

'Cat got your tongue, lad?'

Kyran set the glass down, then reached for a crisp in feigned nonchalance. 'Tongue's fine, thanks, Jim.'

'For now.' A knowing look was cast in both their directions before Jim walked away, tossing a 'have a good night' over his shoulder as he left.

'He knows.' Kenna brought her hand out from under the table and placed it around the stem of her glass. 'Does that mean everyone knows?'

Kyran shook his head, hating the disquiet that eddied low in his stomach. Kenna sounded so fearful, so cautious. Like she was ready to pull away before they'd fully dived in.

'Jim's not a gossip. At least not when it comes to me. Your secret is safe.'

Kenna angled towards him, the colour draining out of her face. 'What do you mean "your". Don't you want to take things slowly as well? Aren't you afraid of what people might say?'

'I don't care what they say. I stopped caring what people around these parts thought of me years ago.'

'I don't understand? You're the most private person I know. What would they know about you that would put you on the defensive like that?'

The beer that had gone down so easily seconds ago decided to make a return trip. Kyran focused on the dartboard on the far side of the pub and swallowed the sour, acidic bile. This was why he kept out of people's way. This was why he kept himself to himself. People pried, they asked questions, they figured things out. They looked down on you, or pitied you. Both sometimes. He wanted neither. Especially not from Kenna.

203

The temptation to brush away their conversation, to tell her he was exhausted and not thinking straight, loomed in his mind. An easy way out. Except easy ways out often ended being anything but. Soon enough the truth would come out, and it was better from him than some busybody.

Pushing the beer away, he stood and offered Kenna his arm. 'Can we go for a walk? I need to clear my head.' *I need to get the truth off my chest.*

Relief surged when she stood and linked her arm through his, apparently deciding the locals wouldn't think anything of the two of them leaving in such a companionable fashion.

'Of course. Fresh air would be good right now. People have been overly generous and my head is feeling it.'

Waving goodbye to Jim, while keeping his gaze firmly above the rest of those gathered, not wanting to see their knowing looks or whispered words, he escorted Kenna outside, and turned towards the wharf. His home. His safe space.

'I get the feeling you want to tell me something.'

Kenna's words, quiet with understanding, sent a shiver rattling down Kyran's spine.

'You don't have to tell me anything if you don't want to. I'd understand.'

'Would you? Now, maybe, sure. But you'd always wonder about what I'd planned to tell you, and it would eat away at you. Eat away at the possibility of us.'

'Maybe, or maybe not.' Kenna inhaled deeply, then pushed the breath back out. 'I mean, we all have pasts. And just because we have pasts, it doesn't mean we can't have a future. It doesn't mean we need to bring the past into our future, either.'

The iciness of the shiver penetrated deeper as he pondered her words. For as long as he could remember he'd believed his past meant he didn't deserve a future. Not after Jen's life had been stolen away from her.

Because of him.

The dark of the night couldn't hide the sound of waves shushing up and down on the beach, and he let the sound soothe him, prepare him, give him courage.

'I came from not the best family in the village. Mum took off when I was a toddler to who knows where, leaving me and Dad alone to muddle along together and, as you know, he left me too when I was sixteen.'

Kenna's hand slipped into his and squeezed. 'That must have been hard. I'm so sorry.'

'It was what it was.' Annoyance at how flippant he sounded saw him briefly close his eyes, then shake his head. 'And I've really got to stop doing that. Making out like hard experiences are no big deal.'

'Can't say I blame you. Sometimes it's easier to make out that what really mattered didn't matter much at all.' Kenna tipped her head towards the beach. 'Shall we? It seems to me being near moving water helps the words flow a bit better, you know?'

Kyran couldn't help but chuckle at her words. 'I spend hours every day out on the water. Do I seem all that chatty to you?'

'You spend hours stuck with a bunch of strangers on the water, and when you're not working you're out there alone, and somehow I don't imagine the birdlife offers the most sympathetic or patient of ears.'

'This is true.' Stepping off the boardwalk onto the sand, Kyran toed off his leather sandals and let the sand envelop his toes. If only burying his feelings was as simple.

Beside him Kenna giggled as, hopping from one leg to the other, she pulled off her canvas shoes. 'How is it

205

I've been here for a month and I've yet to go barefoot on the beach?'

Plonking herself on the sand, she reached up and tugged him down beside her. Whether she'd meant to have him sit so close, Kyran couldn't be sure, but he wasn't about to move away, to create space between them, when all that was keeping him focused on the task ahead was the feel of her soft, warm thigh against his.

'Sonia wasn't much of a beach person, either. Funny, considering where she chose to live.'

'She fished though, right?' Kenna's head nestled against his arm, further fortifying him for what was to come.

'In the early days she told me she worked on the boats to make money to put food on the table and pay the bills, but she confessed to me once that she hated it. Hated regular fishing even more. Said she'd rather be killed by a million pricks from the dull end of a paperclip than sit still and be patient while waiting for the fish to bite.'

Kenna leaned into him, her head resting against his bicep. 'And yet she chose to run a fishing supplies shop. Something I'm glad she did, even if she wasn't all that fond of fish.'

'And why's that?'

'Because if she'd not have done that then I'd never have met you.'

Kenna turned towards him and Kyran could see what she wanted to happen. A kiss. Connection. Understanding. But how could he oblige her when he'd not been honest about who he was. About what he'd done. Kenna deserved that before she and he became more.

Forcing himself to not give in to the urge that begged him to take her into his arms and show her how much he cared, he focused on his knees and prepared to tell a tale he'd only ever told one other person.

'She certainly had a way of making things happen. For a long time after she invited me to stay with her, she left me alone. Didn't pry. Didn't try to cajole me out of my shell. She let me be. Until, one day, out of the blue, she introduced me to Jen. She'd come into what is now Marie's cafe and Sonia did something very un-Sonia-like and offered Jen a seat at our table.'

Kyran drew in a quivering breath, then pushed it out. Even though years had passed, that moment felt fresh. He could still see Jen with her gleaming blonde hair cascading down her back, her clear blue eyes directed at him, open to getting to know who he was, not narrowing in his direction like she'd come across dog poo on the pavement, as so many of their classmates' eyes did whenever he and his too small, age-stained clothing entered their field of vision.

'I'd seen her around at school and in the village, but I never thought someone who came from a family like hers – a proper, well-respected one – would want to get to know me. Would want anything from me. But she sat down, and she talked about her day, then stayed when Sonia left – saying she'd forgotten to turn off the oven at the cottage, or some such lie – and slowly I found myself opening up to her. Then she asked if she could meet me again at the cafe the next day. And so that became our thing, until one day the cafe was followed by a walk, or a swim, until eventually we were inseparable.'

'It sounds like true love. Or, at least, like how I imagined true love should go.'

Kyran found the courage to look at Kenna, knowing what he'd say next could change everything. Needing to see her reaction.

'It was. Until it wasn't.' He gritted his teeth, closed his eyes and willed the strength to keep going. 'Her family embraced me like she had. I was at theirs for dinner most nights. Invited to family celebrations. Everything was perfect. And then, one day she brought up the idea of us moving away together. I got scared. I couldn't imagine leaving Dolphin's Cove, leaving Sonia, leaving the closest thing to security I'd ever had. We argued. Well, Jen argued, I stubbornly refused to engage.' Kyran pinched the bridge of his nose, recalling the public argument, in front of Fishful Thinking, with all the villagers looking on. Jen's tears. His shutting down emotionally. 'And when I could see she wasn't going to back off, I did the only thing I knew to do – I broke up with her. In public. And that was the day she went to the beach and never came back.' He brought his knees up to his chest and wrapped his arms around himself as wave after wave of self-hatred and despair crashed down upon him. 'And it was all my fault.'

Kenna didn't flinch at his confession. There was no wrinkling of nose. No furrowing of brow. No shock. No disgust. Just silence. Long, painful silence.

Kenna inhaled, whisper-quiet, and Kyran prepared himself for the worst. For her to tell him to get out of her sight, that he repulsed her, that he was wrong to treat someone who loved him so much so terribly, that he deserved to suffer in silence for the outcome of his actions for eternity.

'Could Jen swim?'

Kyran nodded once. Not trusting himself to speak. Not sure he even could with the boulder sitting in his throat.

'Could she swim well?'

He nodded again.

'Was she, er, mentally unwell?'

'No.' The word was a quiet croak, but at least he'd managed to get it out. 'She was upset, yes, but not the

208

type to hurt herself. As it was, she told me I'd change my mind, that I just needed time to get used to the idea. But if I hadn't broken up with her, she'd never have gone for a swim, and would never have died.'

Kenna let out a soft, thoughtful 'hmm'.

'So, what you're telling me is that you got scared because you finally had the family you'd always wanted. Sonia, Jim, his wife and Jen, and the thought of upping and leaving them was unfathomable to you. So you broke up with Jen, rather than leave the people who'd shown you love?'

Kenna bum-shuffled around until she was in front of him, then rearranged herself so she was sitting on her knees. Her hands fell upon his knees as she leaned in, her eyes searching his.

'What you're telling me is that you've blamed yourself for an accident you had no control over, that you have tortured yourself due to the guilt you've felt for all these years?'

The boulder in his throat, that he'd only just managed to dislodge, returned.

'Did Gran know?'

Kyran nodded.

'Did she tell you to pull your head in? That this was not your fault. That you were a hurt and scared young man who was trying to protect yourself the only way you knew how? That Jen going for a swim, running into trouble and meeting a truly tragic end could've happened on that day whether or not you had told her you didn't want to leave Dolphin's Cove? That none of this. None. Of. It. Not your mother leaving, your father leaving, or Jen dying is your fault?'

Kenna's hands pressed down on his knees, emphasising the seriousness of her words.

Kyran tipped his head to the inky-black sky pinpricked with glittering lights. He knew what Kenna was saying was logical. He knew because Sonia had tried to verbally beat the same message into him as often as she could. But his heart refused to align with the truth.

'I take it Jim has no idea about what happened?'

'I was sure he'd find out, but for once the villagers said nothing about the argument they'd witnessed. I think they knew it would have killed him to find out the truth. That he'd have lost a daughter and who he saw me as – a son – all at once.'

'Well, thank god for your taciturn nature. Because had you gone in there begging for forgiveness, telling him you were the cause of Jen's death, you'd have lost a great friend. And only further emphasised to yourself that no one could love you, when that's so far from wrong it's not funny.' Kenna sank back onto her bum. 'Not that any of this is funny.' Kenna sighed and shook her head. 'Just what am I going to do with you, Kyran Walsh? How will I keep that inner voice of yours from hitting the destruct button on us?'

Us. Hope swelled in Kyran's heart, then burst out and rushed through his body. Dissolving the lump in his throat. Clearing his head from the mental pain that lived there.

He stared at Kenna. Unable to comprehend how she could be so good. So kind. So open. His confession ought to have been met by rejection. Yet she'd listened and withheld judgement, and come to a conclusion he'd never seen coming: that they should be an 'us'.

Reaching out, he took her hands and brought her to him. Cupping her cheeks in his hands he kissed her, softly, chastely. With the reverence she deserved.

'How did I get so lucky? How have I been given this second chance?' He thumbed the soft velvet of her cheek, laughing as she rolled her eyes.

'You don't remember? There was an interfering old bat who forced me to join you in business? Then forced me upon you at your home? Basically you've been manipulated.' She pulled away a little bit, her expression becoming serious. 'And you haven't answered my question. I don't want your past to repeat. You deserve better than to be in those chains for ever. I also don't want to leave the one place that has felt like home because things go wrong. So we need to set rules if we're going to do us right.'

'More rules? You do remember our original rules, don't you? Keep out of each other's business and what not? I think we suck at rules.'

'We'll do better this time. I just ask that if you ever feel like you don't deserve me, you tell me.' Kenna snorted. 'That sounded far more up my own arse than it should've.'

'Well, it sounds about right to me. I'm still not sure what I've done to deserve you.'

'You've been you. The real you. The Kyran who wants to help out, who wants to do the best by those he cares about. It's impossible for a woman not to fall—'

Kyran couldn't see the embarrassment hit Kenna's cheeks, but he could feel the inferno flaming off her skin. Had she really been about to say she'd fallen for him? Fallen in love with him?

'Impossible for a woman not to fall in like?' He ran his thumb over her lips, hoping his words would make her feel better. Not cause her to retreat. 'I mean, I don't know about that. I can be pretty horrid. You know that better than anyone else.'

211

She kissed the pad of his thumb, then took his hand in hers and brought it down to her heart. 'Only because of what you've been through. What you've put yourself through. But no more, right? Can you promise me you'll stop beating yourself up over things that were out of your control? That you'll let me like you? That if you have second thoughts you'll talk to me first, and not just shut me out? Because . . .' Kenna bit down on her lip, then released it. 'Because I don't want to *not* have you in my life, because you feel like home to me, and I want us to do this right.'

It was like the waves had ceased to meander in then out. Like the faint noise of revelry from the pub had been muted. Like his world had stopped spinning.

Kyran closed his eyes and held onto the words, committed them to memory. He was Kenna's home. He was in her heart. As she was in his. Not just in his heart, she filled it. Gave him a reason to be a better man. To not just exist, but to live.

Bringing her hand up to his lips, he kissed it. 'I won't. I promise. And do you think you could promise me that if you ever want to leave, you'll tell me first?'

'I'm not your mum or dad, Kyran. I would never just take off.' Kenna's eyes shone with compassion.

'No, you're not,' he agreed. 'But there are hints of Sonia in you.' Kyran pressed his lips together and centred himself before carrying on. 'And she didn't tell me how ill she was until it was too late. I had no time to prepare, to be there, to do anything that could have changed the outcome. I don't think I can be left like that ever again. I don't think here,' he tapped his heart, 'could handle it.'

Kenna lifted up and pressed a kiss to his lips. Long, soft, a silent promise that she'd heard him, that she understood his needs.

Breaking the kiss, she bent down, grabbed his sandals and passed them to him. 'I won't. I promise. Now, let's go home. There's so much more of you I want to get to know, to solve, and I think for that to happen a little privacy will be required. First one to your bedroom gets a full body massage?'

With a flirtatious wink she scooped up her shoes and tromped through the sand up towards the boardwalk.

Kyran followed her progress fully intending to let her win; his cheekbones aching from his smile that felt as wide and open as the sea behind him. How was this his life? How had he got so lucky?

And how was he going to make sure he didn't break the promise he'd just made?

Chapter Seventeen

Had the early morning sun ever shone so bright? Had the sky ever appeared so blue? Were the smiles of the villagers she'd passed on the way into Fishful Thinking happier than usual?

Was there magic in the air?

Kenna laughed at herself as she set out the open sign. There wasn't magic in the air, just the tang of sea, the slight pong of sun-warmed seaweed, and the hint of rotting fish guts. Not the most enchanting setting for a romance to flourish, and yet it had. Along with business.

Kenna whistled to herself as she skipped inside and began her daily shop fuss. Making sure all the rods were displayed tidily, that the hooks and feathers were well stocked in the clear display boxes she'd bought, that the new range of fillet knives were still perfectly in line the way she'd left them the day before.

'Morning, Kenna!'

The chorus of voices that came from the door as she checked on the sunblock supplies stretched her smile even wider.

'Morning, Harris family. Are you after your daily bait?' Kenna made her way to the fridge and opened it without waiting for an answer. The Harris kids had become obsessed with fishing after the festival and the family had been popping in nearly every day since. And they weren't the only ones.

There'd been a steady stream of customers in the past month, buying rods and reels, nets and cooler bags. The shop side of the business wasn't bobbing along, it was booming. As was Kyran's charter. The flyers they'd put up around the village and in the villages inland of Dolphin's Cove had worked wonders, with businesses booking charters for team-building exercises, complete with a basket of treats from Marie, which had the excellent spin-off of free treats being presented to Kenna and Kyran from Marie whenever they popped in for coffee as a thank-you for their picnic idea, which had helped to bolster her own business.

Kenna rang up the Harris family's purchase and waved them off, satisfaction filling every cell in her body. How had her life turned around so quickly? How did she have a thriving business, a cottage she was happily settled in, and a man that she adored? Maybe even loved, if she was being truly honest with herself. Not that she'd been brave enough to let the word fall from her lips, especially not since the night at the pub where the wine she'd consumed had nearly spilled the love word beans and he'd made it clear that they were only in the 'like' stage of a relationship. Even if her heart told her otherwise.

Still, she wasn't going anywhere. And neither was Kyran. The words would come out soon enough, and until then she could show her feelings in other ways. As she had been, night after night, and sometimes in the ridiculously early hours of the morning before they had to get out of bed for work.

She closed her eyes and scrunched up her face, trying hard to contain the joy cascading through her. Life was perfect.

'Bloody boat.'

A string of unsavoury words followed the exclamation, followed by heavy, frustrated footsteps.

So much for perfect.

She opened her eyes to see Kyran storming up and down the shop, his face dark with frustration.

'What's wrong with the boat?' She kept her place behind the counter, knowing that in this kind of mood he'd want to be left alone rather than hugged and cajoled into a happier state.

'It's taking on water. Must've got a leak. Again.'

'Can you seal it?'

'Not without bringing her on land, and I've got a group due in an hour.' Kyran let out a string of curses followed by a massive, chest-heaving sigh.

'Is getting them to bail the water out of the boat an option?'

'Not if I want to keep my certification.' Kyran buried his head in his hands and let out a frustrated groan. 'I'm just going to have to cancel the charter. Honestly, that boat will be the death of me.'

He removed his hands to reveal downturned lips and eyes filled with defeat. Kenna knew it was time to go to him. That he wouldn't push her away.

'But it is fixable, right?' She rounded the counter and encircled his waist, bringing him close.

'I should say so. It happens regularly enough, but before now it wasn't a huge deal because I barely had any bookings, and what bookings I had were spaced out enough for me to do maintenance on the old girl.'

'Oh, I see.' A flicker of an idea sparked at the back of Kenna's mind. 'Well, shall I make the phone call to cancel the booking – I'll offer them a discount if they rebook, and then you can get to fixing "the old girl"? And I'll do the same with the charters you've got over the next couple of days, okay?'

'Really? You're okay to do that?' Kyran dropped a kiss on the top of her head and hugged her tight. 'That would be amazing. *You* are amazing. Thank you.'

'No, you're amazing.' Kenna reluctantly pulled away, then picked her mobile up off the counter. 'I wouldn't know the first thing about fixing a boat.'

With a pfft of 'whatever', Kyran left, his aura of irritation now one of determination to fix the boat and get things up and running again.

Making the phone call, Kenna secured a re-booking, then grabbed the laptop she kept under the counter as a fresh idea occurred.

She'd been looking for a better way to express her feelings for Kyran and she'd found it.

Opening up the search engine she typed 'fishing boats for sale'.

As much affection as Kyran had for *Fishful Thinking Too*, it was clear the business needed a new boat. One that was in keeping with the look of a successful business. Less flaking paint on weathered wood and more sleek, aluminium-construction style. Less hard seats, more padded comfort.

One listing caught her eye. Painted white with black accents down the side and aluminium railings, it was simple but chic. Certainly more like the image the business ought to be portraying to customers.

Catching sight of the price, she gulped. Even though the boat was second-hand, it was well out of what she had in mind money-wise, but perhaps with a bank loan she could swing it? Debt wasn't what they needed right now, but then an unseaworthy boat was more of an inconvenience and, in the long run, a money suck. A loan for a new boat was an investment, Kenna decided, as she pulled up the business's bank's website and started tapping numbers into its loan calculator.

Excitement fizzed in her veins as numbers appeared. Numbers that, if sales continued the way they were, made buying a new boat doable.

She went to pick up the mobile but stopped herself. Her mind was screaming yes, but an ache low down in her gut told her no. Buying a new boat was a very bad idea.

Kyran loved his boat. Treasured it. It had been his place of respite for years. Surprising him with a new boat and a whole lot of debt would be unforgivable. As in he would never, ever forgive her. And that would be them done. For good.

Still . . . Kenna turned her attention back to the laptop. There was no harm in considering expanding the business. Looking into other options. Perhaps even going farther afield. If it was too early to proclaim her true feelings for Kyran, then perhaps she could show him just how serious she was about their success, in both business and as a couple, by laying down the foundations for a strong, dependable future.

She wouldn't leave like his mother. Or abandon him like his father. She'd give him every reason to see that she would stay through the bad and the good. She'd proven she was reliable through the bad by not giving up on the business when it was on its last legs; now she'd prove it during the good times by making them even better. By strengthening the ties that joined them.

Clicking out of the boats for sale website, she typed in 'shops for sale Cornwall'. Her plan was to throw the net wide, get a good idea of what the prices to buy buildings were, then narrow the search down to the surrounding area.

Scrolling through listing after listing, her heart began to sink. To own a freehold building was out of the question, especially when you considered the cost of buying stock before you'd sold a single thing. She dropped her head in her hands and massaged her temples, attempting to keep the headache that threatened at bay.

Leasing was an option, but it didn't make quite the same statement: that she was in. All in. Leasing was temporary. Even the longest lease could end, and that wasn't what she wanted to reflect to Kyran.

Raising her head she flicked her fingers up once more on the trackpad, the page coming to a stop on a small, whitewashed, tile-roofed building in Penryn. It was a little further away than she'd planned, but only by fifteen minutes or so. It wasn't the prettiest. In fact it needed cosmetic work. A lot of it. But she could do the work herself. She was sure of it. After all, she'd managed to get Fishful Thinking whipped into shape without hiring in extra help.

Clicking into the listing, she skipped through the pictures. The shop was small, but not much smaller than Fishful Thinking. And above it was a one-bedroom flat.

She tapped her fingers on the counter as the possibilities of owning the property bloomed in front of her. A flat meant regular income if you got the right tenant in. Regular income would offset the cost of the mortgage. Make starting up the business viable. It wouldn't be easy, not by a long shot, but that didn't mean it wasn't possible. If she could make Fishful Thinking a viable business, then there was no reason the impossible couldn't be made possible again . . .

Kenna's fingers flew over the keyboard as she looked up the prices of rent in the area, then played with the bank calculator to try and figure out how much repayments would be. Could she do it? She had no idea. She wasn't a bank manager. It was one thing to run a business, another to be a whizz with numbers and projections. There was only one thing for it. She pulled up the bank website's contact number, picked up her mobile and tapped in the phone number. Her impatience grew as she listened to the robotic voice on the other end of the line instruct her what number to push to get where she needed to go.

Finally a confident-sounding female voice answered and put her through to the bank manager. Taking a deep breath, Kenna launched into the pitch she'd somehow pulled together in the few minutes she was on hold, hoping it was enough to give the bank manager an idea of what she wanted to achieve, and what she had to work with.

Twenty far-longer-than-anticipated minutes later she ended the call and hugged the phone to her chest. Her mad idea to win Kyran's heart for the rest of ever just might work. With the business and cottage as collateral, along with a business plan that she had to create showing financial viability, she could make the expansion happen. There was even enough money available to them to fix up *Fishful Thinking Too* to a standard that meant they wouldn't have to cancel charters every other week in order to deal with a leak or whatever other little problems arose.

Glancing out at the sparkling sea, at the gulls circling above the wharf, squawking at the line of rod-holding villagers trying their luck, a frisson of excitement buzzed through Kenna. Dolphin's Cove today, Penryn soon to come, then who knew? Fishful Thinking could become a huge part of the Cornish fishing community, and Kyran would know she was serious, not just about the business, but about him. That she was going to be by his side through the good and the bad, the ups and the downs, through the low tides and the high.

Chapter Eighteen

Setting their evening meal of pan-fried fish on a bed of mashed potato surrounded by a citrus chilli jus on the table, Kyran couldn't help but notice Kenna, who'd been obsessively picking up her mobile, checking the screen before shaking her head in irritation and setting it down again, turning it over so the screen was hidden from sight.

Disquiet coiled around his heart. Other than Sonia never once mentioning the cancer that took her until it was too late, he didn't know much about the behaviour of those who were hiding something from someone they cared about, but he knew enough that hiding your phone's screen when you usually kept it screen side up never meant anything good.

Fear tangled with the disquiet as thoughts of what Kenna could be hiding flashed through his mind.

She'd changed her mind about him. She'd met someone else. She'd decided life in Dolphin's Cove wasn't for her. You're not good enough and she's finally realised it.

'Dinner's up.' He forced brightness into his voice as he poured them each a glass of Sauvignon Blanc. 'Your favourite.'

'You're my favourite.' Kenna shot him a sunny smile.

One that ought to have allayed his fears, but a split second later the smile was gone and her gaze was once again darting between her phone and the food in front of her, which she was moving around the plate with her fork rather than eating with her usual gusto.

Something was definitely up, and even though he wasn't one for snooping, the fear that suffocated his heart and had his stomach knotted up was insisting he figure out what was going on, if only to save himself from becoming a paranoid mess over nothing.

'You're not hungry?' Kenna reached out and tapped his fork-holding hand, which was hovering over the plate, but had yet to touch any food. 'That's not like you. Normally after a day out at sea you'd be eyeing up my meal hoping for leftovers by now.'

Again the warm smile touched her lips, but never made it to her eyes, forcing Kyran's suspicions that something was up to deepen.

'I could say the same for you.' Kyran nodded at her plate. 'Is everything okay?'

Kenna set her fork down, then took a sip of her wine. 'Just shop stuff, you know? Waiting to hear back about stock that ought to be with us by now. Wondering how much more bait I need to order since it's flying out of both the fridge and freezer these days. First-world problems, right?' She let out a short bark of a laugh. 'Who complains about their success?'

'Human nature, I guess.' Kyran dug his fork into the potato and made himself take a bite. Despite the copious amounts of butter, cream and salt and pepper, it tasted bland. Soulless. Like all the emotion he'd put into making a meal Kenna would love had drained out of it. 'I keep wondering what problem the old girl's going to throw at me next. Her being out of commission can really put a spanner in the works.'

Kenna slumped back in the chair and a small crease appeared between her brows. 'I'm sure it'll be fine. In fact, I know it'll be. You're amazing at getting her up and running again. You got that last leak sorted so quickly. And whenever people come into the shop fresh from a charter, they're buzzing. Saying they've never felt in safer hands, excited to take up fishing, buying up half the shop.' She wagged a finger in his direction. 'Hence my stock problem.' Her frown retreated, replaced with a grin that finally hit her eyes, making them sparkle like emeralds. 'The business is lucky to have you. It wouldn't be what it is without you.'

The business. Not her.

Faking a stretch then a yawn, he pushed his plate away, then scooted the chair back and stood. 'I'm sorry, Kenna. I think the extra charter took it out of me. I'm going to have a quick lie-down and then I'll clear away the dishes, okay?'

'Not okay.' Kenna glared up at him. 'I'll clear the dishes.' She lifted her arm and sniffed, her petite nose screwing up. 'Then I'm taking a shower. I've smelled better, and you deserve more than to sleep next to my stenchy self, let alone do anything else with my stinky self.' She widened her eyes. 'If you know what I mean.'

Kyran pushed away his fears and told himself he was being stupid. Kenna clearly still wanted to be with him, to sleep next to him, to make love to him. They both had a lot on their plates – figuratively and literally – but that didn't mean the end was near. That Kenna was lying to him about how she felt, about what was going on in her life, in her head. It didn't mean she was going to pick up and run away. She wasn't that person. She was too kind, and good. She knew doing that would break him in a way that meant he could never be put back together again.

His fears were further put to rest as she tipped her head for a kiss as he passed.

'There's more where that comes once I smell more like roses and less like twelve-hour-old sweat.' She waggled her brows, patting his bum as he left.

Making his way to his room – their room, since Kenna hadn't slept in her bed since the night on the beach – he lay down and closed his eyes. Quiet footsteps, the scrape of food going into a bin, the sound of running water and the clank of dishes going into the dishwasher, met his ears, followed by more footsteps and the rush of running water in the bathroom.

The sounds of Kenna keeping her word. Doing as she said she'd do.

Before he knew what he was doing, before he could talk himself out of it, his feet were on the floor and he was tip-toeing towards the kitchen.

Don't. You'll regret this.

The words blared like klaxons in his mind as he entered the kitchen and spotted Kenna's mobile, still face down, on the dining table.

What if you see what you don't want to see?

Better to see the truth now than to see a web of lies later, Kyran shot back at the warning voice in his head.

He knew this wasn't right. Knew this wasn't him. He wasn't a snoop. He didn't go through people's personal belongings, but the heaviness in his gut refused to abate, and his intuition – and his sense of self-preservation – insisted he figure out what was going on with Kenna.

If he was wrong? He would learn to live with the guilt, and promise never to go near her phone again.

If he was right and she was hiding something from him? He sucked in a deep breath as he lifted the phone and flipped it over. He'd figure out his next steps then.

Pushing the home button, the screen lit up to reveal the time. The date. The time.

And that was all.

No emails. No messages. No alerts suggesting something was afoot. Or amiss.

Told you so, he rolled his eyes at his inner voice that had him believing the worst. That had forced his deepest fears up and caused him to act out of character.

He went to set the mobile down, but hesitated as an email notification appeared.

Before he had a chance to ignore it, his mind had taken in the contents of the first few lines that had shown up on the screen.

A real estate agency. A time to view. In Penryn.

He blinked hard. Hoping the words might change. That a new email notification would appear saying the email was sent in error. That he wasn't seeing proof that Kenna was moving away. Or thinking of moving away. Of leaving him.

Bone-wracking shudders rattled through him, and he clutched the back of the chair for support, unsure if his knees were up to the job of keeping him upright. Closing his eyes, he clenched his jaw and attempted to get control of himself, of his emotions. Loud buzzing filled his head like a swarm of angry wasps had moved in, and the shaking continued.

How could this be happening again? How could he not only be about to be left without warning, but also lied to? By the one person who'd promised she'd do neither. Who knew how it would destroy him if she did?

The small amount of mashed potatoes he'd managed to eat came back up and he stumbled blindly to the kitchen sink and spat it out. The mouthful of wine, and cup of coffee he'd had earlier followed it.

Gripping the edge of the bench with one hand, the mobile still in the other, he hung his head, gasping for air. Wishing he could wake up to find it was all a horrible nightmare. The darkest part of himself playing a cruel trick.

'Kyran?'

A gentle hand fell upon his forearm, then was snatched away as he whirled around to face the woman who'd lied to him. Who had promised her best and given him her worst. Who'd betrayed him.

As if sensing his anger, she tightened the towel that was wrapped around her, then took a step back, putting space between them. Droplets of water hung from the locks of hair that had come loose from her bun, and she tucked them behind her ears, her eyes darting between the back-door and the hallway.

Kenna was looking to escape? Kyran suppressed a guffaw. Well, if she was already intending to leave, she may as well do so earlier than planned.

'You look . . . angry.' Her gaze fell upon her phone. 'And why do you have my phone? Did someone call?' Spots of red burned high on her cheeks. 'Did you answer? What did they say?' She took a small step forward and reached out. 'May I?'

Temptation to turn on the tap and place the mobile that had shattered his happiness underneath the running water raced through him. The shock of his desire to do so simultaneously brought him back to reality.

This wasn't him. He wasn't vindictive. He wasn't vengeful.

He was solid. Stable. He kept himself to himself. And he didn't let anyone get under his skin.

Ever.

And that meant giving Kenna back her phone, telling her it was over and moving on with his life. Somehow.

He passed over her mobile, careful to keep his fingertips far away from hers. He didn't want to touch her, to risk the tingle that her touch brought passing through him. Confusing him. Making him second-guess himself.

The mobile's screen lit up and Kenna's eyes widened, then slowly, guiltily lifted to meet his.

The tension grew with every passing, silent second.

Kenna wanted him to talk? He wouldn't give her the satisfaction. He wasn't the one who'd hidden something, who'd held back. It was up to her to take the first step.

Then he would have the last word.

'You saw?' She raised the mobile. 'Which means you looked?'

He searched for hints of anger in her voice, but all he heard was caution. The sound of a woman treading carefully, knowing she was in the wrong, desperate for a way to be in the right.

Not going to happen. He'd been a fool to let another person close. *Never again*, he swore to himself.

'I can explain.' Kenna took a step forward, then glanced down. 'But can I change first? This conversation really needs me to be wearing more than a towel. I'll only be a minute, and I promise you it'll all make sense.'

'You can change, but I won't be here when you get back. I know what I saw.'

An impatient huff left her lips. 'Really? You won't even let me get into a T-shirt and shorts? Or a dress? A dress would be quicker if time is an issue?'

'Time's not the issue. Honesty is.' His promises to keep his cool fell to the wayside as his fingers curled towards his palms, the rough edges of his nails no doubt marking the skin as he pushed them into the work-hardened flesh. 'You promised me you wouldn't hide anything. You said you wouldn't leave.'

'I wasn't. I wouldn't. I mean . . .'

Kenna moved towards him and Kyran ducked to the side, not wanting her close. Not wanting to hear the excuses, the lies.

'Really?' Kenna's hands went to her hips causing her towel to nearly fall away. Her eyes widened as she realised she was in danger of exposing herself and she grabbed the thin piece of fabric in the nick of time. 'So you're the one who's going to run? Because it's easier for you to believe the worst of me? Believe that I'd leave you like your family did? That I'd hide something from you like Sonia did? Because you refuse to give up the idea that no one can be straight with you? That they refuse to be, because you're not worth it?'

'I am worth it. That's the thing. I realise that now, and the person who made me realise I was worth something was you, and then you went and did the one thing you promised not to, like this whole thing between you and me was some sort of game. Which maybe it was. Bloody Sonia certainly seemed to think so.'

A fluttering movement out the window caught Kyran's attention, and he spotted the seagull that he swore was the one that had been hanging around the wharf hovering, staring at him in its beady, all-knowing way. Bloody thing. He was starting to feel haunted by it. Haunted, or taunted.

'I didn't know my grandmother well enough to judge her actions.' Kenna tightened the towel around her once more. 'But it seemed to me she knew exactly what she was doing. She somehow figured out that by bringing me here I would have the home I yearned for. The life I dreamed of. That by bringing me here you would have the chance of happiness, because if you liked her then maybe you'd like me. Maybe she meant for us to like each other in a more than friendship way, maybe not. But we do. And we should thank her for it, not curse her.'

'I'll curse her if I want. Her actions have put me right back to square one. And, for the record, we *did* have more than a friendship, but that was then. After what I've just seen on your mobile it can't be now. If I can't trust you, I can't be with you.' Even as the words fell from his lips, Kyran regretted them. Was he really ending things? Just like that? Without giving Kenna a chance to properly explain?

And if he let her explain, then what? She'd think she could do whatever she wanted another time, knowing he'd forgive her? Knowing she could walk all over him, if not out on him?

'Here. Look.' Kenna furiously thumbed at her mobile, then thrust it in his direction. 'It's an appointment to look at a shop down the way. It's a mess. Needs cosmetic work, but it's an opportunity to expand the business. For *us* to expand the business. I'm waiting to hear back from the bank manager about a loan, but—'

Kyran couldn't believe what he was hearing. Did Kenna really think she could do whatever she wanted without his say-so? Without his agreement? Did she think so little of him?

Ignoring the mobile, he took a step forward and focused all his energy on keeping calm, keeping quiet, and ignoring the maelstrom of emotions that swirled through his heart and mind.

'Just so we are 100 per cent clear,' Kyran worked through Kenna's actions, not wanting to muddy the truth. 'The way I see it, this is what you did, and feel free to correct me if I'm wrong.'

Kenna's chin tilted, just a touch, in defiance. Her jaw set, and her chest lifted and held. Ready to defend herself.

There was nothing to defend. As far as Kyran was concerned, she was guilty.

'You went online and looked up shops to buy. Found one you thought was suitable. Contacted our bank manager. Contacted the estate agent. Was planning on going to look at the shop. And then what? Buy it? How? Faking my signature?'

'I wouldn't have done that,' Kenna huffed. 'I was going to talk to you after I'd seen it.'

'Perhaps.' Kyran was willing to give her that point. Even if he wanted to think the absolute worst of Kenna, he didn't truly see a way she could put the business into that kind of debt without his physical presence at the bank providing sign-off at some point or another. 'But, at the heart of this all, you were going to make the first steps in a massive business decision without even consulting me, like my thoughts or opinions don't even matter.'

Kenna's chin remained high but her gaze fell to the floor, and her top teeth grazed her bottom lip.

Kyran ought to have felt a sense of triumph at her silent admission of being in the wrong, but all he felt was cold. Distant. Like he was physically in the room, but at the same time above the room, looking at two people being pulled apart.

'You're not who I thought you were, Kenna. I thought you were honest, and good. Straight up, but sweet. I thought I could trust you. I thought you were better than I deserved. But it seems I got exactly what I deserved.'

'Really?' Kenna's shoulders straightened and her eyes blazed, like a fire had been lit within her. One that threatened to burn out of control. 'Are we back there again? That you don't deserve anyone good in your life? That you're not worthy?' She swiped the back of her hand over her eyes and pushed out a loud, frustrated huff. 'God, Kyran, is this going to be how you live the rest of your life? How my life would be with you if we did work this out? Every little thing I do or say picked over? Every little surprise called a deceit?'

Reaching out she prodded him in the chest. It hurt, but he refused to flinch. Refused to give her the satisfaction.

'I was initially planning on trying to buy you a new boat. One that wouldn't need constant repairs. One that would be more comfortable for our customers. But I stopped myself because I know how much you love that boat. I put your needs over our business.'

She heaved in another breath and Kyran braced himself for another poke to the chest.

'And the reason I thought about buying a new boat is because I care about us. I wanted to prove to you that I was looking long term, thinking long term, and when I realised the boat wasn't a possibility because I cared about your feelings too damn much to tread all over them, I came up with the idea of expanding our business. I was sure if you could see that I was willing to put the work in, to solidify everything we have, that you would see, that you'd believe that I was here – with you – for the long term. That I wasn't going to up and walk out on you. That we wouldn't be just for now but for ever. Yes, maybe I went about it the wrong way, but the good intention was there, and I was always going to tell you, but I wanted to make sure I had all the information I needed. That nothing could fall over. That there would be no reason for you to think I was trying to find a loophole to get out of anything. To get out of us being us. But it's pointless, isn't it?' Kenna shook her head, defeat wilting her body. 'For this, for *us*, to work we were going to have to trust each other. But you were never going to be able to do that. Not fully. So I guess we'll have to figure something else out. Had my plan panned out, I was going to stay here – with you – and continue to run Gran's shop and get someone to run the shop in Penryn, but if this is going to be how things are, I guess, with your permission, should the finances come through, I'll just up and move there. Get the shop fixed up, running smoothly, and make it my new home. You can find someone else to take over Fishful Thinking, and all the profits from it can be yours. All I ask is that you have the decency to allow me to attempt a fresh start elsewhere. I'll work hard to pay everything off as soon as I can, and then we can separate financially, for good.'

Kyran blinked, unable to comprehend what he was hearing. The words coming from Kenna's mouth made it sound like she was ready and willing to up and leave. Not just him, not just the business, but the one place she felt was home.

'And you can have the cottage. I don't care. It's just a house and it's not like it was ever really mine.'

Her trembling lower lip told him she did care, hugely so.

'I'll keep out of your way in the meantime, until everything is sorted with the building and the bank, assuming the loan goes through.'

Kenna straightened up once more, her shoulders square, her arms wrapped firmly around the towel, to keep herself covered as much as to create a barrier between them.

Fear tumbled through Kyran as he realised what was happening. He fought to find the words to tell her he was wrong. He was sorry. That they could work something out. Words failed him. Fear had his tongue.

With a nod, Kenna turned and walked out the door.

And Kyran saw his future disappearing.

All because he'd been too in his own head. Stuck in the past. Afraid to trust. Afraid to hear the truth.

And in doing so he'd created his own reality, predicted his own future.

He was being walked out on, being left, again.

And, this time, it really was his fault.

Chapter Nineteen

Could the day get any worse?

Kenna massaged her aching temples then turned her attention to the spiking pain between her brows. There weren't enough painkillers in the world to deal with this headache. She knew because she'd been dealing with what felt like a drill going to town in her head ever since Kyran had found the email on her mobile from the estate agent.

She squeezed her eyes shut as a fresh stab zinged through her head at the thought.

Even now, a week later, she had no idea what to feel about the situation. Furious at Kyran for not trusting her, for daring to look at her mobile, or angry at herself for not taking his past into account and realising that he needed her to be honest and straightforward about every aspect of their life together in order for him to feel safe, to feel secure, especially when they were in the fledgling stage of their relationship.

Every time she contemplated either option, to be furious at Kyran or angry at herself, she came to the same conclusion: either way they'd have never made it work in the long run.

How could he be with someone when he found it impossible to trust? How could she be with someone who could never trust her? Who was always waiting for her to leave?

And now she was back at square one, which meant she had to go. There was no way she could stay in Dolphin's Cove. Not with Kyran stalking the cottage's hallway in the early hours to avoid her. Not with her skulking about the village, terrified she might run into him.

Two ghost ships in the night. That's what they'd become. Complete strangers to each other. More so than when they'd first been thrust together and were at least capable of civil-ish conversation.

Kenna refreshed her email inbox, fruitlessly hoping that the news she'd received yesterday would be followed up with an 'I'm sorry, we made an error, your loan is approved, go forth and buy your property' message.

As usual no such message appeared.

She was screwed.

The bank had rejected the loan application. The bank manager kindly explained that while the business was on the up, she needed a year's worth of statements that showed growth before the bank could confidently lend them money. Not that Kenna was sure Kyran would've co-signed since he'd never bothered to answer her request to buy the property in order for her to leave and start fresh. Although perhaps, in the end, he would have just to hurry her departure from the town.

Sinking her head into her hands, she groaned.

Her departure.

If she couldn't open a shop in Penryn then where could she go?

She didn't even have to look at her bank statement to know that going elsewhere wasn't an option. She'd sunk what little she had into tidying up Fishful Thinking's interior and exterior, seeing it as an investment in her future.

A bitter laugh filled the small space. Where it once would have echoed, it was now muffled by the stock lining the shelves.

How could she have done everything so right, yet got it all so wrong?

Pressing her palms into her eyes, hoping to suppress the tears that threatened, she turned her mind to her next step: the most logical step she could come up with, even if it was the one she least wanted to take.

Return to Leeds.

Make out to her mum that leaving Dolphin's Cove was no big deal.

Find a job doing . . . something. Anything. So long as it was busy enough that her mind would find it impossible to turn to a tiny fishing village with golden beaches, azure water, crabby seagulls, colourful characters she'd miss dearly . . . and a man who'd managed to steal her heart. But not break it.

She'd done that to herself.

Berating thoughts filled her mind once more, for what must have been the billionth time since she'd cried herself to sleep after their falling out: what had she been thinking deciding that expanding the business without consulting Kyran was a good idea? How did she seriously believe it would have proved to him that she wasn't going anywhere?

Were her actions self-sabotage? Had her years of being moved about by her mother meant she didn't know any better? That when the opportunity to settle down properly was gifted to her, some part of her was destined to destroy it? Because she secretly wanted to keep moving, to keep changing?

Kenna groaned. Asking herself the same questions over and over again wasn't going to get her anywhere. What she needed was answers, and there was only one person she could think of who could give her those. Who might know what it was to feel like Kenna did.

Tapping at her mobile, she brought it to her ear and waited for that person to pick up.

'Darling, it's so good to hear from you! As nice as a message from you is, there's nothing quite like hearing your voice.'

The first smile Kenna had felt in days twitched her lips. She'd forgotten how much her mother loved her, treasured her. How her voice could make everything better, even on the worst days.

'It's good to hear yours too, Mum.'

She lightly kicked the bottom of the counter, not sure what to say next. Just knowing that she needed a kind voice. Soothing words.

'How's Dolphin's Cove today? Sun shining? Sea sparkling? Or is it one of those days where the clouds hang low over the sea, where the water is angry and choppy? Where the gulls look like they'd murder you in your sleep simply for breathing the same air as them? I can't believe I'm saying this, but sometimes I miss them.'

Kenna blinked in surprise. Her mother missed the seagulls in the Cove? Missed Dolphin's Cove itself? This was a first. She'd never spoken affectionately of the Cove. There'd always been bitterness associated with the village.

With the village? Or the reason she'd left? Because of her grandmother?

'It's a beautiful day, Mum. It's been a stunning summer, overall.' Kenna gritted her teeth at the way her last word had come out. Could she have sounded more grim if she'd tried?

'Overall? Had the odd rainy day? Can't be good for business. Is everything okay?'

Of course her mother would notice the change in Kenna's voice and ask after it. Her mother had always done what she thought was best for Kenna, had always wanted the best for her. Wanted her to live a better life than she had.

Perhaps she'd been right all along? That coming back to Dolphin's Cove would only end in misery.

'Is everything okay? Honestly, Mum, it's really not. Things started out fine, got better, got great, even, but then . . .' Kenna paused and tried to get her thoughts together. 'Do you think it's possible for a member of our family to be happy in Dolphin's Cove? I mean . . .' Kenna ploughed on, determined to get answers, to figure out the situation she found herself in, to move on with a clear mind if not a healed heart. 'You left because you were unhappy here. So much so you never ever came back. From all accounts Gran was miserable here. People seemed to respect her but they also feared her. I've never heard a person say she was happy, that's for sure. And me? I was sure I could be happy here, that this was home, that I belonged here, but I've . . .'

A fresh wave of pain rode through Kenna, causing every muscle in her to contract as tight as her heart had felt since arguing with Kyran. Squeezing her eyes against hot tears, she inhaled and counted to five before exhaling slowly while choosing her words carefully.

'I've made mistakes. Things started off well. Well, as well as they can when you discover your grandmother has left you half a business and half a cottage, to be shared with a man who doesn't want to know you.'

Her mother groaned. 'Oh, that's so Sonia. I can't believe you—'

Her mother paused, and Kenna caught an inhale. Knew she'd stopped herself from telling Kenna off from keeping the twists and turns of coming home from her. A slow exhale followed, and Kenna braced herself.

'So, what was the catch?'

'The catch?' Kenna knew the catch, but she had no idea that her grandmother was known for having strings attached.

'There's always a catch, Kenna. It's why I had to leave, why I took you with me. It was better for both of us to go or she'd have spent her life trying to control us, and, knowing your grandmother, she'd have succeeded.'

Kenna pinched the bridge of her nose as a fresh wave of realisation dawned on her. 'From my point of view she's done a great job of doing exactly that. At least when it comes to me.'

'So what was the catch?'

'If I left the business or the cottage, the person I was sharing it with, Ky—' Kenna's throat closed as she tried to say Kyran's name. Still, she'd gotten half his name out, which was more than she'd managed in the last week. 'If I left, my flatmate would get both the cottage and business. And vice versa if he left.'

'Oh, that wretched cow.'

Kenna was shocked at how vicious her usually even-tempered, sweet mother sounded.

'She always wanted us back, but I never thought she'd go that low. Would it have been so hard for her just to let you have one or the other? Give you something to hold onto? To have as all yours?'

Kenna pushed herself up and went to the shop's front door. Leaning against the doorway, she glanced out over the view that had come to feel like hers. She watched as a miniature poodle snuck up on a bucket and pulled a fish out, then raced down the wharf, its prize hanging from its mouth.

Could she really let this go? What would it be like never to see a dog steal a freshly caught fish again? To see a child clap with delight at catching their first fish? To see Kyran's face brighten as a rare laugh boomed from him?

'She also made it pretty clear that she thought me and my, er, business partner and flatmate ought to, er—'

'Get together.'

'You sound unsurprised.'

'Your grandmother, despite her own heartbreak, was a matchmaker, and it was that matchmaking streak of hers that showed me I had to leave. I was happy with you and me being you and me. I didn't need a man, didn't want one, but she tried time and time again to get me to go out with a local boy, to settle down and marry.'

A laugh that sounded sad and amused made its way down the line.

'It was when she told me that if I didn't find someone in the next year – and she had a line of suitors available for me to choose from, not that they had any idea of course – that she'd write me out of the will and leave me without a thing that I decided we needed to go and find our happiness free from her controlling ways.'

Kenna wilted, grateful for the doorframe, unable to comprehend what she was hearing.

'The way I saw it, if I capitulated to her demands then she'd know she could control me for ever. That I would always do as expected. What she didn't realise was that I cared more about you than I did about home.'

Home. Dolphin's Cove was still home to her mother. Kenna had never realised. Never considered that after all this time her mother still held love for the Cove.

'It must've been hard leaving Dolphin's Cove. Leaving your friends. Leaving all you'd ever known.'

'It was, but it was also like being able to breathe properly for the first time in my life. There was no one to nitpick, no one to criticise. My decisions were my own. And, even though they weren't always the best decisions, hindsight being what it is, I hope I did my best. For you. For me. I know I tried to.'

'Oh, Mum.' Kenna wished she could reach across the distance between them and hug her mother. Bring her close and show her how much she meant to her. 'You were an amazing mum, and I'm so sorry I didn't recognise that. All these years I couldn't understand why you took me away, not even bringing me back for a holiday. Now, having been a pawn in one of Gran's games, I understand why.'

Her mother sighed. 'I'm sorry you had to experience it, but don't hate her, okay? Mum was, despite all her faults, a charismatic woman. Beautiful, sharp, funny. It was those faults that drew people to her, and sent them scattering when her best traits twisted into harsh, critical words and manipulating ways. I saw so many people drawn to her flame only to be burned by it. If she'd only let herself be a little softer she'd have been a different person. In fact, I think she'd have been happy.'

Kenna thought of all the people her grandmother must have pushed away. Her husband. Her daughter. Her grand-daughter. The villagers. And yet Kyran had somehow survived. Or perhaps her grandmother had known better than to turn on him.

Could she have realised he was her last chance at having a true connection? Seen the pain in him and understood it, because she too had been abandoned by so many before? Was bringing Kenna back to Dolphin's Cove her grand-mother's warped way of bringing Kyran the love she'd never experienced?

'Mum, do you think Gran stipulated that I must share the business and cottage with my flatmate because she was trying to make amends to those she cared for? That she wanted to bring her family home, one way or the other? Because she wanted to bring . . .' Kenna took a deep breath in and forced herself to get Kyran's name out. 'She wanted to bring my flatmate, Kyran, the happiness, the family, the love she felt she missed out on?'

'I have decided to imagine quote marks around the word "flatmate" because it seems to me you'd not be calling with all these questions if all this Kyran was to you was a person you lived and worked with.'

Kenna let out a dry laugh. 'Fine. You're right. Kyran's more than my flatmate, at least he was.' She forced herself to ramble on with her thoughts before sadness could swamp them. 'Is it a possibility that Gran saw Kyran's loneliness and recognised it in herself, and perhaps decided if Kyran and her could be good, long-lasting friends and business partners then perhaps he and I could be too, but with a little, er, extra attached.'

'Extra attached? Really, Kenna? We're both adults here. You can be honest.'

Her mother tutted, making Kenna laugh. The sound brightened Kenna's soul. Giving her hope that everything would be okay. Even if she never spoke to Kyran again. Even if she left Dolphin's Cove never to return. Even if her heart ached a little for the rest of her life. She had her mother; she had a home in her mother's heart.

'I'm not going into the nitty-gritty of our relationship with you, Mother.'

Another laugh, longer this time, followed. 'Fair enough. Frankly I have no need to hear the nitty-gritty. But I do hear what you're saying, and I wouldn't be surprised if there was something in your theory. Pride has always been a big problem for we Sanders women.'

'Pride?' Kenna pushed herself off the doorframe and began to pace back and forth. Was this the piece of her family puzzle that she was missing? If she could understand what her mother was saying, would her life fall into place? Would she be able to move on with some semblance of peace?

'Your grandmother was a proud woman. She could have missed us more than anything, but she would never have asked us to return. The same way that when her husband, my father, begged to come back after he'd done the foolish, cruel thing of cheating on her, she refused to let him step through the front door. Even though I know she loved him. I'd seen it in the way she looked up at him, coy. Sweet. So unlike her. She thought the moon and the sun and the stars lived in his eyes, in his heart, but the moment he took a wrong step—'

'Cheating on her was a pretty wrong step,' Kenna interjected.

'True, but we all make mistakes, and mistakes can be rectified if understanding of why the mistake was made in the first place is there, and if there's a heart open enough to give the person who made the misstep a second chance.'

Kenna processed her mother's words and saw where she was coming from. She had made a huge mistake going behind Kyran's back, even if she thought it was for the right reasons. But, she believed, it was a mistake that she could come back from, assuming Kyran's heart would be open to giving her another chance.

'My mother's pride stopped her from loving in the way she could. My pride stopped me from coming back. I didn't need to have the cottage, or the business, or anything from your grandmother. All I wanted was my mother's love, but once I walked out that door with you in my arms and her "don't you dare come back here unless you're prepared to live by my rules" ringing in my ears, I swore I would never return. Even though there were times, more than I'd like to admit, that I thought about returning, that my dreams – filled with warm breezes in summer, bone-chilling winds in winter, and crabs nibbling at my toes as I waded in the sea the moment frostbite wasn't guaranteed – begged me to, I dug my heels in. Thought about how she could get to you. What she could do to you. How she could manipulate you.'

An ache surged low in Kenna's stomach, then rose to fill her heart. Her mother had lost so much, had kept so much hidden inside, all for her.

'I had no idea.'

'That's because I never wanted you to know. Another case of that pesky pride. What's worse is that this time it got in the way of us, in the way we communicate. I hated how we left things. I hate that we've only spoken sporadically these past weeks. That I didn't do the grown-up thing and immediately apologise for being angry and behaving badly when you told me you were leaving. That I repeated a family cycle, when I technically know better. I guess some habits, some lessons – like too much pride – take a long time to unlearn.'

'I really hope not or, by the sounds of it, I'm doomed.'

'No one's ever doomed. Not if they're prepared to change, to make amends, to stop the destructive cycles that families can carry.'

Kenna leaned against the counter, the weight of her mother's words heavy on her mind. 'I guess that's my job then, hey? Not letting pride get in my way. Not leaving

Dolphin's Cove because it's easier to go back to what I know, because I'm too proud to try again with Kyran. To risk his rejection.'

'Maybe think of it this way . . . What's the opposite of rejection?'

'Acceptance. If he accepts what I have to say, he'll be accepting me.'

'And all the little Kenna foibles that come with you. Besides, I'm sure he's not perfect either.'

'He farts in his sleep,' Kenna giggled as her mother half choked, half laughed. 'And that's all the nitty-gritty you're getting, I promise.'

She waited for her to mother to stop spluttering before continuing. 'Mum, if I get to stay, if I can make things right, do you think that maybe you'll be able to return? To come home? Even if just for a visit?'

'Oh, my darling, it's not a maybe. It's a promise.'

Kenna smiled into the phone. 'Good.'

'Better than good. Now go take that family pride of ours and throttle it, my love. Send it packing. Live the life your grandmother and I ought to have lived.'

With a flurry of blown, smacking kisses and a handful of 'bye's, Kenna ended the call and set the mobile down.

It was time to sort things out with Kyran once and for all.

She only hoped he wouldn't be the one to let pride get in the way of their happiness.

Chapter Twenty

How many beers were too many beers in the middle of the afternoon?

Kyran had posed the question to himself after his first pint. His second. Then his third.

Turns out his third was one too many. Even though he was only a quarter of the way through it and had yet to feel any sort of buzz. Unsurprising as he'd spent the last week in a numb blur of getting up as early as possible, going to work, taking groups out then sending them on their way, heading to Jim's after work and staying until such an hour that he could be sure Kenna would be tucked up in bed and not waiting for him to have some sort of deep and meaningful, heart-to-heart 'we can make this work if you just give us a chance' conversation.

At least he wouldn't have to fear being pushed into that particular situation. Soon she would get the note he'd left in the kitchen, and everything would be sorted. She wouldn't have to think about him. Nor him her.

'You right there, son?' Jim's bushy brows drew together in the thousandth look of concern he'd given him that week.

Kyran was surprised they'd not become permanently fused together.

'Good, thanks.' Kyran gave his usual non-committal answer. He wasn't going to burden Jim with his falling-out with Kenna. His being Jen's father, his being like a father to Kyran, made doing so all too strange.

Not for the first time, he wished Sonia was still around, then immediately rejected the idea, knowing exactly what she would say to him:

Oh, for Pete's sakes, Kyran. Get over it. There are plenty more fish in the sea, and sitting around moping won't do you any good. If you're going to do something then do it, if you're not then move on.

Even though she was Kenna's grandmother, and his relationship with Kenna might've blurred the lines between he and Sonia, Kyran suspected the advice would be the same.

'Oh, for Pete's sakes, Kyran.'

Kyran blinked and looked around, half expecting the words to have come from his old friend. Except that was impossible. She was gone. She wasn't coming back. She was as dead to him as his relationship was with Kenna.

'God, lad, how many beers have you had? Did you sneak around the bar when I wasn't looking and pour yourself some extra?'

Kyran rubbed his eyes, realising that Sonia's oft-spouted words had come from Jim's mouth.

'No. Just tired. Big week.'

'Is that so?' Jim propped his forearms on the bar and leaned forward, his brows managing to knit even closer together. 'You know what a big week would look like to me? It'd be you not being here because you were too busy living life. What I'm seeing here is you reverting to form. Hiding away. Attempting to bury your pain in the beer you can barely even bring yourself to drink because you're hurting so much.'

The temptation to cover his ears and loudly sing 'la la la' was real, but to do so at the risk of looking like a petulant five-year-old wasn't. Choosing the more mature option – running – Kyran twisted around and made to get off the stool. A large hand on his shoulder stopped him.

'Don't move a muscle. With Sonia no longer here, I'm the only person you've got to talk to. I can't see you going to Marie because she just wants you to be happy and will support you in whatever decision you make, however wrong it is. And I have a strong suspicion that Kenna is the reason I'm seeing you go downhill, so she's out of the running for Listener of the Day.'

Jim's hand fell away from his shoulder as Kyran reluctantly turned around.

'Well, look at you not telling me to stuff off and bolting out the door. That's progress. There's hope for you yet.' Standing up on his tiptoes, Jim cupped his hands around his mouth. 'Drinks down the hatch, folks. We're closing early.'

Ignoring the grumbles from his customers, Jim poured himself a beer, then walked around the bar and sat on the stool next to Kyran.

'There. Now if you try to make a run for it, I'll have a better chance of tackling you and keeping you here until you sort yourself out good and proper.'

Kyran bristled at Jim's assessment. 'What makes you think I don't have myself sorted out? I'm fine. I'm just needing a bit of alone time. That's hardly unusual for me. Hardly unexpected.'

Jim's lips pursed as his brows raised. His expression was screaming, 'I'm not an idiot, so don't treat me like one.'

'Well it's not.' Kyran caught his bottom lip attempting to jut out and pulled it back in. 'I like my alone time.'

Jim nodded. 'You do. But your alone time isn't usually spent staring into a glass of brown liquid looking like you're about to leak some salt into it. Anyone can see you're miserable. That something – or someone – has got you all inside your head and not in a good way.'

Kyran went to fight back, to tell Jim he really was fine, that there was nothing wrong, that he didn't have to be in a good mood all the time, that he wasn't made to be a shining beacon of light and joy, but caught his tongue as he saw the corners of Jim's mouth turn down in defeat, realising that shunning Jim could mean losing the last person who had his best interests at heart.

The one person who he'd hidden his biggest secret from. The one Kenna had told him didn't make him a bad person. The secret that meant he couldn't shake the feeling that he was as bad as he thought. And not worthy of anyone's care.

Summoning what little emotional strength he had left, Kyran prepared himself to lay his soul on the line, and readied himself to be marched from the pub, as well as from the place he held in Jim's heart.

'I'm about to say something, Jim, and you may hate me for it, but if I don't say it now I never will and there'll be little chance of me ever properly sorting myself out.'

Jim nodded, his expression still. 'Go on.'

Kyran took a deep breath in and on the exhale let the words tumble out. 'It's my fault Jen died. The day she drowned I had broken up with her, and if I hadn't done that she wouldn't have gone for a swim and she'd still be here. And I need you to know that. And I will understand if you hate me because I hate myself. But I can't continue to have you be this good to me when you don't know the truth, which is why I'm telling you now, even though I should've told you a long time ago, but I was a coward, and I'm sick of being cowardly. Sick of not doing what's right. Sick of living a lie.'

His inner fear fought with his newfound courage to avert his gaze from Jim's. To hide from what was to come next. But if he was going to be truly brave, if he was going to move on in his life – one way or the other – he had to be up front. Had to lay the past out for Jim to see in order to move on with his future.

'Oh, son.' Jim shook his head, his eyes radiating compassion. 'What you said just now? It's not true. And I can't believe you've carried this burden, this misguided belief, on your shoulders all these years.'

'Stop being nice to me.' Kyran slammed his hand upon the bar, causing them both to startle.

He stared at his hand like it was a foreign object. He may have been known to get angry on occasion, but never violent, not like this.

A ghost of a smile flitted about Jim's lips. 'Would you look at that, son. You're getting some feeling back.'

'I have feeling. I have all the feelings. They're killing me.' Kyran brought the palm of his hand to his chest. 'I'm sick of them. I've tried to ignore them, but they refuse to disappear. I successfully drown them out for a time, then – boom – they float back up to the surface again. And it always, always comes back to me being responsible for the death of the person I loved, for causing you and yours pain, for my not being a good person, being good enough for anyone in my life since pretty much the day I was born.'

'That's a load of codswallop.' Jim shook his head with a sigh. 'You've had a rough go of it, there's no doubting that, but that's not on you. You're good enough for me. Good enough for Kenna, if what I saw between you two was real, which I believe it was. Perhaps *is*. And you were good enough for Jen, too. More than good enough.'

Kyran dropped his hand to meet the other in his lap and loosely laced them together. Inspecting his palms, he couldn't help but notice how much deeper the lines had become over the years, how they crossed each other, a crazy map he could never understand. A lot like life.

'I thought what we, Kenna and I, had was real,' he whispered. 'But we couldn't make it work. We want different things.'

'Sounds to me like you repeated the cycle you started with Jen.'

'I don't understand?' Kyran saw knowing in Jim's face, but couldn't figure out how he had any understanding of what went on with he and Jen.

'We were close, you know, Jen and I.'

'I know. She adored you.'

'So when you broke up with her the first thing she did was come and tell me.'

Kyran knew his mouth was open, that he was gawping, but he couldn't bring himself to close it. He didn't know how to right at that moment. He was struggling enough as it was to process what Jim was saying.

'You knew?'

'I knew everything. That she wanted you and her to travel. That she'd planned to ask you. That she was excited for your future together. I know that she was embarrassed with how she'd behaved when you'd told her you didn't want to leave. That she felt she'd made a fool of herself in front of the village. In front of you. And I know that despite your falling out, she still had hope for your future together.'

An eye-crinkling smile appeared on Jim's face, so gentle it caused tears to prickle at the back of Kyran's eyes.

'When she came to me after you two broke up, she told me that she wasn't going to let you hurt yourself by pushing away the people you loved, so she was going to let you have your time and then talk you round to getting back together with her. Even if that meant staying in Dolphin's Cove. You know, for one so young she was so wise. I'd have told you to pull your head in, lad. Made an ultimatum or some such ridiculous thing.' Jim let out a soft, short laugh, then dropped his gaze as gloom shrouded him. 'Despite Jen's plan to get you back, I could see she was hurting, so I told her to take a dip in the sea, to cool off, that the salt water would wash away her pain, and leave her fresh. So, you see, son, if anyone is to blame for Jen's passing, it's me.'

The tears Kyran had been holding back began to flow freely. He didn't bother wiping them away. Didn't want to hide the torrent of pain being released. Or the empathy he felt with Jim. For so long they'd shared the same secret and never known it.

Jim's hands landed upon Kyran's shoulders, and he gave them a squeeze. 'The difference between you and me though, son, is that while I wish I could take back my words of advice, while I wish that I could have said to Jen to go for a walk around the bay, or told her to buy loads of chocolate and watch a silly movie, I didn't blame myself to the point where I stopped living. Jen wouldn't have wanted that.' Removing his hands from Kyran's shoulders, Jim reached over the bar and tossed him a fresh bar towel. 'Here, let that soak up the last of the guilt you should ever feel. Then tell me, young Kyran, what would make you feel better about everything?'

Taking the towel, Kyran wiped away the tears and took in a shuddering breath as he adjusted to his new reality. He wasn't to blame. He wasn't at fault. Jen had loved him right to the end. She had seen who he was and was prepared to do whatever it took, even giving up her own dreams, to prove that love.

Just as Kenna had been prepared to do the same, until he'd stonewalled her.

Now he'd pushed her away. So much so that Kenna had not once tried to get in touch with him, to make him see that they were meant to be together. That she really had planned everything in his, in *their* best interests. After the way he'd treated her, he couldn't blame her.

If only he'd been able to see past his own barriers, his own stubbornness. If only he could have let Kenna into his heart properly – and that meant accepting and being open to her way of loving, which meant helping others, going out of her way, of building a community. Whether that be with one other person, or with a whole village.

'What I want, what would make me feel better, is for Kenna to be happy. I want her to have the home she always wanted. And Dolphin's Cove is that home. She's done more here, done more for the people in two months than I've done in my entire life. This is her home more than it ever was mine. She deserves it. And if I walk away, according to Sonia's terms, it's all hers.'

'So that's why you've been moping about the place this past week? You've had a falling out with Kenna and you think your only option is to take off? To abandon everything you love? After everything you've been through, after what we've spoken about today, you can't tell me that you're about to give up on the first person I've seen in years who has managed to tug you out of your shell, who you've willingly smiled and laughed with, not out of a sense of duty but because their existence in your life has brought you joy. Surely you're not that broken that you won't even try, or that you don't see what I see – that you are a big part of why Kenna is so happy here. That her happiness lies with you, as yours does with her. '

Panic set Kyran's heart hammering as he thought of the note, propped up against the vase on the dining table filled with dying white roses that Kenna had picked from the cottage's garden the week before.

'Kyran.' Jim's tone held a subtle hint of warning, letting him know in no uncertain terms that he was about to make the biggest mistake of his life in letting the one belief he'd held his whole life get in his way:

That he wasn't worthy of love.

Because he *was* worthy.

He knew that now.

Love had surrounded him his whole life, in the form of a snarly neighbour who'd taken him in when his own family abandoned him. In the form of a kind friend who never gave up on him, in the form of a beautiful girl who'd seen past his pain masked as gruffness. In the form of her father who was currently removing Kyran's pint glass with one hand and pointing to the door with the other.

'We never know when our last chance to make amends will be, so I figure it's best we do what we can to never have to make amends in the first place. But if we find ourselves having to say sorry? We say it sooner rather than later.'

Standing up, Kyran shoved his wallet in his pocket, then leaned over and brought Jim into a hug.

'Thank you, Jim. For everything.'

'Anytime, son. Anytime.'

Releasing Jim, Kyran propelled himself forward, running out of the pub, down the promenade, his brain screaming at his legs to go harder, faster as he hit the incline.

He'd lost the love of his life once.

He wasn't going to do it again.

254

Chapter Twenty-One

Disbelief tore through Kenna as she held the note Kyran had left in her shaking hands. She reread it again to make sure she'd not misinterpreted his words.

Kenna,

It's become clear to me that we can't go on like this any longer, which is why I'm leaving. You can have the cottage. You can have the business. I'm sure you won't mind if I keep the boat.

Best of luck,

Kyran

Best of luck? *Best of luck?* She screwed the note up and threw it across the room.

Who said 'best of luck' to a person you'd spent nights entangled with? Who you'd opened up to about your fears? Your secrets? Who you'd bared your soul to?

Best of luck?

If Kyran was going to bail on her, he was going to have to do it to her face. At least that way she had a chance of convincing him to stay.

Storming out the back door, Kenna rounded the house, ignoring the thorns on the climbing roses tearing at her skin as she rushed past, leaving raw, red marks on her upper arm.

Best of luck, indeed.

She charged down towards the wharf, where she guessed Kyran would be, probably loading up what few possessions he planned on taking with him to wherever he planned to go.

Was this his way of getting back at her? By being the one to leave instead of the one to be left? To leave her in the cold the way he thought she was going to do to him?

A hysterical laugh bubbled up and burst out of her lips. At least she knew the pride that haunted her family, causing them to create lifelong regrets, had passed her by. She was more than willing to make a fool of herself to get Kyran to listen. To stay.

She'd tether herself to the boat if she had to.

Running out of puff, she slowed her run to a jog, then to a power walk. Not noticing Marie waving hello as she passed the cafe. Nor Jim framing the door of the pub across the way, an approving smile on his face.

Reaching Kyran's boat, she saw it was empty bar a rucksack stashed up the top. Probably because he was at the shop getting supplies before he sailed to his next destination.

Bending over, she brought her hands to her knees, and heaved in the fresh, tangy air. At least Kyran not being here meant she had time to compose herself, to figure out what to say, how to say it.

'You all right there, lass? You look like you're about to keel over.'

Kenna looked up to see Old Man Henry, his ever-present dead cigarette hanging out one side of his mouth, staring at her like she was mad.

Which maybe she was. Chasing after a man who didn't want to be chased. Putting her self-respect on the line to win him back.

'Fine thanks, Henry. Just looking for Kyran. Is he about?'

'Not for a bit.' Old Man Henry's gaze moved to something over Kenna's shoulder. 'I'm wrong. Here he comes now. Looks as buggered as you do. Which makes an old seadog wonder . . . What have you two been up to?' With a lascivious wink he shuffled down the wharf, chortling to himself.

Kenna's heartbeat, which had only just settled to a trot, picked up once more.

This was it. Her chance to prove to Kyran how much she wanted to be with him. That they were meant to be together.

But first she had to stop him leaving.

There was only one thing for it. She was going to have to steal his boat. If he couldn't sail away he was stuck on land.

Refusing to overthink her plan lest she decide to try the talking calmly and rationally approach, which would only risk Kyran side-stepping her, jumping into *Fishful Thinking Too* in the graceful way he had and taking off, Kenna leaped into the boat. Untying it from the wharf, she grabbed an oar out from under a seat and pushed off, the boat dangerously wobbling for a moment before righting itself.

'Try and leave now,' she yelled at Kyran, who was racing towards her, waving his arms and bellowing at her to stop.

Stashing the oar back under the seat, she allowed herself a small, triumphant smile. This wasn't quite what she had in mind when she'd decided to talk Kyran round, but it would do. If anything, it would give her time to formulate a better plan.

Or not, if what she saw happening on the wharf – Kyran and Old Man Henry's heads close together in conversation or collusion – was what she thought it was.

Her heart sank as Old Man Henry slapped his back enthusiastically, then, with a nod, Kyran raced down the wharf to Old Man Henry's boat and jumped in.

Kyran was coming after her? To do what? Get his boat back? Turf her out? Force her to figure out how to drive Old Man Henry's boat back to him?

Not happening.

Eyeing the outboard motor, she thought back to the times she'd seen Kyran start it up. Surely it couldn't be that hard?

Conjuring up a mental image of the process, she tilted the engine down as low as it would go. Checking the fuel line was connected and the engine was in neutral, she attached the kill cord to herself as she'd seen Kyran do, and remembered to squeeze the bulb to get fuel through to the engine. Twisting the throttle a few times, she left it in the start position, pulled the choke out, then gripped the handle and held her breath as she yanked it once, twice. The engine revved into life on the third pull. With a howl of happiness, Kenna pushed the choke back, then began buzzing down the bay, relishing the stream of froth she left in her wake.

Her excitement at making her getaway dulled as a rumble from above startled her. Glancing up, a shiver of foreboding scuttled through her as thick clouds, dark and ominous, hovered above. Every now and then she could see a flicker of lightning amongst them.

A sense of foreboding filled Kenna. Even she knew that being on the water in a thunderstorm was a worse than bad idea. It could be deadly.

Despite knowing this, Kenna couldn't help but speed up further as she saw Kyran draw closer. She wasn't ready to face him. She still had to figure out what to say. How to win him back. And if that meant being on the water in a storm a little longer than necessary, then so be it.

Just like that, the huff and puff and determination disappeared as a bolt of realisation hit her hard in the solar plexus. There it was. The pride her mother had spoken of. She was willing to hurt herself, to put both her and Kyran in a dangerous position, in order to win. In order to get what she wanted. In order to come out on top.

Turning off the motor, she raised her hands in surrender.

Kyran acknowledged her giving up with a wave and, slowing his speed, came closer to the boat.

Standing to greet him in the most adult way she could think of possible – her arms at right angles, her palms turned to the sky in a 'what can I say, I'm an idiot' pose – she found herself flying backwards, her arms pinwheeling as she tried to gain balance.

Seconds later, icy cold water surrounded her and sucked her down. Inhaling automatically at the shock, she spluttered as salty water filled her mouth. Panic set in as she found herself unable to figure out which way was up, found herself unable to breathe, to see. Desperately thrashing about, hope came in the form of a series of flashes.

Lightning.

Not good. Not ideal. It meant the storm was worsening. But at least it showed her which way was up.

Kicking hard, Kenna made her way to the surface and glanced wildly around, the water slapping at her face over and over as she tried to get her bearings. The gloom had thickened in the seconds she'd been underwater and she could barely make out *Fishful Thinking Too*, let alone Kyran in Old Man Henry's boat.

'Kenna!'

His voice, a panicked boom, met her ears.

'Hel—' She attempted to call out, but another wave hit her face and inundated her mouth with more water. Coughing, she twisted and turned her legs like egg beaters, the way she'd been taught how in order to stay afloat when she was younger, and waved her arms, not daring to call out unless a wave smashed into her once more.

'Kenna!'

Kyran's voice had taken on a desolate tone.

The tiredness that had begun to settle into her bones was replaced by a desperate need to get to him, to prove she was alive; that she wasn't going anywhere.

Something she could've proven if she'd stayed on dry land and not been so determined to get him by getting away from him.

Kicking her legs into motion, she battled the ever-increasing waves to reach *Fishful Thinking Too*. Her hands clawed at the sides of the boat, but were unable to reach the edge.

'Kyran,' she screamed. 'Help.'

The world went dark as a wave crashed over her. Followed by another. And another.

So this was how it was going to end. They said pride came before a fall, but in her case it was to come before death.

Refusing to give up, to give in, Kenna propelled herself forwards once more and managed to break the surface only to be blinded by a light.

The light at the end of the tunnel? It existed? It wasn't a delusion of those on the verge of death and refusing to leave?

Something hard nudged her shoulder.

'Would you grab the oar, woman.'

Heaven included being hit by an oar and growled at by a pissed off-sounding man?

'Now would be better than in ten years' time.'

Relief swept through her as her brain processed what was happening. Kyran, with an oar in one hand and a flashlight in the other, was saving her.

Wrapping herself around the oar, Kenna found herself being hauled through the water, into the air and unceremoniously dumped on wet, wooden boards that stunk of fish.

No, this was definitely not heaven.

Seconds later she was brought to her knees and crushed to a wet, damp chest, and surrounded by strong, wet arms.

'Don't ever let me go,' she whispered into his chest, squeezing her eyes tight against another flash of lightning.

It occurred to Kyran that if Kenna hadn't very nearly drowned to death, she was about to be hugged to death if he didn't loosen his grip on her.

He commanded his arms to relax, but they refused. If anything, they gripped tighter.

Kyran knew that this wasn't a case of history repeating itself, not in the truest sense, but there had been a terrifying moment when he'd wondered if this was the universe giving him the outcome he'd long thought to be true: that he didn't deserve love, and it would always be taken away from him.

Not today, universe.

He grinned deliriously at the stormy sky. He'd saved Kenna. And now she was in his arms. Happily so. And she'd asked him to never let her go. Which he had absolutely no plans of doing.

After he'd done one more thing.

Pushing her away, but keeping hold of her shoulders, he looked her square in the eye. 'What idiot move was that back there?'

Her face, a ghostly white with a hint of green, found some colour as twin splotches of red hit her cheeks.

'Er, which bit? I did a fair few idiotic things in the last fifteen or so minutes.'

'Damn right you did. Jumping in my boat. Running away from me. Trying to captain a boat you've never captained. In a thunderstorm, no less. Not wearing a life jacket. Standing up in choppy waters. Did you want to die? Was that your grand plan to get my attention?'

Her lips kicked up into a mischievous grin. 'It got your attention though, didn't it?'

Kyran didn't bother to hide his irritation and let out a long groan. 'Woman, if you're not going to be the death of yourself, you'll be the death of me.'

Pulling her onto one of the seats that lined each side of Old Man Henry's boat, he took her hands, still half afraid she'd go overboard on purpose if their conversation went south.

'Can we be serious, just for a minute? You could've died.'

The grin disappeared as Kenna's lips flattened out. 'Like you'd have cared. You were going to leave Dolphin's Cove. Leave the cottage, and the business. Not to mention, me.'

The last word came out in a whisper, and Kyran's heart splintered.

He'd found the note tossed across the kitchen. Known she'd been unhappy, but assumed she'd been more pissed off with the method of delivery than the contents.

'I know you don't believe me when I say that I was trying to prove to you how serious I was about us by looking at expanding the business. That I hoped it would show you I was in this for the long haul, but that was my intention. I don't want to be with anyone else. I don't want to be anywhere else. Yes, I like the idea of growing Fishful Thinking. I've finally found a job that I'm not only good at but passionate about. Not least because I'm passionate about this place and the people in it. Especially one person in particular.'

262

Flipping her hands around so that she was holding his, she sent him the shyest smile he'd ever seen.

'And who was this one person in particular?' Kyran asked, knowing the answer, but wanting to hear Kenna say it.

'This one person, well, when I first met him I thought he was the biggest, rudest, most horrid person I'd ever met. But then I got to know him, and it was a bit like peeling an onion. You have to get through the dry, tough stuff to get to the good stuff.'

'You mean the stuff that makes you cry?' Kyran raised his brows.

Kenna rolled her eyes then playfully punched him in the arm, her hand finding his as quickly as it had left it. 'I mean the stuff that you want to add to all your food because it makes it taste better. I've been taking notes when you cook, you know. I've noticed your affinity for the stuff.'

'Onion doesn't make dessert taste better. So this person can't be all that great.'

'Oh, he's got a gooey, sweet centre. He doesn't show it often, but it's there. He's an onion and dessert all wrapped up in one.'

'Really?' Seeing Kenna shiver, Kyran brought her closer. 'I'm only hugging you because I don't want you to catch your death of cold, okay?'

'Okay. Understood. Crystal clear,' Kenna nodded. 'The thing was, I thought I knew better. Turns out pride is a big thing in our family, and once we decide on something we don't back down. So once I decided on how to show this horrid, tall, grump of a man how I felt, by looking to expand the business I shared with him without telling him, I also chose to ignore the little voice that told me it wouldn't end well.'

A muffled laugh vibrated Kyran's chest, and he glanced down to see Kenna's face buried in it.

'In fact, it nearly ended so unwell I thought I saw the great tunnel of light.'

'Did you?'

'I saw your torch.'

'I'm grateful that you did.'

She tilted her face up. 'Are you?'

'I am. You're not the only person who knows how to make mistakes. I nearly made the biggest one ever by pushing you away, by deciding to run before you could run away from me.'

Kenna reached up and cupped his chin. 'Fat lot of good that did you. I still managed to run away.'

'And I managed to catch you.'

'Save me.'

'Semantics,' he shook his head with a smile. 'The thing is, what I've learned about myself these last months is that even when I think I've gotten over my fear of letting others close, the moment they get closer, the moment I see there's a chance for something more. Something deeper. For love. I kick back, I push hard, I make it impossible to love me. Or at least I try to. That's why I didn't hear you out. It's why I avoided you after our fight. Why I refused to give you a second chance to explain.' He glanced out at a horizon he couldn't see, but found comfort in knowing it was there. Just as he knew that his love for Kenna would always be there, even during the darkest, stormiest times. 'I knew how much I loved you, and knew how much my love for you could hurt me if I let you love me back.'

'If I let you love me back?'

'That's what I said.'

Her arms slid around his waist. 'Well I think things are a bit late for that, mister. I've been falling in love with you for a while now.'

'Just how long?'

'Oh, since about the time you did the one thing you didn't want to do, just to help me out.'

'Sing on stage,' Kyran acknowledged, remembering how much he wanted to help Kenna out, to not see her fail.

'No.' Kenna shook her head. 'I mean, that was great, but it was when you fed me your burnt risotto that first night, that I got the feeling you might well become someone more than just a business partner or a flatmate. That you could be someone who felt like home.' A grin lit up her eyes. 'Even if, seconds later, you annoyed me so much I had to tip it out. Bloody pride.'

Kyran laughed, and held Kenna even tighter as a fresh wave of shivers wracked her body. 'So I feel like home? More home than Dolphin's Cove does?'

'You do.'

'Good.'

'Good?' She cocked her head to the side. 'Is that all you've got to say? You've admitted to loving me, and I've admitted to loving you, and all you're going to say is "good", like it's no big deal?'

Leaning down, Kyran took Kenna's lips with his own, lingered upon them, tasting the salt, the sweet, the hope, the joy. The future.

All too soon for his own liking, he broke away.

'It's a very big deal, but you've been in the freezing water. And we've both been in the pounding rain.'

Kenna looked up, closing her eyes as rain hit them. Turning back to him, she laughed. 'I hadn't even noticed.'

'Love will do that to a person.' Shuffling down the boat, bringing her with him, firmly tucked at his side, he revved the boat's engine. 'It'll also get you killed if you're not

265

careful. And I'm not about to lose the one thing I love most in the world to hypothermia.'

'What about your boat?'

He glanced at *Fishful Thinking Too*, bobbing forlornly in the water. 'She'll come back to me if it's meant to be. That's how love works, right?'

'That's what I heard.'

Kenna cupped his cheeks in the way he loved, and her lips brushed his, leaving him with no doubt that Kenna was as much his as he was hers.

That they would be hooked on each other. For ever.

Epilogue

Would the ticklish bubbles of love that filled her heart whenever she caught sight of Kyran ever pop? Kenna suspected not. If anything, they seemed to multiply day after day, and today they were grander and lighter and more ticklish than ever.

'Remember the good old days when we disliked each other but had nothing better to do than get to know each other?'

She took a moment to admire Kyran's rear end as he bent over to tuck fishing rods away underneath *Fishful Thinking Too*'s seat.

'Stop looking at my bum.' Kyran straightened up, the gleam in his eye as obvious as the smile on his face.

'What do you mean, "stop looking at my bum". I was simply enjoying the view.' Kenna pasted a look of innocence on her face. 'The sea is looking exceptionally stunning today.'

'Pfft.' He shook his head. 'I can tell when you've been perving because you look like that bloody seagull that hangs around stealing freshly caught fish.'

Kenna shrugged and took Kyran's proffered hand, easily setting foot onto the boat. For how much longer, she couldn't be too sure.

'And what are you going on about "the good old days when we disliked each other" for? Do you want to go back to those?'

'No, not at all. More just recalling how back in those days we had the time to spend together. We weren't two successful business owners who barely saw each other.'

Kyran snorted. 'I think we see a lot of each other bare. If you catch my drift.'

Kenna giggled. 'I catch your drift, all right.' She looped her arms around his waist and tiptoed up to kiss his lips. 'It's because of your drift that I've done the unthinkable and shut up shop for the rest of the day to come spend time with you.'

'The locals aren't going to be happy about that.' Kyran clucked his tongue in disapproval. 'That decision you made all that time ago to turn Fishful Thinking into a functioning business has given them expectations.'

'They'll get over it.' Kenna shrugged, knowing that once they heard the news they'd not just get over it, they'd be happy about it. 'We've done well, haven't we? With the business?'

'That we have. Thanks to you.'

Kenna didn't bother to bat away Kyran's compliment. He was right. Since the first fishing festival the business had gone from strength to strength. The only thing that amazed her more than seeing the shelves filled with stock was how often she had to order more in. The community support had been outstanding, and word had spread through the immediate area of the range and expertise – thanks to Kyran schooling her in the ways of fish, fishing, good fishing spots and ones to avoid – and she was seeing new faces come in daily.

'So what do I owe the pleasure of this extended visit?'

'I checked your diary and saw you had a cancellation today.'

'Indeed. Family trip scuppered by a case of food poisoning.'

'No fun being nauseous. Especially on a boat.' Her hand went to her belly as nerves sent what felt like a never-ending line of ants skittering back and forth in her stomach.

'You okay?' Kyran nodded at her hand. 'You seem not your usual self, and not only because you were willing to forego profit in order to hang out with yours truly.'

He laid his hand upon hers, and Kenna smiled at their simple gold wedding bands.

'You've got a Mona Lisa smile going on. What are you hiding? Have you been having secret chats with bank managers again? I know you want to expand the business by buying that run-down shack two villages over in order to work your magic there . . .'

Kenna shook her head. 'No. I mean yes. I'm definitely going to look at getting a loan to buy the business now that we've a year's growth as proof of our viability, but I know better than to do it behind your back. We're a team, remember?' She flipped her hand around and their fingers interlaced.

'How could I forget?' Kyran leaned down, cupping her cheek with his free hand and touched her lips with his own, before sucking her bottom lip in, causing her toes to curl, the bubble machine in her heart to produce, expand and pop at a faster rate, and the ants in her stomach to ditch marching for a dance party.

Releasing her lip, he kissed her once more then fixed a gaze, filled with suspicion, upon her.

'Now, what is it you want to tell me?'

Kenna breathed in deeply. There was no point in trying to hide her nerves. No point in playing down what she had to tell Kyran. Something so life-changing deserved all the emotion and honesty she could give it.

'You know how at our wedding we were all, like I just said, "you and me, for ever"?'

Kyran inched away, the sparkle in his eye snuffed out by a shadow of distrust. 'I remember. Those were our vows.'

'Indeed they were. How do you feel about revising them?'

'Revising them?' His brows raised, corrugating the skin on his forehead.

'To something along the lines of . . . you, and me, and a little version of us . . . for ever.'

Kenna pressed her lips together as Kyran clapped his hand over his mouth. His eyes, as wide as hers, were watery with unshed, happy tears.

'Are you suggesting what I think you're suggesting?'

'I'm not suggesting. I'm telling.' Reaching into her skirt pocket, Kenna pulled out the proof. A plastic stick with double lines that promised to change, to further enrich the future they were building together. 'We're going to be a family.'

The boat rocked as Kyran swooped in, crushing Kenna to his chest before rocking her back and forth.

Squealing, she held on tight, half afraid they'd tip into the sea, half delighted that this was who they were now.

No longer afraid of rejection. No longer scared they didn't fit in. No longer terrified to love.

Steadying them once more, Kyran kissed her nose. Her cheeks. Her lips.

'Silly,' he murmured, his mouth barely leaving hers. 'We already are a family.' Tears flowed freely down his cheeks. 'We're just going to be a bigger one. All three of us, for ever.'

Kenna thumbed away Kyran's tears, laughing as she realised her own cheeks were damp. 'Can you imagine what Sonia would say if she could see us now?'

Above them a seagull circled, its call bouncing around the bay, loud enough to command the attention of those near.

Kyran tipped his head to the sky, let out a soft laugh then turned back to Kenna, his face full of light and love, and hope.

'I don't have to imagine. I get the feeling Sonia already knows.'

He indicated she look up, and together they tracked the gull's progress as it angled away from them and flew towards the horizon, its cry sounding like the laugh of someone who'd got their way.

Finally.

Acknowledgements

To the dynamic duo at Orion Dash, Rhea Kurien and Sanah Ahmed . . . Thank you for all your support, and for your wonderful editing expertise! I love working with you and am so grateful that I get to do so!

To Daisy and Aaron. You're my biggest cheerleaders and I'm so lucky to have you!

And, of course, to you, wonderful reader. Thank you for choosing to spend your time with Kenna and Kyran. I hope you enjoyed your trip to Dolphin's Cove. X